1/7/03

Sue —
Best wishes +
Thanks for your
support!)
— Laura

Ain't Nobody's Bizness

Ain't Nobody's Bizness

Laura Garner

Five Star • Waterville, Maine

Copyright © 2002 by Laura Garner

All rights reserved.

This novel is a work of fiction. Names, characters, places and incidents are either the product of the author's imagination, or, if real, used fictitiously.

Five Star First Edition Women's Fiction Series.

Published in 2002 in conjunction with
Laura Garner.

Set in 11 pt. Plantin by Myrna S. Raven.

Printed in the United States on permanent paper.

Library of Congress Cataloging-in-Publication Data

Garner, Laura
    Ain't nobody's bizness / by Laura Garner.
      p. cm. — (Five Star first edition women's fiction series)
      ISBN 0-7862-4109-8 (hc : alk. paper)
      1. Industrial arts teachers — Fiction. 2. Pregnant women — Fiction. 3. Women teachers — Fiction.
    I. Title. II. Series.
PS3607.A76 A37 2002
    813'.6—dc21   2002017301

Dedication:
To Rosalind, July 12, 1995, 3:40 AM – 1:30 PM

Acknowledgements:

Special thanks to Professor Catherine Houser for her excellent guidance, and to the Graduate Fiction Writing Workshop at UMass/Darmouth; to Joe Sutton for his extensive knowledge of the blues and his smoky voice; and to my friends and family, who are my first and most beloved fans.

Chapter 1

On Valentine's Day I woke up in a bad mood. That wasn't all that unusual, but at least this time I had reason. I was about to dump the guy I'd been going out with, and I'd gone to bed late and a bit drunk, convinced we'd get the blizzard they'd been promising all winter. One look out the window showed me that the Weather Channel had rung my doorbell and run again. Meteorology must be one of the few professions where you can screw up regularly and not get fired; maybe I should've chosen that instead of teaching.

Rolling onto my back to stretch, I pictured myself in front of a weather map that featured a question mark, my oversized mouth glistening with lipstick as I snarled at the camera, "It's New England, folks, what the hell do you want from me?" Damn, I'd been counting on a snow day. My mindset was tuned to a leisurely morning of coffee and trash TV, an afternoon spent fixing the railing on my staircase and maybe putting that new light fixture in the kitchen. Instead, I had to haul my ass out of bed, dress it semi-respectably, and drag it off to work in the sleet. What a drag.

To cheer myself up, I decided to go out for a big greasy breakfast before school. I shivered naked across the cold hardwood floor toward my rickety dresser, tripping over a cat and a few piles of laundry on the way. Since my teaching contract was up for renewal, I tried to put on a halfway decent pair of trousers but found I couldn't button them. Well, that's what comes of closing in on forty and drinking too much Sam Adams ale. I gave up and yanked on my usual weathered jeans and sweatshirt, lurched into the minuscule bathroom, splashed water on my face and stuffed my limp hair into a scrunchie.

My fifteen-pound ginger cat wound himself through my legs and I half-stomped, half-tripped down the narrow stairs. "Damn it, Hairball, what's with you?" I snapped. He studied me with hurt yellow eyes, then collapsed onto his back with an idiotically adoring look on his face. I felt immediately guilty, which was exactly what he'd wanted me to feel, so I dropped to the floor and stroked his belly until his chainsaw purr kicked in. My skinny calico Booger stretched her way down the stairs and joined in with her snuffling, wet purr. My cats are named after their principal by-products.

"Okay, guys, sorry I'm such a crab. It's breakfast time." I yanked on the depressing fluorescent kitchen light and blinked at the sickening brownish-orange Formica counter and curling brick-red linoleum floor. I hadn't owned the house long enough to change some of its most offensive features. The cats crowded me gratefully as I opened the Iams bag and scooped kibbles into a dish on the floor. Without warning, the warm, meaty smell of the cat food punched me in the stomach and I spun around, stuck my head in the sink and heaved.

What the hell was that? I'd had a few beers last night, but that was it.

I stayed there for a moment, but the nausea faded as quickly as it had hit. Rinsing my mouth out under the faucet, I scanned my body for signs of illness, but was disappointed to find none aside from sore boobs. Oh well, guess I couldn't call in sick with that as an excuse, although the idea made me grin a little. "Hey, Ron, could you get a sub? My tits are killing me. I think I need to give 'em a rest." Oh well. I yanked on my battered Celtics jacket and headed out the door, bracing myself for the damp chill of a drab New England winter.

My dad's only tangible legacy was my antique black Ford pickup, Molly — known around town as my twin, since she had appeared the same year I did. She started up reluctantly and I gave her time to warm up as I studied the house. I'd owned it since early fall and it still gave me a shock of pride to look at it. Tiny, ancient, a handyman's special if ever there was one, it looked warm and inviting in the misty morning light. An automatic smile stretched my mouth: my very own home, shoddy though it was, complete with the wraparound porch that I'd always dreamed of. Okay, so the porch listed to one side and contained more splinters than nails. It was all mine, and that's what mattered. I sighed amorously, then forced myself to back out of the driveway into the real world.

Molly rattled along the road, complaining of wet and cold and age. Her bumpy gait jarred my aging joints and sore boobs, and a passing seagull had a Maalox moment all over her windshield. When we hit the main drag, an SUV on its way to Boston wedged itself up Molly's bumper like last year's underwear. Not a good start to an already crappy day.

The lame local radio station droned out a whiney James Taylor song, as usual, after joshing about the non-blizzard and the lack of cancellations. To drown out Molly's moans and my own gripes, I popped sassy Lil Green into the tape deck and helped her belt out "What's the Matter with Love?" I could've given Lil a pretty long list if she were still around.

In what passed for downtown in Hawk Marsh, a road crew was working in the half-light, readying our battle-scarred roadways for the summer season. No problem with inconveniencing the locals trying to go about their lives, but God forbid we should give a cash-carrying tourist any reason to complain. Damn, some of those construction guys looked fine in their winter jumpsuits. A particularly muscular specimen bent over to place a pylon and I honked, cranked down my window and whooped at him. He turned, startled and laughing. "Hey, lady, stop sexually harassing me!"

I was feeling better by the time I pulled into a slush-filled parking space across from Daisy's Herb's Diner, my favorite early morning greasy food stop. Through Molly's windshield, I gave the sign out front a quick once-over. The year before, a few of my shop kids made the sign after Daisy decided to keep the diner open in honor of her once crabby, now dead, husband. Sweet old Daisy was moved to tears when we presented her with it, but couldn't bear to obliterate Herb's name. So finally we just stuck her sign above his and everyone was happy.

Jumping from Molly, I sloshed across the street. Just as I stepped up onto the curb behind a seafood delivery truck, a huge headless fish slapped down onto the pavement, missing me by inches. "Whoa!" a male voice called. "Sorry. You wouldn't wanna be hit by that, huh?"

"I've been hit by worse," I answered, giving him a wink. He was cute.

When I opened the diner's fogged-up glass door, the whiff of overcooked home fries and pungent coffee revived my nausea faintly, but not too bad. I stood in the doorway for a moment, squinting under the fluorescent glare, swallowing bile and looking around to see who was there. My retired carpentry mentor Archy Kopp spotted me and waved joyfully. "Hey, Junior!" he yelled, even though I was standing about two feet from him. "How's my gal?"

"Hey, Max," a dozen voices rumbled at me from the claustrophobically arranged stools and booths. "How's it going?"

The queasiness had passed. I stomped the slush from my

work boots onto the saturated welcome mat and yanked off my mittens. "Hey, guys! Where's that freakin' blizzard, huh?"

Voices grumbled back that I could have it, the weatherman was always wrong, third time this year they'd blown it. I sat next to Archy at the smeared green Formica counter and gave him a smacking kiss, which made him blush like a teenager and reveal his adorable snaggle-toothed grin. "Hey, happy Valentine's Day, you old fart."

At the far end of the crowded counter I spotted my buddy Cal Winters, who'd recently closed his lucrative psychotherapy practice to open a bar in nearby Skiff Neck. Same job, different setting. He raised his cup and blew me a kiss. I blew him a raspberry. Taking that as an invitation to join me, Cal maneuvered his Orson Welles bulk through the squashed quarters to my side, spinning skinny old Archy around on his stool. Cal beamed cheerfully at the glaring Archy. "Good morning, Mr. Kopp, how are you this fine day? Ah, Mad Max, president of Underachievers Anonymous. You're looking ravishing as always."

"Yeah, well, jump up my butt, Cal."

Cal gave me a humorous once-over. "You know you're not my type."

Daisy plunked fresh coffee in front of me, smiled shyly and wiped arthritic hands on a grayish-white apron that was as faded as her skin. She made a mean cuppa joe, but her cooking was sub-par. While Herb lived, he knew better than to let Daisy into the kitchen unless it was a dire emergency. We all came now out of habit, and because most of us had been banned from the IHOP for various character flaws.

I turned back to Cal. "What the hell got you outta bed before noon?"

"I'm meeting the seven o'clock bus, can you stand it?" In a

whisper, he added, "We're taking on an ex-con to work at the bar." He preened over his enlightened social consciousness, but rapidly switched gears as his eyes lit on my chest. "My, my, you're looking rather busty today. Did you get implants to counteract the surgery?"

"Jesus, put a sock in it, Cal," I hissed with a hasty look around. I didn't really want these guys to know about my upcoming operation. It's not that I'm prudish; it just wasn't anyone's business. Only my sister, the guy I was seeing, and my two closest friends knew I was getting a partial hysterectomy the coming Friday, when winter break officially started. That gave me a full week to recover at home with no one asking questions, and I knew I'd be back to work on time despite the doctor's "mandatory" two-week recovery period.

"No need to get thorny on me, Mad One." Cal also gave the crowded area a quick scan, but the guys were busy arguing over last night's Celtics game. He took another look at my chest and leaned in closer. "Hm, could you possibly be, um, growing something else besides Curly?"

Curly was the name I gave my "benign uterine tumor" one night after watching a few too many Stooges and drinking a few too many Sam Adams. Cal's words jolted me. "What, you mean like boob tumors?"

"No, no," he reassured me, "I mean like" — he looked around again, and whispered in my ear — "a baby."

I almost laughed with relief. "Well, duh!" This is what comes of hanging around teenagers all day. "Hello, Cal, the doctor said that was impossible, remember?"

Still staring at my chest, Cal shook his head and shrugged. "Well, doctors can be wrong." A painful grinding and gaseous hiss announced the Bonanza bus's arrival, distracting Cal from his study of my boobs. "Whoops, better go greet my prisoner," he whispered, then stopped for a final look. "You might want to take a little test," he teased.

"I'll get right on that," I scoffed, still in teenager mode. But he'd shaken me and I found myself thinking about big, sore boobs, unprotected sex, and this morning's bizarre nausea. My brain hit black ice as I tried to dredge up the date of my last period. I'd pretty much stopped keeping track; they'd been all over the place for the past year because of Curly, who'd gotten big enough around Christmas that Dr. Brand decided he'd have to come out. I had a choice — just the tumor, or the whole works. I'd be forty pretty damn soon, and I'd stopped laying eggs, so what did I want with a uterus anyway? At that point, it seemed absurd to count anything except the days to my hysterectomy.

In other words, four.

"Hey, Max! Hey, Junior, I'm talking to you here!" Archy was yelping in my ear.

I shook myself out of my coma and turned to him. "Sorry. Guess I need this coffee, huh?" Forcing my mind away from pregnancy, I focused on dumping cream into the delicious-smelling brew. "What were you saying?"

"I was asking what that fat faggot wanted, but forget it."

"Cal's a damn good friend of mine and you know how I feel about your anti-gay bullshit." Trying to make Archy socially aware at this stage was nuts, but call me a diehard. I shook a generous helping of sugar out of the greasy dispenser and stirred my coffee.

Archy stared, shaking his head. "Better watch your figure, Max," he chided. "You're not getting any younger, and you're still single."

I snarled, "And I like it that way, so bite me." Archy wheezed out a laugh and slapped me on the back. Apparently he'd been taking geezer lessons.

"You tell him, Sis!" I covered my face with my hands as

the bleary voice lurched closer. "Hey, Max. You ignoring me or what?"

It was my chronically drunk, older brother Michael Maxwell Junior, also known as "Junie." We were known as the family with two juniors: Junie, who was officially named after our dad, and me, who inherited his nickname when I took up carpentry. My longhaired brother got the femmy nickname and I got the butch one, which should give you an idea of just how broad-minded Hawk Marsh is. I gave Junie a wary look, hoping he wasn't going to hit me up for money. "I'm not ignoring you, I didn't even see you."

"Yeah, right." Without asking, he grabbed my coffee and took a hefty swallow, then set it back in front of me. "How ya doin'?" His red-rimmed brown eyes and sallow skin indicated a bender of major proportions. Imagine Bambi with a hangover, and you've got Junie.

"I'm okay," I said neutrally, "How are you?"

"You don't look okay." He sipped my coffee again, and his eyebrows formed a concerned arc. "Come on, Max, what's up?" Yeah, he was being unusually interested in my well-being, which meant he was going to ask for a handout. Normally he didn't give a shit how I was.

"Nothing," I said, mentally adding, oh, except I'm having major surgery in a few days and what if I'm pregnant by some guy I was about to dump for God's sake I'm 39 years old you think I'd know better . . .

Junie finished off my coffee and signaled to Daisy, who bustled over with the pot. "I hear you been seeing a certain delivery man. That true?"

"No comment." It was impossible to keep a secret in this friggin' town. Bart Fulton was in the midst of his second divorce and I thought we'd been obsessively discreet. Guess not.

Junie nodded solemnly. "Well, you be nice to him, okay? He's a good guy and he's had more than his share of woman trouble."

"Yeah, I know, he's just a poor helpless man victimized by female nutcrackers." I'd already heard the sob story from Bart a few dozen times, and I wasn't buying it. Besides, all this meant was that Bart bought Junie a drink once.

"You stop picking on your sister," Archy commanded. When my dad was alive, Archy was his rival; when he died, Archy took over fathering me. He also taught me all about carpentry, something Dad had refused to do.

"I'm just giving her a little advice, Arch, so chill out." Junie leaned toward me, wobbly but stern, and I winced and swallowed hard to ward off the stench of his breath. "I mean it, Max, if I hear about you breaking my buddy's heart, I'm gonna break something on you." A ghostly *ooooh* rose from the counter.

"Yeah, you and what army, wienie boy?" The background *ooooh* dissolved into chuckles. We sparred for a couple of seconds, till Junie lost his precarious balance and grabbed the counter to keep from falling on the filthy linoleum.

"So what happened to that married guy you were boffing last year? He go back to his wife?" Junie squeezed my arm in a familiar, bully-big-brother way. "Guess you still got that commitment problem, huh?"

"I don't have a commitment problem, I just have crappy taste in men," I snapped. A couple of ex-boyfriends were sitting at the counter. Two hurt pairs of eyes fastened onto me; I winked and shrugged. "I rest my case."

"Or maybe you're a ball-busting bitch." Junie punched me on the arm, then remembered he needed money so he backpedaled rapidly. "Naw, just kiddin', sis. You're a sweetheart."

I shook my head. "Don't even bother, Junie. Payday's not till Friday, and I got a mortgage now."

Junie held up his hands in feigned shock. "Hey, did I ask for anything? God, you *are* a bitch." He and his wounded dignity returned to his seat, and I ordered a number two over light from Daisy.

"I'd like to smack him, Max, so help me," Archy muttered, glaring at Junie's back.

"You're not alone," I grumbled back.

As I caught up with the guys and devoured greasy eggs and home fries — so much for morning sickness — Cal came back inside with a damned interesting stranger. He limped along with the aid of a cane. Gangly limbs, tousled iron-colored hair, and a scarred, baggy-eyed face underscored his outlaw quality. He looked me over appreciatively as he came near, then gave me a slow, lopsided grin and deliberate wink. A bad boy, no doubt about that. In a town full of blue-collar bozos, fishermen, and marine biologists, genuine bad boys were an endangered species . . . and they were definitely on my list. My eyebrows twitched upwards and I half-smiled back.

Cal caught the look, rolled his eyes, and brought the stranger to me. "Jackson O'Brien, I'd like you to meet Maddie Maxwell. You'll find her number on the men's room wall."

I put up my hand as if to smack Cal. "He's just jealous 'cuz his number isn't there." I grinned as long-lashed, gunmetal eyes fastened onto my brown ones, which I hoped weren't too bloodshot for a change. "Hi there. Welcome to Wal-Marsh."

O'Brien grabbed my raised hand and brushed whiskery lips across my knuckles. "Pleasure," he rumbled in a voice straight from the TestosterZone, and he pressed my fingers warmly before Cal yanked him away to a back booth. I was left tingling in his wake. Damn, my hormones were in overdrive.

Cal turned back to me, made a loudspeaker with his hands, and mouthed "E.P.T." I flipped him off.

"Well, I gotta go corrupt young minds," I announced to my cronies. "See you around, guys." I took another quick look at Jackson O'Brien and got a lascivious wink in return. Trouble. I could smell it.

I got out of there quick.

Chapter 2

Thanks to Cal's insinuations, I couldn't concentrate for shit at school. Not that that was anything new; I was a crappy teacher. I left the carpentry trade and got certified to teach because I wanted shorter hours and summers off, and also, weirdly enough, because I really liked teenagers. But that wasn't enough to make me a good teacher — especially when it came to dealing with the parents and the school administration. My patience and interest were worn to a cracked veneer after twelve years. Lately I'd had to remind myself about a hundred times a day that it paid for my house.

After fourth period I charged for the bathroom, and it was kind of an emergency — which refueled my pregnancy paranoia. Since the shop area hadn't been updated in about fifty years, there was still only a boys room in the basement, and I had no compunction about using it.

To my disgust, art teacher Nick Jurgliewicz was lurking by the water cooler near the battered door. When he gave me the I'll-die-if-we-don't-talk look, I snarled, "Excuse me, I have to take a piss."

The big brown eyes pleaded. "I'll wait."

"Don't bother." I slammed into the bathroom — which probably should have been condemned years ago — furious that I'd been caught off-guard, and reflected on my short-sighted stupidity. Last year's doomed affair with Nick had been a huge factor in making my job even less appealing. When things were hot and heavy it had made the school seem dangerous and exciting and even recharged my interest in teaching, but once it died it effectively stunk up the entire building for me. Nick still tried to run into me, while I purposely tried to avoid him. Since I was smarter, most days I was successful.

I'd never gotten to know Nick as much more than a sex toy; our relationship was pretty much limited to boinking in the auditorium storage closet after school a couple of times a week, on the pretext of building sets for the drama group. If we'd had time to get to know each other, I probably would have dumped him in two months, the average length of my so-called relationships. As it was, the thing had dragged on for over a year, ending abruptly last fall when his wife tried to kill herself.

I flushed and absently rinsed my hands under the rusty faucet, staring in the cracked, clouded mirror at the bags under my eyes and pondering escape routes. Since I was in the basement, I was pretty well screwed. I sighed, looked in vain for towels, dried my hands on my jeans, and faced the inevitable.

"What?" I snapped as I slammed back out into the hallway.

Nick cowered further into the cement wall as if I'd slapped him, which didn't seem like a bad idea. "Max, please. I don't understand what happened to us! Why are you so mad at me?"

This was too bizarre. "You don't understand what happened to us? Um, how about you dropped me like a rock and refused to talk to me for a month?"

His eyebrows threatened to merge with his hairline. "But Max — what could I do? Heather was freaking out. I couldn't just . . ."

"You couldn't just tell her there was someone else."

"She'd tried to kill herself! I mean, that would have

finished her!" He grabbed my hand and squeezed it hard enough to hurt. "Honey, listen, just be patient a little longer and we'll . . ."

"Too late, Nick. Unlike you, I've moved on." Oh really? my conscience asked me. Then why are you still punishing this poor slob? It's not like you loved him. Shoving that thought aside, I added smugly, "I'm seeing someone else now." Yeah, my annoying conscience taunted me, another married guy, and you're about to dump him. You've *really* come a long way, baby.

Nick stood there with his mouth hanging open, horrified and crushed at my statement. "But, Max," he whispered, "I thought . . . I can't believe . . . I mean, don't you still love me?"

I furrowed my brow, pretended to think about it, then shook my head, but the gesture wasn't strong enough to discourage Nick. He launched into a begging, pleading, wheedling monologue about his undying love for me and if I could only wait a little longer he'd tell Heather and then we'd be together forever . . . an idea that almost brought back my nausea. As he whined on and on, I realized that our lack of communication had indeed been the key to our affair's longevity. If I'd had to listen to this, it would have been curtains after about ten minutes.

The look on my face must have tipped him off that his begging wasn't going over very well. He sputtered to a halt and settled on looking at me all spaniel-eyed. I realized I was still shaking my head, so I just went with that. "Um . . . no," I said, turning on my heel and walking away.

After several more mind-numbing classes in the dusty air of the shop, lunch period arrived. I immediately hunted down my best friend, Libby Langley, who taught a couple of noncredit acting classes and directed the Hawk Marsh High

Thespians. I found her in the school's lame excuse for an auditorium — an old gymnasium with a stage at one end and basketball hoops at both — where she was holding court with two breathless teenage boys.

Who could blame them? Lib's picture should be in the dictionary next to *Junoesque* — she has the kind of body pygmies like me could only envy. Okay, so she gained a few pounds in the process of having three kids. I thought she looked lush, voluptuous, and more beautiful than ever. She, of course, thought she was fat.

When she finally managed to shoo the little hornballs away, she bustled toward me triumphantly. "God, they really want to do Shakespeare. Do you believe it? I'm finally reaching them." In a lower voice she added, "Can you imagine that big one in tights?" She licked her lips, the proverbial wolf in sheep's clothing.

Only Cal and I knew of the filthy mind lurking beneath Libby's peaches-and-creamy skin, tumbled blonde curls, and angelic blue eyes; she certainly didn't share it with her ultraconservative husband Morris. But I'd known Lib since junior high school. We'd developed our dirty minds together, and still nurtured them when we got the chance.

When I didn't respond with my usual joke about it's-not-Shakespeare-they-wanna-do, she stopped and studied me. "Okay, Max, what is it?"

"God, what a fucking day!" I exploded. "For one thing, I got cornered by Nick and he wants me back."

"That pig!" Libby spat.

The little hypocrite had stolen her husband from his previous wife, but she frowned self-righteously on my affair with Nick. "And . . ." I prepared to run the pregnancy thing by her, but it suddenly seemed unlikely. "Well, you're going to think I'm nuts."

She patted my arm. "I already know you're nuts, so what's up?"

"Look, this is Cal's idea, okay? But I think maybe I should take a pregnancy test."

A former semi-professional actress, Libby was given to dramatics. In a gesture worthy of Vivien Leigh she gasped and clutched her ample bosom. "Oh my God, what about Curly?"

"I don't know. I mean, it's probably just Cal's usual bullshit, but . . ." My symptoms sounded weak when I said them aloud, but Libby listened soberly then snapped into controlling woman mode.

"I'm about to run home for lunch. I'll pick you up an EPT on the way back." She grabbed her coat and purse, dismissing my objections. "Max, if you even think you *might* be pregnant, take a test. Woman's intuition is not a myth."

"Yeah, well, everyone says I take after my dad, so I'm kinda screwed in the woman's intuition department. Anyway, the doctor said I don't have any more eggs."

"Doctors can be wrong."

Cal's exact words. And he was a doctor of sorts himself.

My heart plunged somewhere into my work boots.

I had sixth period free, so I once again locked myself into a cubicle in the basement boys room and read the instructions on the EPT. My hand shook as I peed on the stick for the obligatory six seconds — not a particularly charming way to check for motherhood — then sat on the toilet and stared at the "indicator window."

It was one of those deals with a minus for negative and a plus for positive. To my surprise, lines were already appearing very lightly.

Wait a minute — LINES?

Yep. Two of them. Crossed.

As in positive.

I stared and stared, not breathing. It's not possible, I thought as the lines grew clearer. The horizontal one was darker. I grabbed the directions and found the words, "Even if one line is faint, the test is positive."

Holy shit.

Chapter 3

This was so fucking typical.

When I was fourteen and announced I wanted to be a carpenter like him, my dad explained it all for me: "You can't be a carpenter, you're a girl. You can be a secretary, a teacher, or a housewife." For good measure, he added, "Though who'd want to marry you, I don't know." So I marched out and apprenticed myself to his biggest competitor, Archy Kopp, who thought it was a hoot to have old Max's middle brat working for him. Years later, when I got certified to teach, Dad was long past saying "I told you so," or was doing it in some other dimension where I didn't have to listen to it.

After my soccer coach raped me freshman year, I went the slut route with great gusto and very little common sense. But somehow I never got either knocked-up or an STD, and that was a quarter of a century of asking for it. I figured I'd suck at motherhood anyway so why bother? It didn't stop me from fantasizing during those pesky monthly hormonal surges.

So it figured that there I was, thirty-nine years old, in a relationship I was about to end, on the brink of a hysterectomy, happily resigned to never being a mom . . . and I was pregnant.

Apparently all I'd needed was to be told it was impossible.

This was the crap running through my head as I sat on the cracked toilet in the boys room, staring at that little pink plus sign. It was too much. I started laughing.

It started as a silly grin and erupted into a side-aching guffaw, an animal bellow, a huge noisy hysterical release:

"Jesus, Max, *now* what have you done?" Good thing no one used that bathroom when there was no shop classes, or I'd've been hauled away.

I couldn't imagine what Dr. Brand would say about this. I mean, he'd made a big point of how there was no room for a baby. I pictured him frowning and concerned, telling me the baby would have to come out with the tumor. At that thought, my laughter was strangled by a sharp ache in my throat. What the hell was that about?

Wobbly-legged, I wandered back to the shop and called Dr. Brand's office. Apparently he was still away on his extended vacation — who other than doctors can take six weeks off at a time? — but the recording said he'd be back in the office tomorrow. A student came in just as the answering service picked up, so I left a terse message and hung up.

Somehow I made it through my final class, then took off before Libby could descend on me with questions I wasn't ready to answer. I had to be alone with this for a while, before I saw Bart that night for the hollow ritual of Valentine's Day. I didn't think he even suspected that I'd been planning on dumping him . . . but maybe I should postpone that plan a bit longer.

Damn it.

Early that evening I lay on my rumpled bed, staring at the water-stained ceiling and wishing I could fall asleep and escape. Deep in some realm of satisfaction that eludes humans, Hairball and Booger weighed me down with feline warmth. I touched Booger's head and her characteristic wet purr sputtered out, vibrating my hand. "Hey, fluffy buns," I rasped. With a strangled yawn and a juicy sneeze, Booger sagged against me like a warm sack of flour. Seduced by her affection, I turned over to cuddle her and check the time. God, I'd better rouse my sluggish ass; Bart would be here any minute.

I took a moment to place droopy Booger next to gigantic Hairball, who turned upside down with pleasure at the sight of his honey. Chainsawing madly, he wrapped his front legs around her and licked her ear. Their mutual affection made me smile. Then I heard the front door opening downstairs and Bart's nasal "Hello?" floated up the stairs.

"Uh — hi, I'll be down in a sec, okay?" I'd decided not to say anything to Bart until I knew what was going to happen next, but I felt panicky at the sound of his voice. There'd been a message from Dr. Brand's office on my answering machine when I got home; I called right back but they were closed for the day, so it would have to wait until morning. Easier said than done.

In front of the mirror, I yanked on a bulky sweater to hide my hooters, which seemed enormous since I saw that little pink plus sign. To me, I was all mouth and boobs and butt. I wondered how the hell I was going to keep Bart from guessing something was up. I wasn't that great an actress. Libby could've pulled this off, no problem. I remembered watching her "prepare" backstage when we were in college, when I'd headed the set construction crew for a musical she was in. I straightened, took a breath and forced my oversized mouth into a vivacious smile.

Yikes! It was Mary Tyler Moore meets Dr. Ruth. I decided it was best not to try, so I galloped downstairs and practically knocked over Bart, who was hovering creepily on the landing. I shoved past him and his puckered lips to grab my keys off the kitchen table. "Hi there. Happy V.D. Let's take Molly, okay?"

I was so spaced I turned the truck toward Skiff Neck, where Bart worked in shipping and receiving at the big research lab and had a cheap winter rental from a summer resident. He tensed when he saw where we were heading. "Uh — Max?"

"Yeah?"

"Aren't we going to that Mexican place in Abneyville?"

"Huh? Oh, yeah. Crap." There was nowhere to turn a truck the size of Molly around on the narrow, twisting road to Skiff Neck. Scrub pine gave way to stately maple and working streetlights as I looked for a convenient shoulder.

"Jesus, Max, can't you turn around?" Bart pulled up his coat collar and hunkered down nervously. "All I need is for Irene to hear I'm seeing someone."

"It's dark already, who's gonna see?" I was sick of Bart's paranoia about his upcoming divorce. "Anyhow, she left you, so what's the problem with you seeing someone?"

"I'm the guy, that's the problem. No matter what, I get screwed." He turned resentful basset hound eyes on me. "Every way but literally, that is."

Oh for God's sake, this again. I swear that bonehead thought I'd invented the tumor as an excuse not to have sex with him. He probably thought I'd faked hemorrhaging and blacking out after our last attempt, in late January. That was when the doctor shut Bart off, and he resented the hell out of it.

"Max!" he bleated as the harbor lights of Skiff Neck appeared on the horizon.

Without even looking, I pulled an illegal U-turn. I was damn lucky no one was coming, or they would've been dead; Molly was pretty much uncrushable. Thank God it was February or the traffic would have been hellish — although taking out a few tourists wouldn't have bothered me in the least. God, I sounded like my dad.

At least the crazy U-turn shut Bart up. Women's moods scared the crap out of him; he was silent as we headed back through the intermittent streetlights and scraggly pines of Hawk Marsh.

Hot Tamales pseudo-Mexican décor practically blinded me, so I chose a shadowed booth in the back. When Bart interpreted this as a romantic gesture, I forced a smile and winced inwardly.

It became clear pretty quickly that I didn't need to worry about Bart picking up on anything. Although he liked to believe he was deeply tuned into me and a sensitive New Age guy, he was neither. I sat across the table from him, listening to him complain between gulps of Corona and mouthfuls of beef enchilada, as I queasily sipped water and nibbled at a lukewarm, chewy quesadilla. Normally I could scarf Mexican better than a lot of guys I knew, but that night I could barely choke it down. Libby's morning sickness used to go on all day . . .

What Bart finally noticed was my lack of sympathetic attention to his moaning about Irene and her new lover and her lawyer and devious women in general. "Hello? Is something on your mind or what?"

"Oh . . . you know. The operation and stuff."

Bart pursed his lips. "I thought you were resigned to it. You've known for a couple of months."

I glared at him. "How long would it take you to get used to the idea of losing your dick?" It came out like a threat.

He considered this, then grabbed my hand and apologized. "Look, I'm just under pressure. I mean, God, with Irene yelling at me about meeting with her lawyer — I'm guessing she's going to try to get as much out of me as she can." He peered into his empty bottle. "That bitch is lucky I didn't pull an O.J."

Whoa, did he really say that? I yanked my hand away from him. "What?"

He seemed puzzled. "What?"

"She's lucky you didn't pull an O.J.? Was that supposed to be a joke?"

"Of course it's a joke. I didn't mean it. Not really."

My heart pounded so hard my whole body quaked. Hormones? I shook the thought off and said, "A joke implies funny, Bart. That was not funny. Not even a little."

He peered around as nearby diners turned to check out the raging hell-beast across from him. "Uh, Max — I'm sorry, okay? Sit down." After an apologetic smile to the next table, he stage whispered, "God, what's with you tonight? Is it that time of the month?"

My mouth dropped open. Where had I found this guy? What was I doing with him? I stood there for a moment, considering, staring, struggling not to throw a complete tantrum. Still shaking, I reached for my coat and pulled it on. "Look, Bart," I growled. "I've been doing some thinking, and it's starting to dawn on me that you're really kind of, um . . ." I struggled to come up with a better word, but had to settle for the one that drummed in my head. It came out a bit louder than I intended: ". . . an asshole."

And I grabbed my bag and started for the door.

Behind me, I heard Bart start to yelp, so I practically ran out to the parking lot. I knew he didn't have enough cash to cover the check, I knew his credit card was maxed out, I knew I was stranding him — but Goddamnit, I needed to get away.

I scrambled into Molly's bony seat, peeled out of the lot and hit the road. To drown out my burgeoning panic attack, I cranked the tape player and got my ear blasted by Etta James inviting me to jump into her fire. No thanks, got one of my own here. I slapped her into silence.

After a few minutes on the twilit road I was kind of sorry for walking out on Bart — but not that sorry. I wanted to leave everything behind me and drive like a fiend until I was ready to go home again. Instead, I headed for the ocean, which was sure to be deserted at this time of year. My favorite winter beach, with lots of crashing waves and a big-bouldered jetty, is behind Cal's recently-opened pub, the WunderBar, in Skiff Neck. I was pretty sure no one would spot me there, and maybe the wild surf would make my own turmoil seem small.

Screeching into the vacant parking lot, I rammed Molly into park, shouldered her door open with a loud creak, dropped onto the pavement and pounded toward the sound of waves rushing the shore. The sharp shock of the chill salty air made my head feel light and clear, and a flood of new thoughts jumped all over my case and wouldn't let up.

Why was my life one stupid mess after another? Why did so many of my choices have their roots in rebellion, obstinacy, or pointless rage? Guess I could thank my parents for that. But when do you stop blaming your genes and start getting your shit together?

Frankly, thirty-nine seemed a bit late in the game.

And what a thirty-nine I was! Unmarried and unexpectedly expecting, like something out of one of my own high school classes, bombing around town in my dad's truck with music blasting loud enough to shake the windows. Okay, so it was blues instead of hip-hop. The difference began and ended there. *I Was a Middle-Aged Teenager*. Great title for a horror flick. The story of my life.

Well, Christ, the doctor didn't even know I was pregnant yet. Why was I worrying? I had no idea if the EPT was even accurate. Maybe my hormones were playing a big joke on me; maybe my uterus had to get in one last prank before it was history. Frankly, that wouldn't have surprised me.

Clouds scudded over the full moon as I neared the jetty. I

wanted to get as close to the water as I could, to sit on the big rough boulders and let the cold waves surge around me like I did when I was a kid and things got too rough at home. Maybe that would calm me down. Or maybe a passing seagull would drop a clam on my head and kill me. Keep a good thought.

I couldn't see a damn thing without the moon and I was freezing my ass off, but I followed the sound of the waves around the jetty and groped my way onto the sea-slick rocks. Wet sand clung to my sneakers and I could feel my socks grow cold. My numb hands encountered barnacles, seaweed, and something that felt like the sleeve of a discarded sweatshirt, except for one thing.

There was an arm in it.

Chapter 4

"Shit! Oh God, I'm sorry!" I hollered, freaked by the feel of solid flesh under the cloth. "Jesus, you scared the crap out of me! I can't see a thing, and . . ."

My babbling trailed off as a few things registered. First, the owner of the arm hadn't reacted to my touch in any way — no gasp, no "hey," no yanking away from me . . . not even a twitch.

Second, the sleeve was drenched with cold spray. Who would sit around and let themselves get that wet in February?

Gingerly, I groped the rocks and found the sweatshirt sleeve again.

Okay, third, that arm felt stiff. Rigid. As in dead.

Shit.

Let me say right here, I'm not someone who's scared by death. Maybe it's weird, but I think it's because I saw so many people close to me die when I was young. It all seems pretty natural and not like the huge traumatic thing that everyone else makes it out to be. Everyone does it, so what's the big deal?

But even I had to admit this was a bit creepy. It was dark, I was alone, and I had other things to think about right now.

It didn't seem real at all. Maybe a seagull *had* dropped a clam on my head. Or maybe this person was just asleep. Yeah, right. They found themselves some nice comfy rocks to snooze on. In twenty-five degree sleet. Uh-huh.

"Huh . . . hello?" I managed to croak out as I prodded the unmoving arm. Icy water squelched from the sweatshirt and further froze my fingers. I ran my hand up the sleeve and found what felt like a shoulder. Well, at least it wasn't a severed arm. My fingers traveled the other way and found a hand that felt like a dead fish. I could feel hair on the knuckles and figured it was probably a guy, although you never know around here. Steeling my nerves, I pushed my stiff fingers around the stiffer wrist in search of a pulse just as the moon broke from behind the cloud.

No pulse, and the wrist was so rigid it felt like it would crack if I tried to move it.

My eyes reluctantly obeyed my command to look up the arm toward the rest of the body. The dark blue sweatshirt hood was pulled up over the head, and the corpse lay facedown on the boulders. No way to figure out who it was without moving the body, and I didn't really want to know anyway. I backed away on legs that felt like they needed new shocks, then turned and stumped toward the WunderBar to call in the authorities.

The WunderBar, or Wonder Bra, as I'd nicknamed it one drunken night, was unusually deserted even for the nontourist time of year. The 1930s-Berlin-meets-Yuppieville pub was open for business; Marlene Dietrich smoldered over the bar, Joel Grey winked false eyelashes and puckered rouged lips at me, but no three-dimensional help appeared. Neither Cal Winters nor his partner, rich bitch Alison Shipwood, was anywhere in sight. The place might as well have had tumbleweeds blowing through it. Where the hell was everyone?

"Hello!" I shouted, pissed off at the whole situation. "Could I get some service, please?"

"Hmm. Sounds like someone needs a drink." The husky, Southern-tinged voice came out of nowhere, practically giving me a heart attack on top of everything else. My bug-eyed stare took in the tousle-haired shadow rising from behind the bar. "Didn't hear the door and — hey, you okay?"

I mustered what composure I could, which was never a whole lot. "Uh . . . is Cal here?"

Recognition lit the scarecrow's face as he stepped from behind the bar, leaning on a cane. "Hey, you're Maddie Maxwell!" I was blank. "We met at that greasy spoon this morning, remember?" His crooked smile mixed shyness with lewdness. "Damn, I sure do."

"Oh. Uh, yeah." Of course. Cal's newly paroled employee. I couldn't remember his name, could barely remember my own. Wondering vaguely what he'd been in jail for, I asked, "Uh, so where's Cal?"

"He's off doing some damn thing or other since it's pretty much dead here." I winced at the word "dead" but he didn't pick up on it. "And Alison ran home to check on her kids, so it looks like you're stuck with me for now." He swiped a stripy towel over the bar and leaned toward me with a lean and hungry look. "Jackson O'Brien, at your service. What'll it be?"

Normally my panties would hit the floor with this kind of come-on from this kind of guy — like I said, it had been ages since I'd seen anything other than nerds and losers — but extenuating circumstances put a damper on my libido for once. "The phone."

He cocked an eyebrow. "Local call?"

"Nine one one. I need to report a dead body."

O'Brien started to laugh, but then saw the look on my face. "Shit," he breathed. After a moment, he grabbed the phone from behind the bar and handed it to me, listened in on my report with a deep-furrowed frown. When I hung up, he repeated, "Shit."

"Yeah, that pretty much sums it up." I pulled a cocktail napkin from the pile on the bar and shredded it as I talked. "He said the cops are on their way."

O'Brien picked the phone up gingerly and put it back behind the bar. "You want a drink or something?" he offered. Anxiety had replaced flirtation, which was just as well given the situation.

I considered a nice frosty Sam Adams ale, then decided I didn't need the local law enforcement agents smelling liquor on my breath yet again, especially under these circumstances. "Naw, I better not."

"Coffee? Coke? Water?" I shook my head, seeing the soggy blue sweatshirt in the moonlight, feeling the ice-cold wrist between my fingers. An involuntary shudder almost knocked me off the stool, and O'Brien leaned across the counter to steady me. "Shit. Herb tea, that's what you need. There's some in the kitchen, if you wanna hang on a minute." As he limped from behind the bar, a flash of blue pulsed against the window and he froze in his tracks. "I hate fucking cops," Jackson muttered.

I knew how he felt, but couldn't resist snapping, "Then don't fuck 'em," as I went back out into the cold to greet Hawk Marsh's finest.

They'd arrived surprisingly fast. Around here, dead guys on beaches aren't all that uncommon, but this was a boring time of year and the cops were probably sick of channel surfing at the station by now. Plus it was Skiff Neck, the rich neighborhood, and they knew which side their bread was buttered on.

Police Chief Rolly Yergins heaved his bulldog body out of the squad car and swaggered up to me. "You found a stiff?" His tone implied I was probably responsible.

I pointed down toward the beach. "I'm pretty sure he's dead."

"Know who it is?"

I shook my head, again flashing on that chilling moonlit glimpse. "He's lying on his face and it's pretty dark down there."

Yergins nodded curtly. "Stick around, we'll be talking to you later."

I rolled my eyes. "How long?"

"As long as it takes. Just go inside, we'll get back to you." With that, he walked toward the beach, bellowing out instructions to his officers. There was nothing for me to do but wait. If I took off, Yergins would have my ass. He had a long-standing grudge against my whole family; I think he'd actually enjoyed forcing me to identify my dad's body when the old man finally managed to blow out his liver.

I pushed my way back into the pub, where Jackson O'Brien hovered tensely behind the bar. An ambulance arrived, plus a few more cop cars and, finally, the County Medical Examiner's van. Multicolored flashing lights splashed through the mullioned windows, bounced off the mirror, and twinkled on the polished liquor bottles as O'Brien and I got acquainted.

"So, how do you like it here so far?" I asked.

O'Brien tore his gaze from the lights and focused on me. "Pretty cool. It's a nice place, even though the decorating scheme's a bit weird." I nodded in agreement; Nazi Berlin wouldn't have been my first choice for décor. O'Brien continued, "And they're both good people." I guessed he meant Cal and Alison, which kind of surprised me. I knew Cal was a cool guy, but Alison Shipwood was not exactly Miss Congeniality. She always looked like she'd just smelled a fart and was trying to figure out who let it.

"So you like Cal, huh?" I asked.

O'Brien made a wry face. "Yeah, he's great, but he's not my type."

I chuckled. "He came on to you already? Well, don't worry, he's just checking you for homophobia. It's a game he sometimes plays. He's happily married to Arthur, trust me." I sipped the herb tea he set in front of me. "So you like Alison okay, too?"

"Yeah, she's a real lady," he mused, to my disgust. "Real generous, real . . . you know, gracious. You know her pretty well?"

I mulled this over. Alison had been a total bitch to me more often than not, and I returned the favor in spades. "We knew each back in high school, but we kinda hung out with different crowds."

"I bet." An amused smile creased one side of his face in a way I found appealing. "So, she was the cheerleader and you were the bad girl?"

I frowned. "No, she was president of the National Honor Society and I was a jock. But I did my share of smoking in the girls room, if that's what you mean."

"What sports you play?"

"Field hockey, softball."

"Too short for basketball, huh?" I shrugged. That was still a sore point. He leaned toward me over the bar, temporarily forgetting about the cops, and murmured, "I bet you were fierce out on the field." The look in his eyes raised hairs on the back of my neck as some familiar hormones kicked in. Damn, was this actual chemistry?

Cal burst through the front door with a grocery bag in one hand, clapping his other hand against his leg and stomping his feet as if to thaw out. "Well, hello, Mad Max! I should've known you were around when I saw all the police cars. What's going on down there?"

"Maddie found a body on the beach," O'Brien announced.

"A dead one? Good Lord!" Cal's eyes narrowed. "I thought you were going out with what's-his-name tonight. What did you do, off him?" He looked around. "Where's Miss Alison?"

Jackson shrugged. "Gone to check on her kids a while ago. One of 'em called and she ran home."

Cal set the bag on the bar and unwrapped about a mile of burgundy cashmere from his neck. "A likely story," he scoffed. "She probably sneaked out for a quickie with Mr. Mystery." Cal insisted that Alison had a secret lover — God knows why he had to be a secret, as she'd been widowed about six years. Even the wily Cal hadn't been able to figure out who it was, which made him very resentful. "Nice of her to leave our brand-new employee all on his own, I must say."

O'Brien looked around at the empty tables wryly. "Well, the joint ain't exactly jumping, so no problem. There was just those suits at the end of the bar. After you left, some drunk came in and started shmoozing for drinks, drove the yuppies away."

Cal glanced at me, then back at O'Brien. "A drunk? Which one?"

O'Brien shrugged again. "A guy, kinda long hair, way out of it, hard to tell how old he was. He was pouring it on thick, telling Alison how beautiful she is and stuff. She handled him real well. I showed him the door about an hour ago. Think his name was June, something weird like that."

Both men turned as my head thunked against the counter. "Sorry," I muttered. "Just a little tired. Are those freakin' cops ever gonna come in here? I want to go home."

"What in heaven's name is going on?" Alison Shipwood's accusing Seven Sisters voice sliced the air like an icicle. "No one's going to come in for a drink with all those police swarming around." She turned imperiously to Cal. "Can't you tell them to move, or at least be more discreet?" Then she noticed me and her jaw snapped shut like something out of *Jurassic Park*.

I couldn't resist needling her a little. "Yeah, some idiot thoughtlessly died out there on the rocks. I'm sure they'll clean it up with as little inconvenience to you as possible."

"Me-ow," Cal whispered to O'Brien, whose mouth had dropped open at my unbridled bitchiness.

"Max! How nice to see you!" Alison returned in a transparent tone. "Your brother was in earlier for cocktails, but I'm afraid we had to turn him down this time." She swung her expensive coat onto a hook and sashayed into the kitchen, leaving us in a wake of subtle, expensive perfume.

I wondered if the guys had noticed the puffy eyes and smeared mascara behind her designer frames.

The Black Forest cuckoo clock over the upright piano ratcheted ten times and I yawned loudly, feeling like something the cat had dragged in, eaten, and then puked onto the rug. Makeup freshened and every hair in place, Alison hummed tunelessly as she checked the liquor stock behind the bar. Cal wiped the spotless counter and brass rails for the fortieth time, and O'Brien fiddled with the piano and stared nervously at the flashing lights out back. Jesus, what was taking the cops so long? I had to teach in the morning. Plus . . . oh shit, I had to get this alleged pregnancy checked out.

Why did I have to find a body at a time like this?

"Hey, they're coming up here," O'Brien announced, sidling toward the rear exit. "Okay if I make myself scarce?"

Alison turned to him with a warm, understanding smile. "Of course, Jackson. You must be exhausted." Her tone sounded patronizing to my ears, but O'Brien looked grateful.

"Yeah, I'm beat. So, see y'all tomorrow." He saluted Cal and Alison, then paused and gave me a raunchy wink before he took off for the hallway. Alison peered at me over her glasses and made a face.

Yergins banged through the front door as O'Brien's cane clunked up the back stairs. "Maxwell," he barked, making me think of police dogs, "how good a look did you get at the corpse?"

"Not too good. Like I said, it was facedown, and I didn't want to tamper with the evidence or whatever."

"Yeah, you're a model citizen." Yergins narrowed his eyes at me and scrunched his cold-reddened jowls into his parka. "Can you come out here for a sec, before they take it away? I want to see if you recognize him."

An overpowering feeling of déjà vu washed over me. My heart thumped thickly somewhere in my midsection. "Sure," I muttered, sliding from the stool.

Cal was at my side in a flash, and we walked out to the medical examiner's van together. The cold had intensified since I'd been out earlier; a steady wind blew off the water. I shivered and Cal put a warm, heavy arm around me. Yergins nodded to the guy behind the body bag, who unzipped the top section and held a flap of plastic over the side of the face away from us. "It's pretty mutilated over here, but your side's not bad."

Cal inhaled softly and murmured, "Dear God."

I chewed my dry lips and focused on the bruised face. My eyes closed without my consent and I locked my knees to keep them from buckling under me. God, I was tired. "It's him," I rasped.

"Who?" Yergins prodded, even though he knew damn well.

Asshole, I thought as I took a deep breath. "It's Junie." My voice cracked. Cal's arm tightened around my shoulders. I raised my head and forced the name out in a strident, angry voice. "Michael Maxwell, Junior." I glared at Yergins. "My big brother."

Chapter 5

Thank God Bart's car was gone from my driveway by the time I got home; I couldn't face explaining anything yet. I staggered into the living room and slapped the answering machine, wincing as it broadcast Bart's whine: "Jesus, Max, what the hell was that all about? I had to call Jeff to come pick me up and . . ." I smacked the volume control down to zero so I didn't have to hear any more, and collapsed on the sofa without even bothering to take off my coat.

Needless to say, I couldn't sleep for a while. Around two in the morning, I was lying punch-drunk on the floor by my stereo listening to *Jail*, my favorite Big Mama Thornton album. As she hollered out the blues, I spoke to my belly. "Hey, you in there?" There was no response from the phantom embryo, but I continued, "Well, if you are, I have no idea how long you're gonna be there. If you're smart, you'll get the hell off this planet before you get on it."

Big Mama backed me up, bellowing about her ball 'n' chain.

The phone jarred me awake. I wasn't sorry; my dreams were grimy with symbolism, but it took me a few moments to figure out where I was. The phone rang again, inches from my head, which meant I was on the living room sofa. I groped around and lifted what I hoped was the receiver and not a half-full beer bottle. "Hello?" I yelped, then remembered to punch the "Talk" button. Damn newfangled phones. "Hello?"

"Madeleine Maxwell?"

"Yeah?"

"Police Chief Yergins here. We need you down at the station A.S.A.P., to answer some questions related to your brother's death."

The mantel clock read five of seven. Shit, I'd overslept. "But I gotta go to work."

"You're going to *work?*" Disbelief underscored his usual disdain. "Jesus, Maxwell, your brother's dead. Maybe you could take some personal time. Anyhow, get down here. Something's off about this whole thing."

I blinked and spat a strand of hair out of my mouth. "But I thought he'd just passed out on the rocks and froze to death, something like that."

"Yeah, that's what we thought." Yergins obviously enjoyed messing with my head. "But the M.E. says those injuries couldn't have been caused by a simple fall. It looks like someone pushed him pretty hard, probably bashed his head against the rocks a few times."

A memory of my father beating teenage Junie's head against the floor made me wince. But Dad was dead, too; he hadn't done it this time. "On my way," I growled.

They called it an interview, but it was actually an interrogation. No question about it; I was a possible suspect in my brother's death. In the ridiculously large interview room, rancid with the smell of bad coffee and nervous sweat, Yergins and my former student, Gary Cullinane, asked when I'd last seen Junie alive, was it true we'd traded punches at Daisy's Herb's Diner the previous morning, how'd we get along these days, and so forth. I tried to keep my persistent queasiness and the infamous Maxwell temper under control, telling myself it would be over soon, but around eight-thirty the latter got away from me and I snapped, "Look, why would I bother killing Junie? Why would anyone, for that matter? At worst, he was annoying. And I've learned to say no to him, which is what I did yesterday morning. So can I go now?"

"You don't seem very upset by your brother's death," Yergins observed. "You weren't even planning on taking the day off, were you? Who's taking care of the funeral arrangements?"

I buried my face in my hands. "You know as well as I do Junie's been a walking corpse for years. The only difference is that now it's official."

Cullinane took over, his tone far more respectful than Yergins. "Miss Maxwell, what were you doing on the beach at that time of night?"

I peered through my fingers at the boyish face. "Please, Gary, drop the Miss, okay? Didn't I teach you anything?"

Yergins rolled his eyes. "Answer the question, Maxwell. What were you doing on the beach?"

"Thinking."

"Thinking?" Yergins' suspicions clearly grew. Thinking is kind of a revolutionary activity around these parts. "Thinking about what?"

Whoa, I really didn't want to share that with him. "Y'know, just . . . stuff. Job stuff. I always go to that beach to think. Junie and I used to go there together on our bikes when we were kids." I chewed my lower lip and scowled at the scarred table. I didn't want to remember that right now.

Gary took over again, leaning toward me across the worn metal table. "How long had you been there before you found your brother?"

"Maybe ten minutes? I don't know."

He nodded encouragingly. "And where were you before that?"

Oops, this was a sticky wicket. Bart would not appreciate being implicated in a murder while he was going through his divorce. "I was, um, having dinner with a friend."

Noting my hesitation, Yergins narrowed his eyes and thrust his bulldog face toward me. "Valentine's Day dinner, huh? With who?"

I grimaced. "Do I have to say?"

Yergins snorted. "If you want an alibi, it might be a good idea to give us his name. Or hers," he added with a pseudo-tolerant sneer. Like most of the locals, he thought a female carpenter had to be a dyke.

I sighed. "Okay, I was with Bart Fulton, but please try to keep him out of this or I'll never hear the end of it."

Gary jumped in. "Bart Fulton works for the big marine lab in Skiff Neck, right?" I nodded. "I thought he was married." Little Gary was still so innocent.

"Yeah, well, talk to him about that." I yawned violently and tilted the folding metal chair back to stretch my legs. "We went to Hot Tamales for dinner. I got mad at him and walked out. There are witnesses."

The folds of fat around Yergins' eyes squeezed closer together, reminding me of a blob of Play-Doh in a kid's hands. "So you were pretty worked up when you got to the beach, huh?"

"What? Oh. Yeah, I was, but mostly at myself." If I hadn't been so damn tired, I wouldn't have been so frank.

"And there was your brother . . ."

The harsh lighting and guacamole green walls were starting to give me a headache. "Yeah, but I didn't know it was him, and he was pretty obviously dead."

"So you say."

I bit my tongue. "Then I went to the Wonder Bra — I mean, the WunderBar — and called you guys right away. End of story."

"Who'd you talk to in the WunderBar?" Yergins pronounced it *wundabah*.

I rubbed my eyes again. I was in dire need of caffeine, but they hadn't even offered me a crappy cup of cop coffee. To my disgust my voice came out almost whiney. "I dunno, the bartender. Alison and Cal were out and the new guy helped me."

Yergins and Cullinane looked at each other knowingly. "Jackson O'Brien?"

"Yeah, that sounds right."

Yergins gnawed his pencil. "Had you met O'Brien before?" Wearily I told him about our brief meeting at Daisy's. "So, did he see the altercation between you and your brother?"

An irritated sigh escaped me. "It wasn't an altercation, it was just . . . you know, brother-sister crap. No big deal. And no, O'Brien didn't see it because I don't think he'd come in yet."

Bulldog mouth twisted to one side, Yergins studied me. "And did you and O'Brien flirt?"

My chair made a rude noise as I scuffed it up close to the table. "Jesus, who told you all this shit?" I pictured the guys at Daisy's — all friends of mine, I thought — happily telling Yergins that I'd punched my brother and tried to pick up an ex-con within the same five minutes. "Okay, yeah, we kinda checked each other out, but that's it."

"And you knew he was on parole before you met him?"

"Yeah, Cal told me. Can I go now?"

"One more thing. What was O'Brien's attitude when you told him about the body?"

I furrowed my brow, trying to remember something other than my own huge troubles. "He was . . . I dunno, worried I guess. Then he was worried about me. He made me some tea." What a sweet guy, I thought, squashing down a little smile.

"How'd he seem when you first came into the bar?"

"Fine. He was cleaning, and seemed okay until I told him about the . . . about Junie." My mouth trembled and I looked down at the floor. "Can I go?"

The officers glanced at each other, and Yergins shrugged. "Yeah, okay, but don't plan any trips for a little while."

In the police station hallway, I wasn't surprised to see Jackson O'Brien sitting dolefully on a battered wooden bench, looking a lot worse for wear. With him was a petite blonde, chirpy as a canary, who appeared to be lecturing him in a strong south Boston accent on the virtues of positive thinking. "That's what I'm sayin', Jackie. You say it's the truth and I believe you, but you gotta convince everyone else by the way you act. This negative attitude isn't gonna get you anywhere."

O'Brien frowned, then noticed me and stood. "Hey, Maddie." He came toward me, leaving the peppy little blonde in mid-cliché to put a hand on my arm. "Jesus, I'm sorry about your brother. I had no idea that's who it was."

Good Lord, was this sympathy? There'd been so little I hardly recognized it. My eyes stung, but I shrugged it off. "Yeah, well, what are you doing here?"

The tiny blonde bounced between us like a miniature guard dog. She looked about fourteen, tops. "Who's this?" she demanded. Few people over the age of ten have to look up at me, but I had a couple of inches on this one.

"This is Maddie Maxwell. Maddie, this is Debi." The way he pronounced it, I just knew it was spelled with an "i." "My parole officer."

Debi, who smelled like a Nilla Vanilla wafer, gave me a

sympathetic smile and stuck out her hand. "Maxwell, huh? Was it your husband who died?"

"Brother." I let her wring my hand as I studied her face. Okay, she was at least twenty. Probably older, if she was a parole officer. Standing next to the jaded, long-limbed Jackson, she looked like a doll fresh out of the box. I wondered how they'd gotten paired up.

"God, I'm sorry. That really sucks." Hm, maybe she was fourteen after all. "But look, Jackie here says he didn't do it, and I know he's telling the truth, so . . ."

"Wait a minute, they think *you* did it?" I asked Jackson, who nodded miserably. "God, I thought they thought *I* did it. They were sure implying it in there."

"I'm sure it's just a routine investigation, nothing to worry about for either of you." Debi smiled and patted us both. "They're not gonna hold Jackie. No evidence, just routine when a parolee moves to town." She gave 'Jackie' a chipper punch in the arm and he winced and gave me an embarrassed smile. "No problem, huh, Jackie? I'm gonna hit the little girls room and then we better get you home. I've got a four-month-old who needs his Mommy." I was amazed that a woman with a small baby could have any energy at all, let alone this mind-numbing level. With a sick pang, I remembered my own potential little bundle. Shitstorms happen. Guess I was overdue.

O'Brien wilted back onto the bench and patted the space next to him. "So, Maddie, how ya doing?"

Trying not to worry about how awful I must look in the unflattering yellow glare of the hallway lights, I shook my head. "I dunno. Just numb right now."

"Were you close to your brother?"

"Not since we were kids." Picturing Junie's fourteen-year-old face, fresh and freckled, I flinched and O'Brien put a long, tattooed arm around me. "It's fucked up what happens to people when they drink," I growled. I thought about my dad, I thought about Junie, I thought about me — not that I was an alcoholic, but — anyway, then I thought about that positive pregnancy test, and I thought about drowning myself in the water fountain down the hall. "Jesus. Now there's only me and Gabe."

"Gabe?"

"Our little sister — holy shit, Gabe!" I almost knocked the bench over as I jumped to my feet. "I've got to call her and let her know what happened. She's going to freak. And I've got to see a doctor."

"Whoa, hey, okay." O'Brien helped me on with my jacket. Down the hall, Debi came out of the ladies room, saw us, and paused discreetly by the fountain for a drink of jet fuel-laced town water. "Why you gotta see a doctor? You okay?"

"Yeah, just . . . God, sorry, really, it's probably nothing." Jackson O'Brien buttoned the top button of my coat and looked down at me, that devilish half-smile on his face again. Something deep inside me convulsed . . . something strangely warm that I hadn't felt in ages. Damn, damn, DAMN. "I gotta go."

Those warm gunmetal eyes riveted onto mine. "Just for the record," he drawled in a soft voice, "I didn't kill your brother."

Chapter 6

After leaving a terse message on my baby sister's answering machine — just saying I had bad news about Junie so call me back — I aimed Molly at the office of Dr. Cory Brand, ObGyn, where I loudly demanded immediate attention. To keep me from upsetting the serenity of the cozy pink waiting area full of pregnant women and mothering magazines, the nurse whisked me into an exam room and shut the door.

After a twenty-minute wait, an irritable PA took my blood. I was staring at an oversized plastic womb with a removable baby when she returned and confirmed my pregnancy. Her eyes had widened and her manner was suddenly sympathetic. Was she worried about a lawsuit? I wasn't going to reassure her. She rushed off to get the doctor, thrusting a magazine at me on her way out the door. Like I wanted to read *Good Housekeeping* right at that moment. Thank God Dr. Brand appeared immediately, with a cheery, "Well, well, well, Max, let's give you an ultrasound!"

I squinted at the computer monitor as Brand glided his greased-up ultrasonic mouse over my belly. A classically good-looking guy with beach boy hair and eyes, he enjoyed a reputation as the best gynecologist in the region. I'd suspected for a while it wasn't his clinical skill that had the local females flocking to him. Now I was pretty sure of it.

"There's the tumor, hasn't changed much since the last time we looked . . . oh, and there's your baby." He wiggled the mouse to focus on a peanut-shaped object. "My goodness, you're further along than I thought. I'd say about two months, give or take."

I battled down a bunch of confusing emotions and cut to the chase. "Excuse me, but didn't you say I'd stopped ovulating?"

"Well, apparently, you started again." He gave me a boyish grin that made me want to smack him. Hard. "Let's see, it's mid-February, and you're not sure when your last period was? By the look of the fetus, I'd guess you're due somewhere in September, but that's subject to change." He patted my knee and winked. "Congratulations."

I felt like I'd crash-landed in the Twilight Zone. "But — what about the operation?"

His baby blues widened. "Oh, we'll cancel that. We can't operate on a pregnant uterus."

I struggled to a sitting position, trying to absorb this mind-blowing reversal. "But you said the tumor had to come out. You said there was no room for a baby. How can it survive with that thing in there?" I was on the verge of tears, which pissed me off.

Another reassuring smile, this one with appropriate clinical concern. "It'll be a high risk pregnancy due to the tumor and your age, but Max" — he rested a manicured hand on my forearm — "many women with larger fibroids have carried full-term babies."

I counted to ten. "So everything you've told me over the past few months just flew right out the window, huh?"

The blue eyes grew wary. "Is this an unwanted pregnancy, Max?"

My blood pressure shot through the roof. "Well, it's a big fucking surprise based on your diagnosis, *Cory*." Fury dried up my tears.

Now guardedly neutral, he handed me a towel to mop the goop off my belly. "I'm as surprised as you are, believe me."

He didn't seem sorry when I asked for a referral to another ObGyn.

I had a meltdown in my truck on the way to Hawk Marsh High. It involved a lot of variations on "Oh my God": repetitive chants, sudden bursts, long drawn-out moans. I thought about babies, tumors, malpractice suits, Junie, Bart, Nick, Dad, God knows what. I had to get it out of my system quick. I had to leave my raging hormones in the parking lot so I could talk reasonably to the principal, who hated my guts, and my students, who for some fucked-up reason liked me. Maybe because they sensed I was as clueless as they were.

When I entered the school, it felt foreign to my overloaded mind. I crept down the institutional beige hall to the main office, seeing every crack and stain with unaccustomed eyes. The fourth period bell shrilled, startling me. Trying to act normal, I struggled toward the office against a surge of students.

Lizard-faced principal Ron Gorman happily granted me the rest of the week off. He and his appropriately named secretary, Dolores Bagg, didn't even bother to express insincere sympathy about Junie's death. I left the office wondering what I had done to earn myself so many enemies in such a small town.

In the dust of my woodshop classroom, Libby was supervising a study hall for my automotive class. She swooped down on me and hugged me, as the kids stared and whispered among themselves. They must have heard about my brother. Libby dragged me out into the hall for some semblance of privacy. "Oh my God, Max, I'm so sorry about Junie! How are you doing?"

"Fucked if I know. I haven't even talked to Gabe yet, and the police just interrogated me like they think I killed him or something." Libby put a hand to her mouth in a silent-movie gesture of shock. I took a deep breath and went on. "And you know that EPT you got me yesterday?" God, was that yesterday? It seemed like ages ago.

Libby looked ready to pass out as she squeaked, "Positive?" I nodded and filled her in on my meeting with Dr. Brand. She kept herself under control for once, probably because the kids were watching us. When I was done, she breathed deeply and whispered, "How do you feel about it?"

"I . . . don't really know. I mean, how the hell am I supposed to know? I should be happy, I guess, but . . ." I shrugged, indicating I wasn't sure what *happy* felt like, which was unfortunately true. "I'm still freaked. I mean, I thought he'd say I had to have an abortion or something. And by the way, that fucking doctor . . ." An immense junior sitting near the door looked up at me and clucked his tongue prissily. I lowered my voice. "I've just got to take some time off, so I can sort it all out, deal with Junie's funeral, whatever. And I really have to tell Bart, even though I kind of dumped him last night."

She frowned. "You have to tell Bart about this? Why? He'll just freak out on you, won't he?"

"No, Lib, it's only fair. I have to tell him." I was very, very rigid when it came to rights, and I felt strongly that Bart had a right to know about this. His reaction was his problem.

At least, I wanted to believe it was.

"Well, have it your way. I'd better get back in there before they start copulating on the drafting tables." Libby smiled. "I'll call you later, Mama Max." She gave me a parting squeeze before she swung back into the room.

Back at my tiny fixer-upper, I flopped onto the creaky sofa and forced myself to behave like a semi-responsible adult for once. I called Bart's machine and asked him to stop by after he got off work, then made an appointment at the funeral home. I hung up wondering again where the hell my brain had been lately. Or rather, most of my life.

To distract myself, I wandered into the underused kitchen and, wonder of wonders, washed the stack of dishes moldering in the sink. Even this novel activity couldn't stop the nagging in my head.

The affair with Bart was unintentional; I practically sleepwalked into it. I was pissed — hurt pride, most likely, since I was usually the dumper, not the dumpee — when Nick Jurgliewicz ditched me after his wife tried to kill herself. It was all a big control move; she knew if she acted crazy enough he'd run to her rescue. A couple of weeks later, Bart started flirting with me at the WunderBar, and the next thing I knew I had a boyfriend. I didn't even want one, but sometimes I'm so half-assed . . .

The phone rang. I dried my hands on a ragged towel, ran to the living room and answered, "Yeah?"

It was my sister Gabe, returning my call. I quickly filled her in on the Junie situation, which some old friends had already called and told her about. Naturally, she was furious not to have heard it from me first. She cried a little, not knowing him as well as I did and being a diehard traditionalist. When I told her my plans to have him cremated with no ceremony, she practically jumped through the phone at me. "He has to have a Christian burial!" she wailed.

Good Lord, how could I have forgotten Gabe had been born again back in high school? And that Junie, human waste product that he was, was her precious kiddies' uncle? Granted, they never saw him; even Gabe's level of denial didn't stretch that far. But family was family, and Gabe insisted on making all the funeral arrangements to give him a fighting chance at the pearly gates. Thank you, Jesus.

I actually felt sick when Bart knocked on the door at twenty minutes after five. I opened the door to accusing eyes. "What the hell are you thinking?" he demanded, pushing past me and parking his non-existent butt on my favorite chair. "The police called and asked me if I was with you last night."

Wow. What a difference between Bart's unsympathetic reaction to my brother's death, and Jackson O'Brien, who had been considerably more inconvenienced. "Holy shit, Bart, Junie's dead and the police needed my alibi. Isn't that, you know, slightly more important than your paranoia?"

"How am I supposed to know where you went after that stupid fit you threw?"

Sitting on the edge of the swaybacked sofa, I swallowed hard. "What did you tell them?"

"I told them you'd been on edge all evening, then suddenly freaked out and took off for no reason." He looked smug, as if pleased that he'd been able to make me look like a homicidal maniac.

My jaw hit the floor. "You said that?"

"Yeah." He shrugged. "You're supposed to tell them the truth, right? Well, that's the truth."

I blinked hard. "Bart, um, first of all, that was my *brother* whose body I found. I'm kinda depressed, and now you're making me look guilty to the cops. I'd like to thank you for your sympathy and support, but we really have to talk first."

"What? It's not like you were close to Junie. Anytime you talked about him you were bitching. And I wasn't making you look guilty, I just told them the truth." He looked at me with baggy, red-rimmed basset hound eyes and added, "Hey, it'll probably be in the papers that we were together, and it's not going to help my divorce. So maybe we're even, huh?"

My eyes squeezed shut against his smug, resentful face.

"Forget about Junie for now. We need to talk about something else."

"I'm grabbing a brew first." He shuffled into the kitchen and returned a moment later sucking on a Sam Adams. I was aghast at how at-home he was, after just a couple of months. Did I allow that? I grabbed the chair while he was gone and leaned forward as Bart spread himself across the sofa. "I'm sorry to be such a bitch, but this is kind of serious," I blurted as I clenched my shaking hands.

"Was I right?"

I was blank. "Right about what?"

"That message I left. You were pissed because I was talking about my ex?" He looked smug again.

"Oh, God, I haven't even listened to my messages." I glanced over at the machine on the end table and saw the blinking red light. "Anyway, why would that piss me off?"

"You know . . . maybe you were jealous."

It was a real struggle not to laugh or puke. "Uh, no, that wasn't it. Sorry. It was . . . it's the way you talk about her. It's the way you always talk about both your wives, like everything was their fault." He didn't get it so I tried again. "There's a point where you stop being a victim and start being an asshole." I should know, huh?

Bart spluttered indignantly over his Sam Adams. "Hey, you can ask both my exes. They'll tell you I was a great husband!"

"Even the one that's ditching you now?" He barked an affirmative; I got up and wandered to my miniature fireplace, poking at the fluffy gray ash with my foot as I shook my head. "Well, Bart, that's more than I can claim for myself. I mean, my exes would happily fill you in on what a pushy bitch I am, my nasty temper, et cetera. I'm no better than them, and I won't pretend I am." I realized I had completely derailed.

Talk about avoidance.

"Jesus, Max, you're not that bitchy." Relaxed now, Bart took a pull off the bottle and smiled beerily. "I mean, you've got a temper, like last night, but you're usually pretty easy-going."

Ambivalent is the word you're looking for, I thought. Shit. I was dismayed by how distant and cynical I felt. Had I felt this way all along? Why had I been seeing him? What was wrong with me?

Summoning my inner Scarlett O'Hara, I postponed introspection. "Look, Bart, this is really hard, so let me just say it."

"Yeah, Max, go ahead." He leaned back on my sofa, his linty black socks resting on my homemade coffee table. Ugh.

I sank back into my chair. "Okay, here goes." I sighed. "I had to see the doctor today. For another test."

"Another one? Has something changed?"

My heart pummeled my sternum. "Yeah, you could say that. It turns out I'm pregnant."

Bart stared at me like I'd suddenly turned inside out. Goldfish eyes protruded, chinless jaw hung slack for at least a full minute. Finally he managed to gasp out an unsurprising, "By me?"

Opening my mouth would have been a mistake, so I just nodded with clenched teeth.

"Oh Christ. Oh God. Max, how the hell did that happen?" He slammed the beer bottle onto my coffee table and leaned toward me. "You told me you couldn't!"

"The *doctor* told me I couldn't. Apparently he was wrong."

His eyes got slitty and suspicious. "Are you sure?"

"Yes. I took two tests and both were positive."

"I mean, are you sure he said you couldn't get pregnant? Last month you said you never realized how much you wanted a kid."

"I was drunk when I said that." I didn't remember, so that was pretty likely.

"How do I know you didn't just use me as a sperm bank?"

I forced myself to think before I spoke. After all, it wasn't his fault he was so ignorant. "I promise you, Bart, I did not lie to you and I did not use you. The only fucked-up thing I did was to trust this alleged specialist. I assure you I did not develop a tumor just to fool you into knocking me up. Okay?"

He was clearly unconvinced as he paced the scarred hardwood floor, running his fingers through his thinning hair. I guiltily forced down the fear that my baby would have no chin and no brain.

"Christ, what if Irene finds out?" He stopped to glare at me. "Have you told anyone?"

"Just the doctor, Libby, and you."

"See that Libby keeps her mouth shut, okay? The last thing I need is Irene getting a hold of this." His face darkened with anger. "Jesus, Max, you *know* I already have two kids I'm paying child support for. Christ, I told you I'm *done* having kids!"

I closed my eyes again to shut out his damp red face. "Then maybe you should've had a vasectomy when you were *done,* or at least insisted on using birth control. I wouldn't have objected." I waited to see if that sunk in, then decided not to waste any more time watching Bart's synapses misfire.

There's no need to immortalize the rest of the conversation. It went on far too long and accomplished little more than giving Bart another reason to hate women. I finally threw him out, telling him we both needed time to think about it.

Well, at least now he knew. The worst was over.

Chapter 7

After Bart left, this weird feeling kicked in. It was vaguely familiar, but I couldn't put my finger on it right away. All I knew was I felt like the biggest piece of shit that ever saw daylight. Again I paced the house, but there was no music this time. In the silence, a voice pounded at me about my bad attitude, my big mouth, my drinking and screwing around, and most of all, my unbelievable stupidity. Yeah, now I recognized the feeling: guilt. Blast from the past. I dialed Libby's number, fast. Unfortunately, her tight-ass husband answered, sounding harassed as always. "Yes, hello?"

"Yeah, hi, Morris, it's Max. Is Lib around?" Without answering, he set the phone down and muttered something.

I missed the long cord on my old phone; it gave me something to futz with while I waited. Instead I chewed my lip and wondered if there was any beer left in the fridge, then remembered I shouldn't drink . . . or did it matter? I beat myself in the head with the phone, but didn't manage to knock myself unconscious before Libby picked up. "Hi, Max, what's up?"

"What fucking kind of mother will I make? Answer me honestly."

"Fantastic. Why? You having second thoughts?"

"Try twenty-second thoughts. Jesus, I'm thirty-nine, I hate the father, two people in my family have now died of alcoholism and I'm starting to wonder if I'm headed that way myself. Aside from the drinking, look at the role models I have, I mean, my God, Dad practically killed me and Junie when we were teenagers, and Mom was on some other planet entirely, and . . ."

Libby was gently repeating, "Max . . . Max . . . Max . . ." throughout this tirade, and when I stopped for breath she murmured, "There are options." I didn't respond, still breathless from my outburst. I could hear Morris nagging in the background and Libby sighed into the phone. "I'm sorry, but Morris is leaving on business tomorrow and I've got to get him and the kids organized." In a lower tone she added, "There's a really good clinic in Abneyville . . . Yellow Pages, women's health, something like that. And for God's sake, make an appointment with Cal. You've got issues, girl." And she hung up.

I slumped onto my worn brown La-Z-Boy in front of the cold fireplace, staring into the ashes. I hadn't thought about Mom in a long time, except fleetingly whenever my little sister called. Little Gabe, who didn't remember Dad's drunken rages and thought Junie and I were making things up . . . kinda like my mother, who always said we must have provoked him or he wouldn't act like that.

I switched my gaze from the empty fireplace to the silent TV perched in the corner. Mom. Good Lord. The woman who lived vicariously through television, preferring its brightly colored, laugh-tracked version of reality to the dull horror of her own life. Who could blame her? I remembered my conviction that she'd died to get away from Dad, and my adolescent fury that her death had removed the one protective barrier between him and me. And another vaguely familiar feeling gnawed my gut and stung my eyelids. I liked this one even less than guilt, and I shook it off angrily.

I thought about it — no, I agonized about it — and finally reached what seemed like the only conclusion. At that point, my accustomed numbness returned. I couldn't even tell how I felt, other than relieved to make a decision.

The next morning, my first appointment with Dr. Geary, my new ObGyn, confirmed that decision, although I didn't want to say anything without talking to Bart first. Subdued but resolute, I called him. "Why don't you stop by tonight so we can talk?"

When he showed, he looked extremely wary. Who could blame him? He'd been dating Exorcist Broad for two months and had only just found out. Wondering if he actually thought I'd killed my brother, I led Bart into the kitchen, handed him a Sam Adams, grabbed one for myself — what did it matter now? — and plopped down at the card table and chairs that served as my dinette set. "Look, I'm sorry I put you through all that. All I can say is, I'm really freaked here."

Bart looked at me morosely. "You're freaked? How about me?"

I closed my ears to his me-me-me stuff. After all, was I any better? "Yeah, I know, but think about it. I mean, I was told no way was I ever going to get pregnant, I was about to lose my organs, and suddenly, oops, I'm knocked-up. It's enough to push anyone over the edge, and I'm only about two inches away from there on a good day." That roused a weak smile from him, which made me feel slightly less horrible. "And then, fuck, I find my brother's body. It's been a teensy bit tense. Can we just call that forty-eight hours of temporary insanity?"

His face was unreadable. "What about the baby?"

My eyes slid from his as I drank deeply from the bottle. "Well, actually, it's pretty iffy."

"Meaning what?"

I played with a scrap of plastic peeling from the tabletop,

striving for nonchalance. "My new doctor says this baby might not stick. The tumor's a big problem. So's my age. And it's my first pregnancy. Three strikes. He said even if it survives the first trimester, it could still be really premature. Also he said the placenta might attach to the tumor instead of the baby." Bart's hands twitched toward his ears. Men just can't handle that shit, can they? "Anyway." I took a deep, shaky breath, knowing I had to ask. "What do you want to do?"

"I can't support another kid, Max." His tone was rigid.

I made myself say it, since I knew he wouldn't. "So you think abortion?" The word came out harsh and jagged.

We looked at each other a long minute. Bart set his beer down and sighed. "God, I couldn't ask you to do that."

"I know, but . . ."

His eyes snapped back to mine. "Would you consider it?"

I'd only considered it nonstop for twenty-four hours. I thought I'd made up my mind, but the words staggered from my mouth. Who knew I was such a sap? "Seeing as this baby's chances are pretty crappy, maybe it'd be best." My throat hurt as I spoke. "Plus I think I'd be a really shitty mother. I'm too much of a fuck-up to have kids. Plus I've been drinking, like, almost every night lately, which is really bad in the first months. Plus I'm old and it might have other problems even if it survives the coconut." Why did I sound like I was trying to convince myself? Another long drink of Sam washed the hurt down into my chest.

Bart's spaniel eyes were hopeful but concerned. "You sure?"

I shrugged and nodded, keeping my lips pressed tightly together. He pulled his chair next to mine and put his arms around me. "God, Max. Thank God."

For what, I wondered as I wrapped my arms around Bart, chugged the remaining ale behind his back, and rested my head on his shoulder. What the hell? I could use some comfort. Without another word I led him upstairs.

Our lovemaking was more passionate than usual, probably because Bart was so relieved and because I wanted to smother the ache in my chest. How was he to know my cries were not ecstatic moans, but bursts of emotion that had nothing to do with sex? When we lay back on the pillows, damp and exhausted, he glanced at the clock. "I've got to run. The girls are coming around seven."

Bart's two daughters, Rachel and Sally, stayed with him three nights a week. My relief that he was going gave me a guilty twinge. "Look, go ahead, I'm just gonna stay in bed. I haven't slept much the past two nights."

Bart dressed, gave me a quick kiss, and took off. I went to the bathroom, completely drained and numb — until I glanced at my panties, then at the toilet paper, and finally into the toilet itself.

Blood. Big gobs of it, dark and thick and scary.

When the harried emergency room nurse saw all the blood and I told her I was pregnant, her forehead creased with sympathy. "Oh my God, I'm so sorry." Her immediate assumption that I'd miscarried chilled my gut. Bizarre.

It turned out my new doctor had just delivered a baby and was still around somewhere, so the nurse sprinted down the surreal hospital corridor to find him. Pretty soon gray-haired, bespectacled Dr. Geary arrived and peered up my crotch, making little *mm-hm* noises. "Any cramping?" I shook my head. Speech was impossible; I held my breath the whole time, shoving down the ache that was trying to overwhelm me. I just lay there, feet in the stirrups, waiting for the bad news. Bad? Isn't this what I was going to do anyway? Hey, this way it was free.

Finally he whisked me to an ultrasound machine, squirted silicone gel onto my belly and shoved the little mouse around until he found what he was looking for. "Ah, there it is."

To my amazement, the peanut appeared on the screen.

I stared at it, bewildered, with a surge of something very much like . . . joy?

"Everything's okay, Madeleine. Your cervix is still closed up tight and your baby's just fine. Let's take a picture, okay?" He jabbed a few keys, waited a moment, and with a weary smile handed me a shiny gray printout of the peanut. I couldn't take my eyes off it as he talked. "What's happening is normal. The tumor is breaking up a little due to the pregnancy hormones. It'll grow again, probably even get bigger during the pregnancy, so this doesn't mean it's going away." He paused, fixing doubtful blue eyes on me. "I want to emphasize that this is a high risk pregnancy. Yes, as Dr. Brand told you, it *is* possible to carry this child to term, or close enough, but you'll have to make some sacrifices if you want that to happen."

"Like what?" All I could do was stare numbly at the peanut's image and wonder at the intense wave of emotion washing over me.

"Did you have sex recently?"

"Yeah, tonight." I turned the picture another way, barely breathing, as I contemplated the minuscule, blurry smudge that was my baby's head.

"Well, I strongly advise you to avoid intercourse for now. Definitely for the next few weeks, then we'll see. The tumor is positioned near the cervix, which could cause some serious problems. Also, don't lift anything over, say, twenty pounds. Finally, and this is a tough one, especially for someone in your situation: do whatever you can to keep your stress level down. Meditation, naps, time off from work, massages, whatever you need." He sighed and frowned at me worriedly. "Do you understand?"

My head independently nodded agreement to all of it. When I tried to bring up abortion, the words stuck, wouldn't budge. I finally just thanked Geary, who told me to go home and put my feet up and the bleeding would stop soon. He patted my arm absently and bustled off.

I sang the "oh my God" chorus again as I drove from the hospital in the frosty gloom. I had to, had to, *had to* talk to someone right this fucking *minute*. I thought I'd made up my mind, but now I was wondering if I even had one.

I drove by friends' houses in search of a shoulder. The best possibility, psychotherapist-turned-bartender Cal, had his porch light on and an empty driveway. Damn. All the lights were out at Libby's; her husband was traveling so she'd probably tucked the kids in early and rented a porno flick, knowing her. At Bart's house, right around the corner, TV colors played on the curtains. But his kids were with him, and I was a big secret, so that was another dead end. And come to think of it, he was the last person I wanted to talk to.

As my truck bumped down Skiff Neck's main drag, I saw the lights of the WunderBar glowing pinkly down the block. Relief whooshed through me; the pub was still open even though the streets were dead. And if Cal wasn't there . . . maybe Jackson O'Brien would be. Hopefully Alison wouldn't.

I screeched into a parking space on the street, praying for Cal. My anxiety level had hit the sky again. How the hell was I supposed to avoid stress?

As I slapped the heavy wooden door open, rollicking blues crescendoed at me; Percy Mayfield's *Nothin' Stays the Same Forever* struck me right between the eyes. I stood dumbstruck in the middle of the floor, a chill shuddering my insides. A premonition? The last three words of the song echoed in my brain as I scanned the darkly paneled, dimly lit décor for help, comfort, reassurance, another warm body. And that's when Jackson O'Brien stepped from the shadows near the bar and rumbled, "Hey, it's you again."

I waved weakly and slumped onto a chair, dizzy and exhausted. Jackson frowned worriedly. "You okay, Maddie?"

"It's Max," I corrected. "Is Cal around?" Jackson shook his head, still frowning. I debated for a moment whether to stay, whether I could keep it together, and mostly whether I wanted to be alone with this guy. I mean, they suspected him of killing Junie . . . but hey, they also suspected me. Finally I thought, hell, if he kills me, he'll be doing me and countless others a favor. I hauled myself up onto a barstool and almost ordered a Sam Adams, until I remembered something about alcohol and fetuses. So why was that stopping me? What the hell was going on?

My admirer leaned on the bar and spoke with mock-formality. "What'll it be, ma'am?"

"Uh, how about a club soda?" I wasn't even sure what that tasted like, but at least it resembled a drink.

"Sure thing." His smile returned as he spritzed soda over ice cubes and chucked in a lime wedge. "How you holding up? You still seem pretty shaky."

As if I needed a reminder. I buried my face in my hands as the stress I was supposed to avoid swelled inside me. "Don't even ask, okay? Jesus, I find Junie dead, funeral's tomorrow, I have to deal with my wacko, born-again Christian sister, for Christ's sake, and now . . ." I smacked the bar with my fist as questions I thought I'd already answered bombarded my useless brain. "Agh, I'm sorry. You really don't want to know."

"Sure I do." Jackson spoke in a suitably *film noir* tone. "No one else is in the joint, it's almost eleven thirty, we're both stone cold sober, so I say spill."

Despite my angst, a smile quirked the corners of my mouth. I liked his style. "But I hardly know you," I answered melodramatically, adding, "and I really was looking for Cal."

"Aw, I thought we'd kinda bonded a little already." Jackson raised his crooked eyebrows. "And not to be harsh, but if I were you I wouldn't confide in ol' Cal too much."

"Yeah, I know he's a gossip, but . . ."

"Gossip ain't the word." Jackson tugged a pack of Camel Regulars from the torn pocket of his threadbare T-shirt and eased his jean-covered haunches onto a stool. "I already know more about you than I should so early in our acquaintance." He somehow implied he expected to know me pretty damn well, as he tapped out a cigarette and lit up.

"What the hell's Cal been telling you?"

Jackson took a long, deep drag. "Oh, let's see. I know about your old man."

I rolled my eyes. "Who doesn't? It's hard to keep town drunks a secret." I drank from my glass and almost spit it out, then remembered it was club soda, not beer. Man, I was going to have to get used to that.

He settled back on the stool, his voice matter-of-fact. "I know he used to beat the crap out of you. And" — a dramatic pause for tobacco inhalation — "I know you put a teacher away for rape when you were just a kid." He blew smoke out the side of his admiring smile. "That musta took some balls."

"Ovaries," I corrected automatically, shaking my head. "Cal told you all that, huh?"

"Yeah, 'bout five minutes after we met. He's like a psychological tour guide to this place. For every face, there's a few dirty little stories." Taking another deep puff from his unfiltered Camel, Jackson leaned his head back and examined me from behind a lush fringe of eyelashes Libby would have killed for. "He tell you anything about me?"

"All I know is, you're an ex-con working here on parole." Somehow this seemed mild after listening to him recite my past. "But he didn't tell me what you were in for."

The scarred face clouded. "I was in for the same thing everyone's in for. Stupidity." He took a final puff from the remaining inch of Camel. "Okay. So now we're better acquainted. Talk to me. I promise I'm way more trustworthy than Cal." He gave me a friendly what-the-hell grin and crossed his heart with the smoking stub before squashing it in the ashtray.

Suspicious as always, I looked through the smoke at Jackson's tarnished silver eyes. I was about to say thanks-but-no-thanks when I saw something behind the wry expression and the semi-leer . . . something kind, sympathetic, intelligent, and all too familiar with pain.

And blam, out of nowhere, I had this whoosh of intuition that I could trust him. Maybe it was the seedy past; maybe it was the pain. Or maybe I was just desperate to talk. So I talked.

Jackson listened with gratifying attention as I garbled and raged and moaned my way through the whole convoluted story. I told it for myself; I needed to hear it all out loud, to feel every twinge, to look at what the hell I was going through, to acknowledge at last that I was in some seriously deep shit.

When I finally sputtered to a halt, Jackson stubbed out his third Camel, puzzled and solemn. "So you figured out you wanna be a mom. What's the problem?"

"The father." I sighed. "Jesus, I don't know. He can't help me out — he's already paying child support for two, he's living on the edge, and I . . ." My mouth snapped shut, not wanting the next sentence to escape.

"And you don't love him." His eyes squinted in his gaunt face, and I squirmed, forced myself to focus, to say it out loud.

"I don't love him." It lay there on the dark gleaming wood of the bar, ugly and twisted. I shifted my gaze, but it wouldn't go away, not even when I hid my eyes in my hands again. "I don't even think I like him. Jesus, I'm such a fuck-up!"

"Naw, Maddie, you're not a fuck-up. You just *fucked* up. It's a whatsis — a verb, not a noun." Grimly, he added, "And anytime you want to compete for Fuck-Up of the Year, come see me. I'll make you feel great about yourself."

"But you have no idea how —"

"Rule number one, don't look back. You can't fix the past — God knows I know that. All you can do is keep history from repeating itself."

This from a guy who looked like he'd been on the wrong end of too many drug deals. "Where'd you hear that? Rehab?" Jesus, my big mouth.

To my surprise, he gave a rusty, rasping laugh. "Actually, I think it was Whitney Houston." I couldn't suppress another smile. "So what are you gonna tell the father? What's his name, anyway?"

I shrugged. "He doesn't want anyone to know he's the father; he's made that pretty damn clear."

"That bugs you, huh?"

"Yeah. I mean, everyone's gonna know I'm the mother. What's the diff?"

"Yeah." Jackson studied me for a moment, then glanced up at the cuckoo clock and started. "Jeez, I gotta close up, keep the place legal." He paused in front of me, solemn and thoughtful. "One thing's for damn sure, Maddie." Reaching across the bar, he placed a long, gentle finger under my chin and looked into my eyes. The air between us hummed when I looked back. "You gotta tell that guy the truth. And the sooner the better."

Chapter 8

Bart came over after work the next night. I had a feeling this would be the last time. At least, I hoped it would.

I sat him down on the sofa without the buffer of beer or small talk. When I told him what had happened, I could tell he was disappointed the baby was still there. He seemed almost excited when I told him about the blood, and distinctly unenthusiastic when I told him how it turned out. Especially the no sex part. I found myself getting angry at his callous attitude, but before I ripped him a new butthole I remembered: we'd agreed I was getting an abortion.

The atmosphere solidified like Sakrete when he finally asked, "Max, what's going on?"

"Nothing." God, what a wimp. My wheels spun as I tried to avoid the inevitable.

Would it be right for me to fake it? Should I . . . could I pretend to love him to make my latest decision all right?

Actually, I didn't think Bart would mind my faking it if I could be nice about it. But the longer he sat there, looking at me with dread in his eyes, the less I felt like being nice. And the less I felt like being nice, the more I realized I had some major personality defects that I'd better work on pretty damn fast, if I was going to be a mother. Abruptly I stood up and walked into the kitchen and pulled the reeking trash bag out of the garbage pail, but that didn't keep Bart from yapping at my heels.

"You've changed your mind, haven't you?" Accusation made his voice even more whiney than usual. I closed my eyes and nodded. "Jesus, Max, why?"

I couldn't speak for a moment; I really needed to collect my thoughts so I wouldn't just blurt it out for once. But all I could think was, God, I'm so tired. Dropping the garbage on the floor, I wandered back out to the living room and sunk onto the sofa.

"Why, Max?" Bart demanded.

"Because — I can't." I choked on humiliation at my weakness, on feelings I had no name for. "I thought I could, but last night when I thought it was gone, I felt . . . well, something happened. And now I just . . . I can't pretend this doesn't mean anything to me." And that's when I lost it.

Bart had never seen me even close to tears, let alone bawling my eyes out. Actually, no one had, not since I was twelve and swore I'd never cry again no matter how hard Dad hit me. He didn't know what to do, so he ignored it and focused on himself, surprise surprise. "What the hell am I supposed to do?"

I grappled for control of my voice. "Whatever you want." I forced myself to look at him. It didn't make me feel any better.

"You want me to get lost, don't you?" Red splotched his cheeks. My eyes wanted to drop but I wouldn't let them. They just kept leaking as I gazed at Bart. "Jesus, Max, I thought we had something good here. I was really falling for you. What the hell happened?" His bewildered, hurt face — however stupid — made me hate myself.

"I can't explain it. I sure as hell can't justify it. All I can do is say I'm sorry. Again." Suddenly I was drained beyond belief. "Look, Bart, I'm so fuh . . ." I stopped, feeling the bizarre need to censor my foul tongue for once, then tried again. "I'm so fried I can't think straight. This has been the week from hell. The doctor told me to rest and avoid stress, and so far I've done anything but."

"You used me." His voice shook.

I squeezed my eyes shut. "It wasn't deliberate."

"How'm I supposed to know that?"

My eyes opened again to take in his confusion. I considered his question, struggling to be fair, then decided I'd been sensitive enough for one day. I needed more practice to be able to keep it up this long. "You're not. Think whatever you like. Do whatever you like. Make me the villain so you can hate me, if it helps. I've got to get some rest before I drop dead." I blew my nose on a crumpled paper towel. "We'll talk sometime soon. Just no more tonight, okay?"

After Bart stormed off into the sunset, I stretched out on the sofa and breathed deep and long. Hairball belched as he settled fifteen warm vibrating pounds on my legs while Booger chewed her rear toenails lustily on the floor near my head, but these familiar comforts didn't soothe me.

Junie's memorial service the next morning — sans guest of honor, due to the ongoing homicide investigation — was mercifully short despite my Jesus freak sister Gabe's involvement. I guess some part of her acknowledged that there really wasn't much to say, although I found myself choking up when Gabe herself read some psalm or whatever. Maybe it was because she still seemed so young to me, despite having been married six or seven years and spawning two little Baptists of her own. I hadn't told her about my own impending heathen bastard; frankly, I was postponing it because I could imagine what she'd say.

It was hard to focus on the service, or even remember what I was there for. Motherhood was distracting, and I actually found myself smiling as I pictured my little peanut curled up in there. Curled up next to the giant monster Curly. I sniffled and Cal patted my hand. I'm sure he thought my tears were for my brother.

After the service, the guests — mostly friends of Gabe and me — gathered in the dank, under-heated church basement for coffee and donuts. Gabe must've had cops do the catering. Well, Dad and Junie had certainly kept them in business for the past thirty years or so. I spotted young Officer Cullinane casing the crowd. At least he wasn't in uniform. He caught my gaze and came over, wiping crumbs from his mouth. "Hi, Miss Maxwell. How you doing?"

"Okay." I shrugged. "It's kinda weird."

He slurped his coffee. "Hey, we're holding someone on suspicion." With an earnest nod, he whispered, "Jackson O'Brien. You know, that guy who's on parole, working at the WunderBar?"

My mouth hung open in dismay, long enough for Cal to waddle up and interpose his enormous gut between me and Gary. "Thanks for taking away our help," he complained. "We hadn't even had him a week yet."

"But he didn't do it," finally burst from my gaping mouth.

Gary shrugged. "They matched some footprints on the beach with his only pair of shoes."

"Oh for God's sake!" I yelled, causing heads to turn. When they realized it was me they turned away again, unsurprised. "You never checked *my* footprints."

"You told us you were there. You found the body. He never even said he'd been down the beach." Triumphant, Gary polished off his coffee and crumpled the cup, making an easy basket in the nearby trashcan.

Cal sighed. "I could've told you Jackson was there. He went down earlier to look at the ocean. It was all new to him."

"Gary, you've been with Yergins too long. Don't jump to conclusions like that. What the hell was his motive?" I insisted.

Gary looked a bit shaken — like we were ganging up on him, which we were — but his voice remained firm. "Look, O'Brien has a history of violence, okay? Bad enough to serve time for it. That's one of the first things we look at when someone like him moves to town."

I looked at Cal, dismayed by this bit of news. Jackson didn't seem like the violent type to me, but then again I barely knew him. And although I thought I'd seen something I could trust in his eyes, God knows my instincts weren't the best.

Cal made a regretful face and stroked his graying beard. "Well, yes, there is that."

Point gained, Gary nodded and went on. "Okay, well, as you know, Junie was in the bar earlier, being a . . . you know, shmoozing for drinks. Did you know he was completely sober when he died? He was probably going nuts with the DTs." Wow, Junie sober? That was a scary thought. No wonder he was hitting me up for cash so early in the month; he must've blown through his disability check in record time. Gary continued, "Anyway, I guess he drove some customers away and started bothering Ms. Shipwood to give him a drink, and O'Brien got mad."

Cal and I exchanged skeptical smirks. "So he killed him?" I scoffed. "God, Gary, if people got killed for being annoying there wouldn't be many of us left."

"True enough," Cal agreed, looking pointedly at me.

"Oh, bite me," I responded, but it had a hollow ring. "I need some coffee, damn it."

I made my way to the white-clothed table that held plastic coffee carafes, Styrofoam cups stuffed with sugar packets, used creamers, and a platter featuring a couple of squashed donuts. Most of the attendees were still hovering despite the dismal layout. After shaking a few carafes, I found one that still had a little coffee in it. I poured it into what I thought was a clean cup, but when I smelled the coffee I set the cup back down and walked away hastily, overwhelmed by nausea and confusion. Junie was dead, Jackson O'Brien had a history of violence, I was pregnant, and coffee made me puke. Life seemed pretty awful at the moment. I sank onto a folding chair against a flimsy divider covered with pre-school drawings of Jesus on a donkey and muttered, "Shit."

Gabe was close enough to hear. She spun around and hissed, "Max, would you please keep your voice down and stop swearing? Have some respect for Junie."

I made a rude noise. "Why? He never had any for me."

"Max!" Gabe squeaked, horrified — God knows why she expected anything different. "He was family!"

"Yeah, and that makes him worth respecting?" I snapped. "Or is it just because he's dead? He's been killing himself for years; we should be happy someone finally finished the job for him."

After a breathless pause, Gabe burst into tears and ran away from me out into the hallway, probably toward the ladies room. "Nice one, Max," Cal murmured.

"Well, she knows it's the truth." But I thought again of the tiny thing sprouting limbs and organs somewhere inside me, and I felt an unaccustomed rush of sympathy for Gabe and her delusions. I don't know what it was, but it made me want to apologize.

As I pushed through the swinging door out into the hall to pursue my little sister, a hand reached out of the shadows of an empty Sunday school room and seized my arm. Startled, I found myself staring into a familiar pair of brown, pleading eyes. Nick Jurgliewicz, my former married lover and fellow teacher. I groaned, "Oh, for God's sake, what are you doing here?"

Alarmed, Nick pulled me into the darkened end of hallway

near the back exit door and whispered, "Max, I'm so sorry about your brother. I just wanted to, you know, let you know I'm here for you."

"You didn't even know I had a brother." My hair fell into my eyes and I pushed it out irritably. "No, Nick, this isn't for me, this is for you. Something for me would involve *you* leaving *me* the hell alone." I tried to pull away, but his hand clamped desperately onto my arm. To avoid making yet another scene, I stopped struggling and summoned a shred of patience. "Okay, what? Make it fast."

Someone pushed through the swinging door into the hallway and headed for the mens room. Nick gasped anxiously and dragged me further into the shadows. If he thought he was being subtle, he was even dumber than I thought. "Max, my God, I love you so much," he choked. "I need you. I can't stand not being with you. I think I'm losing my mind."

"Well, that'll make you and your wife an even better match, won't it?" I blurted.

The big brown eyes watered and he sniffled wetly. Yuck. "What?"

"Nothing. Sorry, that was mean." His spaniel eyes overflowed and he wiped them on his sleeve roughly. A tiny worm of pity squirmed around my heart, but I stomped on it. "Look, Nick, you made your choice a few months ago and I think it was the right one for both of us. I mean, I was pissed at the time, but I got over it. Plus, it's kinda weird for you to be lurking around me like this. I'm sorry to be so blunt, but would you please get the hell out of here?"

"Max? Is that you?" Libby's mellifluous voice floated from the hall doorway, causing both of us to jump and separate. I suddenly flashed back to those overheated after-school sessions with Nick in the auditorium closet, which Libby did her damnedest to disrupt. Nick blushed deeply as Libby wafted over and gave him a saccharine smile. "Nick, how sweet of you to be here. But shouldn't you be getting back to school now? It's almost time for third period." She stood there and stared, arms folded imperiously.

With one last longing gaze and brokenhearted sigh, Nick released me and faded out the back door. Libby sneered, "What did that little weasel want?"

"Oh, the usual." I shrugged. "Me."

"Well, we're about to leave and I wanted to say good-bye. Morris is getting cranky," she sighed. I followed her back into the reception, where Libby's husband Morris waited holding their youngest, a chubby toddler named Tucker. I'd tried to warn Libby that kid would be in for some major humiliation in junior high, but her tightly clenched husband had insisted on using a family name.

Slick, handsome Morris nodded at me politely for a change. "Hi, Max. Sorry about your brother," he said with no attempt at sincerity, and Libby looked embarrassed. Seeing as he'd been an actor when they met, I knew he could fake it. I also knew his opinion of my brother, so I tried to appreciate his integrity rather than resenting it.

After thanking Morris with matching indifference, I found myself staring at Tucker like I'd never seen him before. So this was a baby. I'd have something that looked like this, only smaller, before the year ended. Damn, what a totally weird thought. As I stared, angel-faced Tucker stuffed a slimy powdered donut into — and all around — his mouth; a large chunk broke off and bounced off Morris's starched shirt onto the mildewed carpet. The kid's screams could have woken Junie down at the morgue. Filled with misgiving, I gave Libby a hurried hug and wandered away to find Gabe.

She was sitting disconsolately on a folding metal chair, far away from the refreshment table and the straggling guests.

Without a word she reached up to me, just like she used to when she was a tiny kid. My tough old heart twisted around and I hugged her for a moment, then sat next to her. "I'm sorry for being such a bitch, Gaby-baby," I muttered, "but we have radically different philosophies."

She sniffled. "You scare me, Max. I worry about you."

"Well, same here, kiddo, so live and let live, huh?"

Her delicate face creased with worry, no doubt contemplating the hellfire in my future. "I don't understand you. I mean, you're so smart, you could do anything you put your mind to. Why do you . . ."

I couldn't take this right now, so I cut her sermon short. "Not today, Gabe, please?"

She sniffled again and found a tissue in her dress pocket. "Junie," she gasped between nose-blows. "I haven't even spoken to him in, oh God, months."

"It's not your fault his phone service got shut off."

"But I should have helped him. We can afford it. I just thought . . . I thought I'd be enabling him." Apparently my little sister had been reading some twelve-step books or some other source more contemporary than Jesus.

"Look, hon, Junie having a phone or having money or whatever wouldn't have saved his life. He started drinking when he was fifteen, for God's sake. That's over twenty-five years of nonstop abuse. He was probably dying anyway, just like Dad. That was what I meant to say in there, but it came out all wrong, as usual." I squeezed her shoulders. "It's better this way, Gabe, believe me."

"But he died not knowing Jesus," she whimpered. "I should have tried harder to reach him . . . I should have . . ." Guilt overwhelmed her and she wailed on my shoulder. Cal had lumbered up to us and was listening gravely, stale coffee in hand.

"Gabe, sweetie, you don't realize how far gone he was," Cal said. "There was no reaching him. God knows I tried to get him into a program. And you tried to talk to him, didn't you, when you'd come home from college?"

Gabe nodded, shivering. "When he was in the hospital that time . . . I sat with him and tried to tell him . . . Jesus loved him and forgave him . . ."

I rolled my eyes, not eager to hear Jesus-talk. "See, Gabe, that's what I mean. He was drinking bad enough to be hospitalized back then, and that was what, twelve years ago?" Something vague stirred in my memory; I found myself squinting to bring it into focus. "Yeah, that's when he really started getting crazy. He'd drive around wasted out of his mind, until they took his license away. I remember one night, just a few years ago, when he came over to my apartment about two in the morning and . . ."

Gabe and Cal were silent as I stared at the picture in my mind as if it were right in front of me. I trailed off as the memory replayed, something I'd tried hard to forget and obviously succeeded, until now. I winced and looked away, then looked back, my hand pressed hard against my mouth. "Oh shit." Fingers muffled my moan; I removed them from my mouth and looked at Cal, enunciating clearly this time. "Shit! Cal, is Gary Cullinane still here?"

Cal looked surprised. "The baby policeman?" Looking around, Cal nodded. "Yes, but he's putting on his coat."

"Get him." I sat frozen, my eyes drying up from not blinking as I stared at the memory.

Gabe tugged at my arm. "Max, what is it? Are you all right?"

"Yeah." I inhaled tightly. "I think I just figured out who killed Junie."

Puffing like an elderly walrus, Cal returned with Gary.

Gabe announced, "She says she knows who killed Junie."

Gary sat beside me and waited. When I didn't say anything right away, he prompted me gently. "Miss Maxwell, who do you think killed your brother?"

I closed my eyes as the image returned. "He . . . Junie, I remembered he came over my apartment one night a few years back, when I still lived in town. He couldn't get any booze and he said he was going nuts. I couldn't help him; I didn't want to. I even locked the door and turned out all the lights. But . . ." I swallowed as the donut I'd eaten earlier threatened to reappear.

"What?" I don't know who said it. Maybe all three of them.

"He sat down in the driveway and started . . . banging his head against the pavement. Really hard." My eyes were squeezed shut so tightly that I was giving myself a headache, but the image was still there. "He was bleeding pretty bad. I had to take him to the emergency room. He'd given himself a serious concussion." I looked up at the open-mouthed Gary, heard Gabe whimpering at the description. With an effort, I asked Gary, "Those gashes and bruises — were they definitely caused by someone else beating Junie's head against the rocks?" Helpless, I felt tears flood my eyes and dash down my face. "Or could he have done it to himself?"

Chapter 9

Jackson O'Brien was released from custody when the M.E. admitted that there were no signs of force or struggle on Junie's corpse. In other words, it looked like I was right. It didn't make me particularly proud or happy, but at least an innocent — and, I had to admit, very appealing — man was free.

I was wise enough to stay away from the WunderBar for a couple of weeks while I tried to undo the damage I might have caused during the oblivious first two months of my pregnancy. Actually, I preferred to stay out of the public eye those days; Junie's bizarre death gave Hawk Martians and Stiff Neckers another reason to look at me funny.

After February vacation ended I went back to teaching, but the vibes had changed radically and I felt like an alien. I couldn't look at the kids without thinking about my own burgeoning bundle. My language and attitude cleaned up almost spontaneously as I pictured a wide-eyed infant watching my every move, hearing my every word. My emotions wore me out; I was either grinning like a moron or teary-eyed, either excitedly marking days on the calendar or morosely wondering how long I was going to be allowed to carry my baby before the inevitable loss.

The first Thursday in March, my phone rang just as I settled in for another dull night of TV and cats. "Grab your coat," Libby commanded. "Morris is staying with the kids, Tucker's off the nipple at last, and I'm drinking. Wonder Bra, 8:30, no excuses." She hung up before I could object, so I yanked on a coat to ward off the legendary March wind and headed out to warm up Molly.

When I pushed through heavy oak doors of the WunderBar, Cal greeted me from behind the bar with a delighted smile and wave. Beside him, Alison Shipwood rolled her eyes and turned away. In the words of Jackson O'Brien, the joint wasn't exactly jumping. As Libby beckoned me from the table with the best view of the dance floor, I spotted two people staring me down from the bar. One was Bart, who eyed me dolefully over his pint and looked away when I caught him. The other was Jackson, who toasted me with club soda and beckoned energetically. Bart noticed and glowered even more. I manufactured a glassy-eyed half-smile and headed straight for Libby.

A bouncy young waiter pursued me with a white wine and a Sam Adams ale. "First round's on the house, ladies," he bubbled with a cheery wink. "Dr. Winters orders."

I looked worriedly at the ale, but Libby scoffed, "God, one beer isn't going to hurt. Just wait till you're breastfeeding — it's friggin' torture." She tapped her glass against my bottle. "Bottoms up." Libby took a mouthful of wine and looked like she was having a celestial vision . . . or an orgasm. I tried to wave the waiter back and order a club soda, but he'd vanished as quickly as he'd appeared. Libby murmured, "Oh God, did you see who's at the bar?"

"Yep."

"Do you want to go somewhere else?" Libby's imagination had convinced her that NRA member Bart would go on a killing spree and I, of course, would be his first victim.

"Hardly," I scoffed. "If he has a problem with me, he can talk to me about it. I've been as nice as I know how."

"Yeah, and we know how nice that is, don't we?" After another swallow of wine, Libby tossed her hair back and leaned toward me. "So you've almost made it through the first trimester. How are you feeling?"

Over the past two weeks, I had pieced enough information together to come up with a rough conception date of . . . well, sometime around Thanksgiving; I was either nearing the end of my first trimester or in the beginning of the second. I shrugged and smiled. "Kinda freaked. But mostly happy." Staring at the beer, I rubbed my forehead and looked around for the waiter again.

Libby grimaced sympathetically, resting her still-swollen breasts on the edge of the table. "Are you sure you want to do this? I mean, look at me."

"I am looking at you." I gazed into her cleavage and waggled my eyebrows.

"Oh, stop. I'm serious. I mean, do you have any idea of how exhausting mothering is? And I've had Morris! I don't know what I would have done without him; probably pulled a Medea."

"Huh?"

"She cooked her kids and served them for dinner. How the hell do you think you're going to do this alone?"

I felt myself getting tense and defensive. "Other women have."

She leaned back and took a long sip of wine. "I'm sorry, I have no business lecturing you. I mean, God knows you are the master of achieving the impossible." Another sip. "Maybe I'm just jealous."

I was stunned. "Jealous? Of me? That's a laugh."

"Girls' Night Out at the Wonder Bra? How perfect." After setting a second round in front of us, Cal planted a fruity concoction on the table and lowered his bulk into the chair on the other side of Libby. "I'm taking a break. Let me know if I'm interrupting anything," he said with an air of martyrdom.

"Hey, Mad Max, did you notice my partner staring you down?"

"No," I lied, "but I wondered why my hair was smoking."

"Oh, she's just jealous of you. Don't be so mean."

Why did all these rich women envy me all of a sudden? "You think Ms. Trust Fund is jealous of the town tart?"

"Of course," Cal said. "You've made your own way, you're successful in two professions — teacher and carpenter — and no one handed you a thing. And you openly defied your father to go after what you wanted. She knows she couldn't have done any of that. What do you think she was trying to do, opening this bar and all?"

"I thought she decided it would be kooky fun to work like the rest of us," I sneered. Libby choked on a mouthful of wine. The way she was sucking it down, she'd be loaded in no time.

"No, no, no. The lady's bored. Her husband's long gone. Her kids are all in college or high school now; her job with them is pretty much over. She probably feels useless, and she's only a little older than you, Mad Max."

Holy shit. I realized I'd be retirement age when my kid reached college . . . if I wasn't dead, that is. I seized one of the untouched bottles of beer, then pushed it away again. I hadn't had a drink in two weeks and I wasn't going to screw up now.

Libby started to chime in, but she was interrupted by strident piano music. I perked up as I recognized the opening bars of a blues tune, and peered through the dimness to identify Jackson O'Brien at the keyboard. His weedy hair waved rhythmically and a harmonica perched mouth-level on a stand next to him, but that's about all I could make out so I just sat back and listened.

For openers, he rasped his way through *Built for Comfort*,

loaded with the perfect genitally-generated sound and feel. I glanced at Libby to see how she was taking it; her mouth hung slightly open and she fingered her neckline idly as he broke into a languorous ivory-tickling interlude. When harmonica joined the keyboard, she licked her lips and murmured into my ear, "Mmmm, mmmm, a man who can multitask."

I murmured back, "I like what he can do with his mouth."

Cal took in our lust-glazed stares and shook his head. "No no, ladies, you don't want to go there. Listen to Auntie Cal." We leaned in, ready for some hot gossip. "First of all, that's Jackson O'Brien, he's out of prison on parole — as you well know, Max."

Libby glared resentfully at me, then her two empty wineglasses. I looked longingly at the two bottles of beer and waited for the second shoe to drop. Cal's dramatic timing was almost as good as Libby's.

"Second, he's otherwise occupied." A triumphant, catty smile lit Cal's face as he leaned in closer and stage-whispered, "I get the distinct impression he's been spending time in my partner's pants."

Wow. Now *that* was a surprise. An even bigger surprise was the dart of jealousy in my solar plexus at the idea of Jackson with Alison. "Alison and Jackson?" I scoffed.

Cal shrugged. "She's slumming. I get the feeling her regular squeeze pissed her off and this is her revenge."

"Oh, Alison's mystery man," Libby snorted, her normally proper diction ragged with wine. "I don't believe it for a second. Who'd want to do Alison? Must be like humping a bag of coat hangers."

I pushed back from the table, feeling oddly prudish about Libby's inebriation. Maybe it was jealousy. To distract myself from several uncomfortable feelings, I focused on the music.

I'd had no idea Jackson was a musician. I didn't know a lot of things about him, aside from his sympathetic ear and the strange connection between his eyelashes and my nipples. He was good. He was damn good. His voice was rough but comfortable, like a really satisfying back scratch.

When Cal returned to the bar, Libby leaned over to me and breathed wine fumes in my face. "You know that guy?"

"We met." I blamed my blush on hormones.

Libby studied me with the same cornflower eyes that had been studying me for twenty-five years. "You're hot for him, you little slut. Is he the reason you dumped Bart?"

I scowled. "No, Libby, Bart is the reason I dumped Bart, okay?"

"Jeesh! Sorry." She sucked the last two drops from her wineglass and blew some blonde tendrils from her forehead with a little upward whoosh of breath. "Which way's your sex drive going these days, Max?"

"Huh?" It had been through the roof for the past month, but I wasn't going to share that with Libby. Plus, I was trying to ignore that along with my desire for booze and my penchant for strong language.

"I mean, when I was pregnant with Ceci, Morris and I couldn't get enough of each other. It was incredible! With Hettie, things slowed way down. And with Tucker . . ." She made a little raspberry noise with her pink lips, seized one of my untouched beers and took a moody swallow. "I'm still waiting for things to start again."

"You're kidding me. You? Libby Libido?"

She gave a sharp, cynical laugh. "Oh, my libido is fine. It's Morris. I guess I just don't turn him on anymore. He keeps telling me to lose weight."

"Screw him."

"I'd love to, believe me. Or someone." Over a longer sip of

ale, she gazed at some guys at the bar as they roared over a great Celtics play. The thrusting opening bars of *Spoonful* pumped out of Jackson's keyboard, embellished with harmonica grunts. Libby grabbed my hand and almost knocked her chair over when she stood. "Let's go get another drink." She practically dragged me to the bar, then wiggled her way through a couple of Celtics fans to place our order.

At least I got a good look at Jackson in action, and it was a sight to see. His love of playing bordered on hedonism; he swayed as his long-fingered hands moved over the keys. Occasionally he blew into the harmonica with lascivious enjoyment. When he caught me looking, he winked and nodded, and I got the strangest sensation in my gut.

Gas? I thought unromantically. But no — there it was again, a feeling like a tiny fish wriggling right above my pubes. And suddenly I knew what it was.

Libby returned holding a glass of wine and another damned bottle of Sam Adams, which she handed to me. What's a girl gotta do to get water in a bar, I wondered. I grabbed her for a quick consultation, and she chided, "No, there's no way you could be feeling that this early. It's just gas."

"It doesn't feel like gas, it feels like a fish. Like an eel squirming in there."

She made a face, puzzled. "Well, yes, that's kind of what it feels like, but I'm sure it's psychosomatic. There's no way. It's too early."

But I knew better. A huge smile pushed my big mouth to its limits and I thought, Hello, little eel. I looked back at Jackson and he was still staring at me, transfixed, mumbling the sexually syncopated chorus as his skillful fingers fondled the keys. He crooked his expressive eyebrows at me, and I put my hand on my stomach, closed my eyes, and whirled.

When I opened my eyes again, still smiling like a fool, Bart's basset hound glare greeted me. Alison stood near him on the other side of the bar. She shook her head in disgust and gave Bart a sympathetic pat on the arm. I wondered if, despite his bellowing about not wanting anyone to know the baby was his, he had told Alison, and my smile drooped a bit. "I need some water," I shouted in Libby's ear. "I'll be back in a few." I moved to the bar and planted myself on a stool as far from Bart as I could get. Jackson wound up the song with some incomprehensible lyrics and a slow upward arpeggio.

"Thanks, folks, I'm gonna take a break now," he growled into the mic. "Be back soon." And he switched off the mic and grabbed his cane from the floor.

After a bit of shmoozing on the way, Jackson stood right next to me at the bar, and I mean *right* next to me. He deliberately pressed his leg against mine, then gave me a knowing, " 'Scuse me, ma'am," and moved about one millimeter. Closer.

"Nice set," I murmured as Alison glared in our direction. If they had something going, it seemed pretty one-sided to me.

"Why, thank you, ma'am. Hey, Ally, two club sodas here." Alison spritzed, dealt up lime wedges and slammed the drinks in front of us without making eye contact. "Thanks, babe." I had to stifle a guffaw at anyone calling Vassar-educated Alison Shipwood 'babe.' "So, Maddie," Jackson growled, "I never got to thank you for getting my butt outta jail."

I grimaced, preferring to forget the whole thing. "It's nothing."

"Nothing my ass," he countered. "Not many people woulda done that. Y'know, come out with something like that about their family." I looked away and he changed the subject. "So what's doin'?"

"Not a whole lot, how about you?"

He looked me up and down as he sipped his soda. "Believe it or not, I been doin' some thinkin'."

"Yeah? What about?"

"You." Good God, he was coming on strong. "You have an amazing face."

I wasn't sure how to respond to this, so I opted for funny. "Yeah, it always surprises the hell out of me."

"No, really, look at me."

I looked at him. He scrutinized me in the dim light, then smiled. I smiled back, feeling foolish, and he looked at me even harder. Okay, now I felt really uncomfortable. "What, do I have something between my teeth?"

"No, would you like to?"

"Oh, gross. No thanks, you fucking pig."

He shook his head, clicking his tongue. "Ooh, that mouth. It'll get you into trouble."

Oops, I'd forgotten my resolution about swearing. "It already has, believe me. It's too damn big, for one thing."

"It's more than big . . . I mean, it's not that it's big, it's . . ."

"Huge," I said helpfully.

"No, it's just incredibly . . ." He breathed out, concentrating on summoning the right word. "Sexy. Erotic. Makes me wanna do some serious kissing."

He was pretty close to my face as he said this, and I felt the effects of his words and wondered if he was going to try anything. God, I hoped so. Then I remembered this was a pretty screwed up thing to be wishing for, so I crossed my eyes at him and sipped my soda. He cleared his throat and buzzed into my ear. "Cal told me you teach shop. Must be tough on those horny teenage boys, watchin' you handle power tools."

I stifled a nervous laugh. "Well, Jesus, Jackson, I don't

wear a bustier and thong when I'm working, okay?" God, why did this sleazy bum get me so hot? I was tingling like mad.

"Oooh, you wouldn't have to," he rumbled. "I can see you in one of those . . . whaddyacallums, coveralls . . . pair a' safety glasses . . . maybe a hardhat." His words buzzed in my ear, with a hint of chuckle.

That did it. Even mothers-to-be need a little lust fix every now and then, and I'd been feeling distinctly deprived for the past few weeks. I swiveled my barstool to face him, trapped his leg between my knees, plucked the cigarette from his mouth and rested it between my lips. With a deep puff and a suggestive downward glance, I said, "Oh yeah? And what kind of work would you want me to do for you?"

His eyes gleamed. "I thought maybe . . . drill holes in some sheet metal?"

I thought it over, nodding and exhaling smoke. "Mm-hm, mm-hm. Then what?"

"Well . . . whaddaya got?" he drawled lasciviously, using his other leg to trap me in return. He stared me down like a ravenous coyote. I glanced toward the bar at Alison, who looked like she was shitting ice cubes. Next to her, Bart was just about frothing at the mouth. Rebel Max took over completely, whispering, well, screw them. Even more reason to go along with this game.

I took another drag and beckoned Jackson closer. His aftershave had a warm, spicy scent that almost pushed me over the edge. "I could . . . replace a refrigerator motor for you," I breathed into his ear. "Or put a more efficient . . . water pump . . . in your toilet."

He inhaled through his teeth, a sharp, excited sound. "Oooh, yeah, now you're talking." Another little chuckle shook his words as he leaned in closer. "Then what?"

Another deep drag on the cigarette before I pressed my

mouth to his ear and murmured, "Then maybe I could . . . flush the radiator . . . in a 1963 . . . Chevy . . . pickup."

Jackson's next question shuddered with suppressed laughter . . . or something. "What . . . color?"

His whiskers tickled my neck and I felt a hopeful throbbing down below. Aiming to ruin one of Alison's nicely upholstered barstools, I licked my lips and exhaled into Jackson's eager ear. "B-lllaaaaaa-ck-hhhhhh." I drew the word out and explored every syllable with sensual relish, finishing it with a warm rush of breath.

Neither of us moved for a moment. And I suddenly realized I'd just engaged in a form of sex — tongue-in-cheek, perhaps; verbal foreplay, perhaps; but sex nevertheless — in a very public place, with a man I hardly knew. And this while I'm pregnant by someone else.

I was acting less responsible than most of my students. Not that that was anything new, but it sure as hell had to change.

Abruptly I pulled away, stuffed Jackson's cigarette back into his mouth, and considered slipping an ice cube into my panties.

Jackson remained transfixed for another moment, then took a long drag and removed the cigarette from his mouth. As he was about to stub it out, he noticed a smudge from my lipstick on the tip. "Aw, wow," he moaned. "Aw, shit." After a moment of wistfully studying the burgundy striations, he gave me his best slow, mischievous, sexy grin-and-wink combo. "You better watch it, Maxwell. You are dangerously tempting."

Still grinning, he tapped out the cigarette, dropped the butt in his breast pocket, and limped back to the keyboard.

Chapter 10

"Hey, Miss Maxwell, are you on drugs or something?" asked Artie Durang, one of my more ballsy woodshop students, as I showed him the finer points of sandpapering.

"Yeah, really," a couple of other kids chimed in.

"What?" I thought they were joking. "What are you talking about?"

"I dunno." Artie shrugged. "It's just . . . lately you're like all happy and stuff. It's kinda, y'know, weird. So are you like on Prozac or something?"

The class giggled and poked each other. Kerry Sullivan sneered, "Nice one, Durang," and threw a small screwdriver at my accuser.

"Don't throw tools, Kerry." My frown faded. "That's a legit question. I'm not sure I can answer it, but . . ."

"My mom's on some kind of hormone thing because of her age," someone volunteered. "She was getting really crabby, but she's a lot better now."

"Thanks for sharing," Kerry snapped. Her imitation of my voice and attitude was dead-on and disturbing. Why had the power of my influence over these kids never occurred to me before?

Artie looked at me, fascinated. "Is that your deal, Miss Max?"

I smiled. "I'm not quite there yet." Jaded young faces peered at me over their various projects, all wondering why the hell I'd been so nice lately. Supposedly since I'd gotten through the first trimester, it was safe to tell people. So I told them. "Actually, I'm pregnant."

The sawdust-filled air froze and I could hear the huge wall clock ticking in the silence. Some faces looked blank, others amused, most horrified. Artie summed it up for the class. "Holy shit."

"Artie, watch the language."

Hearing that from me shook the class up even more, but Artie persisted, "Sorry. So why are you happy?"

It sucked having to live down a reputation like mine. "Because I am. Because I want to have a kid. It's cool."

Kerry was bewildered. "But who's the dad? Are you married? Are you gonna keep teaching?"

Oh good Lord, even the teenagers were bigger prudes than me. "The dad's not important. No, I'm not married, and I don't want to be. And yeah, I want to keep teaching. Let's get back to work now, okay?"

Police Chief Yergins brought a half-rotten coffin to my house and told me there'd been a mistake, my dad wasn't dead after all. I tried to tell Yergins I didn't want him back, but he told the policeman pallbearers to set the coffin down on my porch. They walked away laughing.

The coffin lid cracked open and a skeletal hand snaked out and grabbed my arm. Then the upper part of the lid snapped open to reveal — not my dad, but Junie, the gashes in his face rotten with decomposition. He sat up and tried to talk to me through his broken jaw as he clutched me with cold fingers. He wouldn't let go, no matter how much I struggled and fought and screamed. A loud ringing jarred me bolt upright in bed, to discover my own right hand grasping and tugging my left arm hard enough to bruise.

For the first time in my life, I was grateful for a middle-of-the-night phone call. At least it had yanked me out of that nightmare, although it threw me straight into another one.

"Hello?" I gasped. Nothing. "Hello?" Again, nothing. "Well, fuck you!" As I got ready to slam the phone down, I heard a quavering male voice whisper something that sounded like my name. I pulled the phone halfway back to my ear. "What? Who is this?" A sniffle. "Oh for God's sake . . . Nick? Is that you?" Another sniffle. "Get lost!" I slammed the phone down hard, then took it off the hook to avoid a rerun. The nightmare and the call had shaken me up, so I turned on the bedside lamp and contemplated my belly.

Three and a half months, and things were lively down there. Earlier that day I'd sneaked into the Hawk Marsh Salvation Army store and bought some maternity clothes, and then on a whim added some tiny outfits, a bib and a Snugli to my load. For some bizarre reason, I'd put an itty-bitty pair of pajamas under my pillow before I went to bed. Maybe that had triggered the nightmare.

I wondered what had triggered the phone call.

I didn't have to wonder for long. The next morning at school, Nick ambushed me outside the basement boys room again. This time he'd apparently lurked around the corner to see if I went in, then waited for me to come out. This guy *really* needed a hobby.

He lunged into my path. "Max, I have to talk to you."

"No." I started to blow past him toward the stairs, but he grabbed my arm and yanked me with surprising force back into the bathroom. At first my natural fighting instinct kicked in and I tried to knee him in the crotch. If maternal instinct hadn't taken over, Abneyville Medical Center would have been extracting Nick Jurgliewicz's nuts from his nasal cavities that afternoon. But then I realized the stress of a struggle could harm the baby, so as suddenly as I'd started fighting, I stopped. My leg dropped and I stood in front of the empty, rusted towel dispenser, glowering at Nick and panting. Warily he waited for another kick before he started whining. Frankly, I preferred the fighting.

"Are you really pregnant?"

The question startled me, but I held my ground. "Is it any of your business?"

He was shaking. "Well, since you told a bunch of sophomores, I guess maybe it is my business." He paused, swallowed. "Is it mine?"

The hopeful look in his eyes gave me a jolt. I leaned my expanding butt against a wobbly sink — not a good idea — and considered the best response. Okay, in retrospect, maybe it wasn't the best. "Nick, when was the last time we fuh— I mean, we, uh, had sex?"

He sniffled again. "We didn't have sex, we made love."

"Don't kid yourself. We had sex. My point is, do you remember the last time?" He nodded, eyes tearing up nostalgically; I restrained mine from rolling. "Do you remember the *date?*" He furrowed his brow, shook his head. "It was early last October. Now it's almost April. Do the math. Do I look six months pregnant to you?" And I walked past him, pushing through the creaky door, trying to slow my heartbeat to match my nonchalant exit.

But when I got home, there was a message from Nick on my answering machine. "Max, I don't get it. I thought we understood each other. I thought you knew I wanted to get back together after things had settled down. How could you do this to me?"

What was it about that message that set off such loud alarm bells? Nick was such a meek little guy, the definition of "he'd never hurt a fly." In fact, he'd probably be scared of it.

So why was this freaking me out?

Oh yeah . . . I knew why.

I'd dealt with psychos a-plenty: stalkers, obsessive types, drunks, druggies, you name it. Guys who for some reason wouldn't take no for an answer, and didn't understand how I could possibly reject them. And suddenly quiet little Nick, who'd put his tail between his legs and backed away from me as soon as his wife caught on to our affair, was sounding and acting like a psycho.

But I was far from innocent in all this. Hadn't I led the poor guy to believe I loved him because I couldn't resist the thrill of illicit sex on school grounds? Hadn't I pretty much convinced a faithful (if miserable) husband that what he really needed was me? And hadn't my selfishness put his wife's tenuous sanity in further danger?

Why hadn't any of this occurred to me before?

When Libby dropped by that evening, I was stretched out on the sofa, uncharacteristically pale and wan. "Jesus, are you okay?" She felt my forehead. "Is it the baby?"

My eyes got all damp, which they had a tendency to do too damn much those days. I rolled over and croaked out some incoherent ravings. "God, Lib, I dunno. The baby, or the big monster that's in there with it — the doctor says I'm supplying blood to both — no wonder I'm so damn tired — did I tell you they had trouble hearing the baby's heartbeat because the tumor drowned it out? — and now — no, God, wait, you have to hear this." And I struggled to a sitting position and reached for the answering machine's play button.

As Nick's message whimpered out of the tinny speaker, Lib pursed her lips. "What an ass," she sneered. "What a self-centered, egotistical, whiney, worthless waste of chromosomes." She peered at me. "How do you feel about it?"

"Not very good."

"Does he know you're pregnant?"

"Apparently it got back to him."

"Well, he should have the sense to leave you alone. Do you want me to scare him?" Her eyes glowed with pleasure at the thought of torturing an unfaithful husband, the hypocrite.

"No, Lib, I'll do this." Filled with a sudden fierce resolve to 'fess up and protect my baby, I picked up the phone and dialed Nick's direct number at the school, which threw me into his voice mail since it was after hours. Despite my quaking guts, my voice came out surprisingly calm and measured; I recognized it as the tone I would take with a suspected lunatic. "Hi, Nick, it's Max. I got your message. Look, I'm sorry about this, but . . . anyway, you know I'm pregnant, but what you don't know is it's high-risk and I'm supposed to avoid stress. I'm sorry if this hurts you or whatever, but I can't talk to you for a while because I want the baby to be okay." My voice started to break when I said that, so I rushed the last part. "So please don't call me or try to talk to me at school, okay? Thanks."

I hung up and looked at Libby, who grabbed my hand and pulled me into the kitchen. "You need some tea." She flicked on the overhead and gasped. The shocked look on her face — dish-free sink, clean counter, no beer bottles or rotting vegetation — was gratifying to my newly domesticated soul. "Lord, Max, have you been *cleaning?* What's happened to my frat-boy girlfriend?" Gently she pushed me into one of the chairs at the card table. "Okay, I can't believe I'm saying this to you, but . . . that was way too nice, Max." She shook her head as she filled the teakettle and lit the burner under it. "What happened to, 'You're a big asshole and I hate your guts'?"

I thought about this. "Well, for one thing, I think he's kinda on the edge right now, and I don't want to push any buttons. And for another . . ." I chewed my lip as I tried to force a generous thought out my mouth; another thing I'd have to work at. "Well, maybe he wasn't such an asshole."

Libby's mouth dropped open. "Excuse me, but when wifey made a fuss, didn't he drop you like a ton of bricks?"

I didn't appreciate the analogy, given my weight gain, but I let it pass for now. "His wife didn't just make a fuss, she slashed herself up with a knife."

Libby's salon-shaped brows arched. "She did what?"

Nick had sworn me to secrecy about his wife's mental illness, but I didn't really give a crap at this point. "She has this . . . thing, this syndrome or disorder or whatever where she cuts herself when she's upset. Nick told me about it and I looked into it for him. Supposedly it's something some women do when they were abused or molested as kids."

"*Cuts* herself?" Libby's nose wrinkled with disgust; she couldn't imagine purposely disfiguring herself. Frankly, neither could I, but I understood the rage and pain that might drive one to that. I'd had my moments as a teen, especially after the rape. And God, look at Junie and the way he'd killed himself. How many people would choose to beat themselves to death on a rock?

I shook off the warm family memories and got back to Libby. "Yeah, Nick said when she was upset she'd just grab a knife or scissors or a razor blade and slice away at her wrist or her arm . . . her breast once, he said. The stuff I read said the physical pain took the edge off the emotional stuff." I felt another pang of sympathy for Nick's wife and another stab of guilt at my contribution to her craziness. Briefly I wondered what was becoming of my stone-cold heart.

I didn't have to wonder for long. It resurfaced that same evening, when a beer-soggy Bart called to whine at me about my fickleness. "I come home from work and there's no one here waiting for me. Three women in a row dump me for no reason. How do you think that makes me feel?"

I tried to follow this line of thought, but logic didn't play a huge part in it. "Well, Bart, it's not like we were planning a wedding or something. I mean, we just went out for a couple of months. That's it."

"But you're carrying my baby and you broke up with me! What am I supposed to think? What am I supposed to do?" He was genuinely confused, and I couldn't blame him. Yet.

I forced myself to respond as gently I could. "Look, I'm really sorry about how this makes you feel. All I'm trying to do here is be honest. This wasn't planned, so . . ." Over the receiver, a sarcastic snort interrupted me, and my patience started to crack. God, I didn't miss his crap one bit. "Look, Bart, there's no way I could have planned this. I explained that to you."

"Yeah, you explained it, all right."

Steam started to build in my head. "Look, you wanna call my doctor? I'll give you the number right now, so you can get the facts from a professional."

"Yeah, like doctors can't be bought."

I burst out laughing. "Bought with *what*, for God's sake? I'm a shop teacher! I'm in debt up to my ass with this house; I'm probably going to have to sell it to afford the baby." That was the first time I'd said it out loud, and it wrenched me.

Predictably, Bart heard a threat and leaped into paranoia mode. "Well, don't you try to come after me for child support! I've got enough women trying to get money out of me. Irene's going after alimony, and now Nina wants more money for the girls. You said you wanted to do this yourself, and I'm holding you to that, so don't . . ."

I finally managed to interrupt the flow of male outrage. "Jesus, Bart, didn't I just say I was going to sell my house?"

"Well, you do that, and don't expect anything from me."

"Don't worry, I don't expect a Goddamn thing from you," I reassured him, adding mentally, except bullshit.

But when we hung up at last, I had to wonder what made the man so much less of a parent than the woman, at least in cases like mine. It seemed like nothing more than biology. I was carrying the child and that gave me a lot of control; it also gave me the stronger connection and sense of commitment.

But it still didn't seem right. And although I meant it when I told Bart I'd take full responsibility and wouldn't ask him for a thing, it felt as crazy as skydiving without a parachute.

As if Bart and Nick's combined weirdness wasn't enough, concern about the baby increased. There I was thinking we'd passed the first trimester test with flying colors and everything was going to be fine, but it turned out Dr. Geary was even more worried about the second trimester.

"We really need to keep an eye on you now," he told me. "The tumor is growing again due to the pregnancy hormones, and this could cause premature labor. We need to try to keep the baby *in utero* as long as possible. Twenty weeks is about the earliest for a baby to be viable, and that's really pushing it."

My heart sunk. "God, what can I do?"

He smiled reassuringly. "You're doing fine. Just keep watching what you lift, and avoid stress. Try meditation."

How was I supposed to avoid stress with that hanging over me?

But the four-month ultrasound gave me some good news. The amused technician chased the fetus around my abdomen with her greased-up mouse to get a glimpse of heart, spine, brain. "Never saw such a hyper one," she said, smiling. "Drink much coffee?" She glided her instrument around and the oversized jumping bean paused. "Hm. Um, do you want to know the sex?"

I was surprised. "You can really tell? I mean, they have little dicks and stuff already?"

The technician chuckled. "This one's pretty much flashing me right now, so I have a good shot. Do you want to know?"

I swallowed and crossed my fingers. "Yeah, sure."

"Well, this isn't one hundred percent certain, but I'm willing to bet we're looking at a little girl here."

Big breath out. I didn't want to admit it to myself, but this was what I'd been wishing for. And I already knew her name.

Rosalind.

There was no other choice. During the first Hawk Marsh High Thespian production of *As You Like It*, I fell in love with the name and its feisty cross-dressing character.

And there was another, less romantic consideration. Bart already had two daughters. He wanted this one to be a boy; he'd said so repeatedly, during our brief, unpleasant conversations. Maybe another girl would keep him from causing big, horrible problems. Maybe he'd back off, lose interest.

Maybe he'd just disappear.

Yeah, right.

To my disgust, Nick called again about ten days after his first message. I was on my guard then so I never answered the phone, I just let the machine pick up. Usually it was a friend or telemarketer or Bart, and I almost decided I was being paranoid until the day I heard his voice again. This time it was completely devoid of emotion . . . at first.

"Hi, Max, it's Nick. I got your message and I've thought about it a lot. I don't understand. I really want to talk to you." His words sounded stilted, stiff, carefully controlled, like

Libby's drama kids when they first put down their scripts and try to act. "Is there a reason you can't talk to me? Please call me back or come to my office at the school. I still care about you." He paused, hesitated, threw in what sounded like an ad-lib, full of ominous undercurrents. "You have no idea how much."

The machine clicked off and beeped at me as I stared at it. My theory that Nick was going psycho took on this new fuel and accelerated. Perhaps he was already gone. Far gone.

Feeling an overwhelming need for a professional opinion, I pulled the tape from my answering machine — it was an old model that used regular cassette tapes — and drove to the WunderBar to play it for Cal. I tried to quash the hope that I'd run into Jackson.

It was mid-afternoon and business was dragging. Cal stared morosely at the TV over the bar, letting CNN inform him of world events. Morris Langley, Libby's handsome-but-dull husband, sat alone at the bar with some legal papers and a cup of coffee. No sign of Jackson, however. I sighed with regret and relief, said "Hey" to Cal, and gave Morris a nod.

Although his firm was in Boston, Morris handled contracts and agreements for his wealthy neighboring Skiff Neckers. There was more than a bit of social climber in Morris; he was strongly committed to achieving Inner Circle status in Skiff Neck's close-knit society. His good looks certainly didn't hurt, and his limited acting ability served him better as a lawyer than they ever had in the theater. Since Alison wasn't around he was almost friendly to me. "Hello, Max, how are you?"

I suddenly realized I'd hit the jackpot: a shrink and a lawyer, right when I could use both. I quickly explained the situation with Nick, then handed Cal the tape and said, "Pop this in the boom box and tell me what you guys think."

When Nick's message finished whining through the sound system, Morris shook his head and smirked. "Where do you find your men, Max? God, what a loser!" Dramatically, he repeated Nick's last lines in a dead-on imitation: "I still care about you. You have no idea how much."

I had no idea if Morris was disparaging the message or me, so I said, "Shit, Morris, you missed your calling. Forget law and go into impersonation." I turned to Cal. "What do you think?"

Cal rewound the tape and listened to it a few more times, then shrugged and shook his head. "Something very strange about that boy," he mused. "Don't respond, just let it drop. He must feel guilty about how he left things and doesn't know what to do about it."

"Is he nuts or what?"

"Um, well, he's borderline. He may just be going through a crisis, but if he's chosen you as his object you'd better stay pretty far away."

"But how could he possibly call me after the message I left? It was very clear, and I gave him a pretty compelling reason not to call me."

"It wasn't a reason he wanted to hear. To find out you're pregnant, and it's not his . . . well, I don't know what to make of it without knowing the guy. All I can say is, he sounds like a loose cannon, at least where you're concerned. I would avoid him at all costs."

"Oh, great. Why don't I just quit my job?" I turned to Morris. "Is there anything I can do legally to keep him from calling me?"

Morris idly stirred cream into his coffee and yawned. "That message is far from threatening, Max."

"But it's stressing me out and I'm supposed to be avoiding stress. It could hurt my baby. Is there anything I can do at all, given the circumstances?"

Morris pondered this as he studied his manicure. "Not really. Not unless he actually threatens you in some way, and even that's tricky legal ground." He sipped the coffee, made a face. "Just do what Cal says and don't respond. Maybe Psycho Boy will get discouraged and give up."

I had a feeling he wouldn't, but decided to give optimism a shot for once in my life.

Chapter 11

You know how it is when you have a sexy dream about someone, then you run into them the next day? Well, imagine that, and then imagine being pregnant at the same time. By someone else.

Despite my resolution to clean up my act, and despite my distracting personal circumstances — or perhaps to distract me from them — I found myself fantasizing about Jackson O'Brien, endlessly recalling our torrid last meeting, imagining a much more satisfying ending than watching him walk away. Thoughts of him playing piano, giving me grizzled but heartfelt advice, buzzing suggestively in my ear, made my pulse speed up in a way that probably wasn't good for the Roz — so I set about trying to calm myself down and figure out what the big deal was.

Why did Jackson O'Brien have this effect on me? I was pretty far from a starry-eyed teenager, to say the least. Was it my usual raging hormones talking, or was it something deeper? Was there any way it could be — good Lord — actual love in bloom? That would figure, given my usual brilliant timing. So one night I stoked up the fireplace, sat myself down in the easy chair and talked to the only person who wasn't going to give me crap about it.

"What do you think, Roz?" I put a hand on the bump in my stomach. "Is Mama just playing with fire again, or is there something more to it this time?" I thought about the men in my life — for the past few years at least they'd been easy to push around, easy to outsmart, easy to forget. "What makes this Jackson guy so memorable, huh? I bet Cal would say he's like my dad." I thought that over: my dad, red-nosed and beer-bellied, swaggering from shoddy affair to shoddy affair. Shit, that sounded like me, and I wasn't too proud of it.

Could it be Jackson wasn't like anyone I'd ever met before? Mysterious, smart, once dangerous but reformed (according to him) . . . and trying hard to start over?

Kinda like where I was now. I sighed and patted Roz. "Maybe it's because we're on common ground or something. Maybe . . . maybe I have something to learn from him." I felt my heart soften toward him even more at that thought, which was the last thing I wanted to feel.

So I begged off Thursday Girls' Night Out at the Wonder Bra for a few weeks. At first Libby was sympathetic, but finally the excuses and her patience wore thin. She stopped by my house with Cal one mild evening and together they dragged my reluctant ass out of the house for a few hours. "But . . . all that secondhand smoke," I objected as Cal wrapped me in my well-worn Celtics jacket and slapped a baseball cap on my head.

"Come on, you need to do something other than teach, for God's sake," Libby chided. "And Jackson misses you." She smirked.

My heart flipped. "What? Did he say that?"

Cal gave me a knowing smile and pulled me out into the moist early April air. He opened Molly's door for me, then hoisted himself into the passenger seat, causing Molly to list dramatically to the right. Libby leaned in my window to answer my question.

"Not in so many words," Libby responded, "but he came over during his break last week and asked about you. Something really subtle, like 'So where's your hot little friend?' He probably fantasizes about you."

"Oh, come on," I protested, dying to hear more despite her catty tone.

"I bet he'd fuck anything that moves." Usually I loved it when Libby swore; it completely contradicted her angelic appearance. But right now it just sounded spiteful and I didn't want to think about what she was saying. "I mean, my God, Alison Shipwood?"

When I asked Libby why she was taking that so personally, she threw up her gloved hands and stomped off to her silver Miata, pausing to scowl at Cal before she got in. "Don't talk about me on the way, okay?"

Cal smiled noncommittally and started gossiping as soon as we were on the main road, with Libby tailgating avidly. "Miz Libido made a little play for Jackson last week, and got turned down flat."

My mouth dropped open. "Libby hit on Jackson? But . . . I mean, my God, he's hardly her type."

Cal peered into the rearview mirror and checked to see if Libby was close enough to read his lips. She was, and she had her high beams on. "I think she was trying to make her husband jealous."

"Morris? Was he there?"

"He was at the bar, talking to Alison about some legal stuff. Libby was all put out that he wasn't fawning over her, so she started flirting with Jackson." He chuckled at the memory. "Too bad you missed it, really."

"What happened?" I was pretty pissed at Libby.

Cal shrugged. "She was doing her usual eye-batting, hair-tossing thing. Jackson seemed amused but unimpressed. Then he went outside to smoke and she tagged along. She came back in about five minutes looking flummoxed as hell, but wouldn't share the story with me." He smiled again. "Oh, and although hubby seemed indifferent to the whole thing,

Miss Alison was unquestionably seeing red." Behind us, Libby tooted her horn and shook her fist. "And green," he added as we pulled into a parking space across from the WunderBar.

When I opened Molly's door, Libby's dulcet voice inches away made me jump. "So, did you tell Max all about last week? Do you want to know what happened, Calvin dearest?" She was in full cat mode now. "Nothing. Nada. Not a damn thing." Libby shrugged at me apologetically. "I thought he'd take the bait and then I could tell you what a worthless piece of shit he is, but . . . well, he didn't bite." She frowned. "He didn't even nibble." She brightened slightly. "But Morris was definitely PO'd when I told him I thought Jackson was sexy. He slammed around the house for about two hours." She smiled at the memory of upsetting her usually composed husband.

I frowned back as I started to ease myself from the truck and set my feet on the wet, sandy pavement. "Why do you feel the need to prove his worthlessness to me?"

She sighed, fixing those innocent eyes on my face. "Well, I got the feeling you like him and I'm worried that you'll get caught up with another loser. And you can't do that. Especially now."

My blood was starting to simmer, but Cal put a soothing hand on my arm. "She's just looking out for you, Mad Max. Don't get all offended. And anyway, she's right."

After a couple more deep breaths, I was able to sound diplomatic. "Don't worry, guys. I've got too much on my mind to get involved with anyone right now."

Except in my dreams, I added to myself.

I finished sliding out of Molly and *umphed* when I stood. Barely halfway to motherhood and God, I felt huge. Already I waddled instead of walked. I didn't really look pregnant — at least not with clothes on — but my body sure was a different shape. My boobs wouldn't quit growing, my waistline had vanished, my ass felt broad and flabby. To me I looked squatter than ever.

Nevertheless, when I walked into the Wonder Bra, Jackson practically flew off his barstool to greet me. "Where the hell you been, Maddie?" he croaked, that fabulous crooked grin splitting his gaunt face.

I bit the insides of my cheeks to keep my own smile under control. "Just taking care of business," I said, patting my belly.

"Damn, look at that. Startin' to show, huh?" He gazed at the insignificant baby bulge, then at the impressive chest bulge, and his eyes bulged in return. "Whoa. Maddie 'Melons' Maxwell."

"Yeah, well, they don't feel so great."

He opened his mouth and from his leer I knew he was going to offer to feel them, but the look I shot him forced a hasty revision. "So, anyway, welcome back to the Wonder Bra." He gave me another huge smile. "Any special requests? I'll play anything you like. You name it."

My mind went blank. I loved a million blues songs, but I couldn't think of a single one. "Uh . . ." I finally dredged up the last thing I'd listened to before I left the house. "How about something by Screamin' Jay Hawkins?"

Jackson looked surprised, but nodded. "You got it, babe." He glanced at Libby, who was staring determinedly at the TV over the bar. "Hey, Lib."

"Oh . . . hi."

"Any idea why your husband hates me all of a sudden?"

Libby turned to him, surprised and obviously pleased. "He does?"

Jackson shrugged. "Yeah. We got along okay till about a

week ago, and now he won't hardly talk to me. I figure someone told him something bad about me." A sarcastic edge underscored his words. "Any idea who mighta done that?"

Wide-eyed, Libby shook her head. "No. Actually, Jackson, I just told him I thought you were . . . very talented." She dimpled coyly, looking like an oversexed Kewpie doll.

Jackson nodded, then shook his head. "Thanks," he growled. "I appreciate it." He noticed me vainly trying to flag down Alison for drinks. "Whaddya want?"

"Chardonnay for Lib and a large O.J. for me." Jackson hustled behind the bar to fill our order, tiptoeing around Alison, who was deliberately blind to his presence. I sensed some very nasty vibes there.

The vibes grew worse a moment later, when Bart Fulton pushed through the front door and took a seat at the bar. Alison rushed over to him with a Sam Adams and a concerned smile, then jerked her head in my direction. Bart's resentful goldfish eyes moved balefully toward me as Jackson hobbled from behind the bar with our drinks.

"Here ya go, ladies." Libby seized her wine and headed for a table without thanking him. Before I could follow her, Jackson took my arm and whispered, "Hey, I got a little present for you." He pressed something soft and squishy into my free hand. Startled, I raised my hand to find a very cute stuffed seal. I looked back up at Jackson, puzzled and touched. He shrugged. "Well, it's for the baby, really."

"Uh . . . thanks." My chest tightened up at this unexpected gift. "Why?"

Jackson studied the carpet. "Oh, I dunno. Just seemed you were getting a lot of negative shit, that's all." Glancing toward the piano, he touched my arm, then whispered in my ear, "I'm done at eleven. Ditch the bitch and come have coffee with me, okay?" With a quick parting wink, he limped to the piano and positioned himself to play.

My arm kept tingling where he'd touched me. I squeezed my eyes shut and rubbed my feverish forehead, trying to erase the inconvenient impact Jackson O'Brien was having on me. Okay, okay, so he was sexy, he was funny, he was smart, he was unexpectedly sweet, he was . . .

. . . fresh out of prison for some kind of violent crime, he was crippled, he was probably unbalanced, he was . . .

He was a damn good match for me.

Jesus.

"Headache?"

My eyes flew open to find Bart's resentful face about six inches from mine. "No thanks, I already have one," I answered, thinking, *and here's* a damn good match for my boot.

"What the hell was that about?" he demanded.

"What?"

"That little interchange between you and O'Brien. Is he my replacement?"

The puffy violet bags under Bart's eyes indicated lots of beer, which generally led to lots of chest beating on his part. And I was not in the mood to hang around the TestosterZone any longer than I already had. "There is no replacement for you, Bart," I sighed.

"What's that supposed to mean?" He was itching to find fault with whatever I said. I struggled to summon a scrap of empathy, but the little I had was soggy with lust so I just shrugged. "Are you seeing that Goddamn criminal?" His voice raised and cracked. "He beat a guy up, you know. A cop. He beat him up so bad he put him in a wheelchair. That's what he was in prison for." He exhaled beer fumes into my face and I grimaced. "Is this some kind of Freudian thing where you want to date your father? Cal thinks so."

Cal had already told me what he thought, but I was a little

pissed that he'd shared it with Bart. Or maybe he'd shared it with Alison who'd shared it with Bart. "Let's take a walk," I suggested.

"Fuck that."

I forced a hearty laugh, slapped his arm pseudo-playfully, and murmured, "Well, you might like to know you're attracting some attention, and I'm pretty sure you wanted to keep our little thing a big secret. What if Irene hears about you fighting with the pregnant town slut in a bar? What's that going to do for her case against you?"

Fortunately our current bone of contention spoke into his mic at that moment. "This song goes out to my favorite lady shop teacher, by special request." Jackson rolled a bluesy chord and nodded rhythmically. I slipped off the stool, waved bye-bye to Bart with the toy seal, and joined Libby at her table.

When Jackson started growling *I Put A Spell On You* into the mic, I realized he was indeed performing a Screamin' Jay Hawkins song just for me. I was touched for about five seconds, until the overall creepiness of the lyrics came across. Reality check time: I really didn't need another psychotic male interested in me. Nick and Bart were more than enough. But I clearly knew how to attract them . . . was Jackson another one? He seemed to be emphasizing the weirdness of the words . . . was it his twisted sense of humor, or was he really disturbed?

Libby glanced at me, obviously having the same thought. "Well!" she yipped into my ear. "Those eligible bachelors are just lining up around the block for you, aren't they?"

"You should talk," I snapped back. "Those yahoos at the bar are drooling in their Buds looking at you." Three heavily plastered men had been staring Libby down since we arrived. She gave me a little what-are-you-gonna-do shrug and dimpled.

Libby's lecture on the dangers of a man like Jackson went on for the better part of his set. "I think he's probably on a few non-prescription drugs. And you know all he wants is a quick screw. Not the type you want getting all hot and bothered about you — especially when you're pregnant, for God's sake." She took a good slug of wine and her blue eyes sparkled with realization. "Hey, maybe that's why he was in prison!"

"What?"

"I'll bet he can get pretty pushy when he's horny, and pretty pissed off if he's rejected." She seemed to have conveniently blanked out her own fouled play for Jackson. Nothing like selective memory. "If I were you, I'd look out for him."

I thought of the most plausible excuse to get away from this. "I have to pee. Be right back, okay?"

In the one-holer ladies room, decorated with an artsy print of a tuxedoed Marlene Dietrich, I locked the door and splashed cold water on my face, then looked in the mirror. God, I looked awful — short and fat and super-stressed. What the hell made me think I was so hot? Jackson had probably been joking with me. I couldn't imagine anyone being seriously attracted to a little pissed-off fireplug. Angrily I wiped my blotchy face off with the rough paper towels and pushed open the door to the hallway . . .

. . . where I ran straight into Jackson, barreling down the hall with a crate full of sound equipment, cigarette dangling from his mouth. In fact, I practically knocked him down with the ladies room door. "Hey, hey, hey!" he rasped, then purred, "Oh, it's you." I nodded and tried to continue back to the bar, but he got a firm hold on my arm and I was too depressed to struggle. He set down his crate and pulled me toward the back exit at the end of the hallway. "I was afraid you'd left. C'mere and talk a minute."

The alley behind the bar was dark and damp; the stars above were sharp points of light. Stale beer and urine permeated the air around us but somehow didn't manage to kill the romance, or whatever the hell this was.

"So." He took a thoughtful drag on his cigarette.

"So." I forced myself to stop, breathe, think. He had his hand on my arm again; the gentle pressure from his fingers started up my tingling again.

"You afraid of me now?" He smiled, a twisted, rueful grimace.

Was I? I didn't think so, but I wondered what the hell I was doing as I brazenly leaned against the brick wall behind me and shrugged. "Should I be?"

He took one last drag on the cigarette and dropped it. "You sure are hard to read, Miz Maddie." He ran one finger down my arm and exhaled a slow stream of smoke.

And my heart was an industrial piston again. Excitement? Fear? I couldn't tell. He must have noticed, judging from the next words out of his mouth.

"Pretty foolish, coming down a dark alley in the middle of the night with me." I gave him a sharp look, but his expression was melancholy, not threatening. He seemed to be looking at his hand, which rested lightly on my sleeve. After a moment, he looked up with a shadow of his usual leer. "After all, I haven't been alone with a woman in years."

Damn, where was this man a few months before? Oh yeah . . . prison. I squashed the thought with a lame, "Really?"

"Mmm-mmm. Not with a real woman." I wondered what the hell that meant, and thought fleetingly of Alison, but Jackson was exuding so much testosterone I couldn't get my talking muscles to function. "Are you wearing perfume?" Without waiting for an answer he raised my wrist to his face and inhaled. "Oh yeah. Just a hint. Mm, nice. Where else do you put it? Crook of your arm?" I'd left my jacket inside. A sigh escaped me as lips and whiskers tickled a path up my arm; little hairs all over my body stood at attention. "Uh huh . . . behind your ears . . . in the hollow of your throat . . ."

His mouth brushed its way around the course as he described it, and my knees prepared to give out. "Mmmmm-mmmm," he hummed into my neck before planting a warm, sensual, brain-fogging kiss on my mouth. Double-minded creature that I was, I worked a couple of his shirt buttons open and nuzzled his fuzzy chest hair with my face. A gruff chuckle made his sternum reverberate.

I had forgotten making out could be so much fun; I was usually too rushed with Nick, too bored with Bart. Although I knew I needed to stop, I couldn't suppress some encouraging sounds.

Jackson was moaning even more strenuously than I was. He rammed one hand under my blouse as awkwardly as an over-stimulated teenager; his mouth on mine prevented me from protesting. I wasn't sure I could anyway. The thing in his pants felt huge, potentially disastrous for the baby. If Bart's little pencil could cause problems, imagine what this could do. When I pushed Jackson away, he clamped a hand over my mouth. "Sssh," he hissed.

Oh God. He was a rapist, he was a murderer, he was going to do something unspeakable, I was going to lose my baby and it would serve me right . . .

. . . then I realized he was standing stock still, listening to something. I heard the footsteps and sharp voices approaching. The door behind Jackson flew open as if a battering ram hit it. Harsh light from the hallway and Libby's shrill voice cut through the mood like a guillotine.

"Oh my God, get him off her! Max, are you all right?"

Chapter 12

Someone yanked Jackson away from me, and I stood there with my unbuttoned shirt hanging out of my waistband, my bra wildly askew. My dazed eyes took in Libby, Alison, Bart, and finally Cal, who hung onto Jackson's arm looking uncertain. Alison glared at Jackson. Bart tried to do the same to me but it came off more sulky than furious. The overriding expression on Jackson's face was outrage.

Libby bustled toward me, all wide-eyed solicitousness. "Max, my God, are you all right?" Jaw clenched, I nodded at Libby as the steam slowly built. "Cal, I think she's in shock."

"Go . . . away," I snarled through rigid lips.

"What?" Libby leaned in closer.

Behind her, Jackson exploded. "Get the fuck outta here! All a' you!" He shook Cal off his arm and smashed his fist against the half-rotten wood fence by the Dumpster; a chunk hit the damp pavement with a hollow sound. "Jesus, just go away!"

"Calm down, Jack," Cal commanded.

"Calm down my ass! Jesus Christ, I moved here a few weeks ago and I'm already suspected of murder and rape. That's what you thought, right?" Again he smashed the fence with his fist, then turned his back to the crowd and leaned his head against the Dumpster. "Fuckheads."

Cal pushed the hovering Libby aside and asked me, "Was he molesting you?"

Even though my mouth still stung from the pressure of Jackson's hand, I held Cal's gaze steadily. "It was mutual."

Sighing with relief, Cal patted my arm. "I thought as much. Okay, Libby, you've had your moment of drama, now let's do like Jackson says and go back inside." Cal shrugged at me helplessly. "I told her, I begged her, but she wouldn't listen to me. I do apologize. Come along, Miss DuBois." Libby was hauled from the alley, protesting that a rape was in progress and she had to do something.

Bart shook his head at me, blearily disgusted and beyond words. After giving Alison a sympathetic pat on the shoulder, he followed Cal and Libby back into the pub.

Alison lingered a moment longer, her eyes still on the motionless Jackson. Her angry expression started to crumble, but she raised her head and commanded, "Jackson, get yourself together and come to my office. I want to speak to you before we close tonight." Her eyes started to shift in my direction, but she sternly refused to let them acknowledge my existence and walked back to the exit, the queen leaving her jesters. Just before she closed the door, she swatted at a wall switch inside and a bare light bulb glared at us from the side of the building.

I walked over to Jackson, who gave the fence another half-hearted smack. His stance reminded me more of a dejected teenager than a tough ex-con. "Why don't you go?" he asked.

"You okay?"

He laughed. "Me? I'm fine. I'm a fucking murdering rapist." His eyes aimed at me, perplexed. "Honestly, did you think I was . . ."

Casually I rearranged my bra so it covered my right nipple, then buttoned my blouse and tucked it in. "I was a little nervous when you put your hand over my mouth," I said, "but I think that had more to do with my dad than with you." The gray eyes questioned me and I scowled. "He used to cover my mouth and nose with one hand while he smacked me with the other."

Jackson slid his back down the side of the Dumpster until his haunches rested just above the pavement. "Jesus. I don't know why I did that. I thought I heard something, is all."

I nodded, shivering in the damp chill. "It's okay."

He took a deep breath. "I guess it looked kinda bad, but . . . God, I feel like shit they'd think that of me."

"Libby's probably responsible for that," I offered.

"Why?"

"Well, before I left the table, she was hazarding guesses about why you were in prison. I think she got a bit drunk and carried away with her fantasy and . . ." I glanced down at him to see how he was taking it. It was not good. "It's just Libby. I mean, she's really . . . kind of . . ." I couldn't think of how to describe my best friend's turn for the dramatic, so I trailed off.

"A bitch," Jackson finished for me. "I figured that out a while back. But I mean . . . what about Cal? And Alison? Did they think . . ."

"I think Cal came to keep Libby under control. And I think you know why Alison came."

Jackson sighed. "She's pissed, all right."

"You going to go see her?"

He snorted. "No fuckin' way. She can't boss me around like that. I got every right to do whatever I want, long as it's legal." He stood and buttoned his shirt defiantly.

I tiptoed up to another landmine. "I kind of thought you and Alison were, you know, together."

"Who the hell told you that?"

"I just heard it."

"Same place you heard I was a rapist?" Jackson fumbled for a cigarette, came up empty. "Shit, I need a smoke. Wanna see my place?"

I didn't really, at the moment, but I felt like he needed someone to stick with him for a few minutes. "Sure. Is it far?"

"We can get there up this fire escape." He guided me to a rickety cast iron stairway and we climbed one flight. At the top, he tugged open a heavy door, fumbled in the dark for the knob to another, then yanked on a string and bare bulb popped on dimly. "It ain't much, but it's all I got."

A garret worthy of a Dickens novel greeted my blinking eyes. A flat, antique mattress lay on the floor under the sloping roof; the skylight overhead was propped open with a chunk of two-by-four. A lopsided bookcase constructed of scrap lumber and cinder blocks took up an entire wall; the battered books, records, and tapes it held threatened to spill onto the threadbare beach towel that served as a rug. Milk crates and cardboard cartons made up the remaining furnishings. This couldn't be kosher. "Do they know you're here?"

"Believe it or not, it's legal. Just needs some work. And hell, it's free. Want some herb tea?" He busied himself with a bottle of spring water and a plug-in kettle while I looked over his collection of used paperbacks. It wasn't what I expected. Philosophy, religion, history, politics, biography, and even some poetry revealed yet another surprising layer of Jackson.

"Got all those for free at that dump swap shop. Pretty good place. Matter of fact, got most of my stuff there." He stooped under the sloping roof to join me at the bookcase.

"Didn't you have old stuff in storage or something?" I couldn't help being curious about his past.

Jackson's jaw tightened and he growled, "Naw, I left all that behind. She prob'ly sold it or something anyway. I just didn't wanna know, y'know?" Having walked away without looking back more than a few times myself, I nodded and let it drop. For now.

The teapot screamed and Jackson limped back over to the stack of boxes that served as his counter, unplugged the kettle, and carefully poured steaming water into two mismatched mugs. "Tea's ready. Take a seat." He offered me the more presentable of the mugs, pulled up a sturdy-looking crate for me, and plonked himself down on the mattress. "Debi tells me I gotta learn to communicate better."

I drew a blank. "Debi?"

"My parole officer. Remember her? Nice little girl." I remembered the tiny blonde coaching Jackson at the police station the day after Junie's death, and nodded. As he sipped his tea, he watched me out of the corner of his eye. I wondered what he was looking for. "Debi says she's trying to get me to stop walking on my knuckles."

"No need to stop on my account," I said, although my curiosity was piqued.

"Well, I feel I owe you some kind of explanation or something." He sighed. "So I guess maybe I oughta tell you about my honorable intentions and all that shit. I mean, I guess I come across with you like I got one thing on my mind, but I don't." With a rueful grin, he added, "Not usually, anyway."

Was this some kind of romantic declaration? "It's okay," I assured him. "I've lived most of my life in the TestosterZone."

He mulled the word over then burst out laughing. "Shit, I really like you."

Baby Roz wiggled violently and I set down my mug on the floor. "You have a john up here?" Jackson's smile faded. "Hey, no reflection on you or what you're saying, it's just . . . you know, the baby."

In a gesture worthy of the Ghost of Christmas Future, he indicated a stained sheet hanging up in a dark corner of the room. "It ain't much, but it serves the purpose."

I approached the sheet cautiously, wondering what I was going to find behind it. A chamber pot? A vase? Perhaps a beer mug? No, by God, an actual toilet, ancient and cracked and in bad need of cleaning. I straddled it, just to be safe. "Does this thing flush?"

"Not exactly. Just leave it, I'll deal."

No way. I was up to the challenge. I removed the cover on the back of the toilet, made a few quick adjustments, and flushed triumphantly. "Fixed!"

I returned to the room more or less in one piece and Jackson nodded toward the door. "Someone just dropped something outside. Probably your purse or jacket or something."

I opened the door and grabbed my stuff from the dark hallway. "Hey, your box of cables is out here too."

"Leave 'em." I slipped into my jacket and shouldered my bag. Jackson's brows furrowed. "You leaving?"

"Yeah, I guess."

"Why?"

"Why not?"

"Well . . . because." He shrugged. "Do whatever you want. No big deal."

"I can stick around a little while if you want." I dropped my bag on the floor and plonked down on the mattress next to him. He looked sideways at me with a sly little smile, then started stroking my thigh with one long, sensuous finger as he nuzzled my neck. I sighed with contentment as the tingles started up again, then I recollected myself and forced the words out at last. "Uh . . . Jackson?"

"Mmmmmm?"

"Look, you know . . . I'm pregnant."

"Yeah." He kept nuzzling me, but his finger paused mid-thigh. After a moment I heard a muffled, "Is it mine?"

I made a face. "And the thing is, well, it's a high risk pregnancy and I can't have sex." I felt a sigh tickle my neck. "I mean, you know, regular sex."

"Ain't been nothin' regular about this so far, so I wouldn't worry if I was you."

He cupped my left breast in a gentle, long-fingered hand. I drew a shaky breath and released it as his thumb caressed my nipple. It took all my strength — and another sharp wriggle from Roz — to stay more-or-less upright and finish what I had to say. "Okay, look, I really thought I'd lost the baby a few weeks back, that time I came in here and we talked. My doctor told me sex isn't such a great idea. If I can get her to stick for another couple months, we might make it."

"Hey, hey, I'm just caressing you here," he purred into my neck. "It's been a while since I played with one of these."

I sighed again. "Well, you're doing great, but it's making me kinda forget my priorities." I reluctantly took his hand from my boob and gave him a squeeze. "Get back to me in October, okay?"

After a moment, Jackson nodded. He flopped back on the mattress and I restrained myself from joining him. "So who's the daddy? Do I know him?"

"Not important."

Jackson stretched and various joints popped. "Y'know, I heard more shit about you, but I didn't believe it."

"What kind of shit?" I had a feeling I knew, especially if he was pals — or whatever — with Alison.

"Oh, I dunno, that you're kind of a wild woman, I guess."

"Town tart? Nympho? Dyke? That kind of shit?"

Unexpectedly, he sat up and grinned. "Hey, don't worry, I don't hold it against you. What right would I have to hold anything against anybody? And anyway, I draw my own conclusions."

"I've got a question for you."

"Yeah, what?"

"What were you in jail for?"

His face darkened and he stood abruptly, then limped over to another corner of the room and fumbled around in a box. "Hungry?"

I thought he was going to evade my question until he handed me a couple of crackers and sat back down. "Why was Uncle Jacko in jail? Sounds like a freakin' country song. Okay. Me and my band was playing this bar, and my girlfriend was in the crowd flirting with this guy. So at break we all kinda wandered over to check things out. The guy asked my girlfriend, quote, 'Why do you hang out with these niggers?' " Jackson chewed his lower lip and stared at the floor. "It was stupid, but I saw red. I mean, I hate that fucking word, and I was already kinda worked up and jealous."

I could understand why he hated the word, but . . . "Your friends were black?"

"Yeah, and I'm probably part black myself, but that's not the point. So anyway, I hurt him pretty bad. Problem was, he was an off-duty cop, all his little cop buddies were there, I was outta control, I had some weed on me, it was my third offense . . . get the picture?"

"Snowball, chance, hell . . . use those words in a sentence?"

"Pretty much." He flashed a crooked grin, which faded immediately. "He ended up in a wheelchair. So they tossed me inside, my girlfriend wouldn't bail me out — in fact, my little rage sent her flying right into that cop's arms. She always went for victims." He chuckled bitterly. "Hell, she should see me now."

"What are you a victim of?"

He thought about it. "Nah, forget the victim crap. You're right."

I yawned, and it hit me I was completely drained. "Shit, what time is it?" Jack shrugged, so I fumbled through my bag for my strapless watch and grimaced at the read-out. "God, I gotta teach tomorrow and it's almost one in the morning. I better hit the road."

"You can stay here if you can stand it."

"Thanks, but . . ."

"Yeah, tell me about it. It's nasty if you're not used to it." He surveyed his room as I yawned again. "You gonna make it home okay?"

"Sure. It's only a few miles." I moved toward the door and he followed me, suddenly shy and uncertain. I turned to him. "So, anyway."

"Yeah?"

"I'll see ya."

But when I started to open the door, he pulled me to him and wrapped me warmly in his arms, his scratchy face against my cheek. We stood like that for a few heartbeats, before I pulled away from his intensity and opened the door. "Bye."

He was reaching for me again as I closed the door behind me.

Chapter 13

The phone's hysterical bell jolted me awake minutes after I drifted off to sleep on the sofa. Years of living with various alcoholics had trained me to race blindly through the dark toward the sound and grab the phone, forcing calm and capability into my voice, but the added weight of Roz left me breathless just struggling to my feet and I barely managed to gasp out, "Hello?"

"Hi, it's me," a somewhat slurred male voice complained. "Hope I didn't wake you." No mistaking the underlying accusation.

I tapped on a lamp and squinted at the clock through sleep-swollen lids. "Um, well, Bart, it's after two in the morning."

"I tried you earlier and you weren't there." Yep, he'd definitely had a few more since I'd seen him in the alley. "Were you with that damn criminal all this time?"

I took several deep breaths to slow my racing heart and clear my mind enough to be kind, to remember Cal's unsolicited advice: "He's your child's father, no matter what else he might be. I have no idea what you were thinking, but now you have to try to forge a working relationship with him for Roz's sake."

"Max? You still there?"

"Yeah, Bart, I'm here, but I'm exhausted. I really need my rest."

"Well, maybe you should get home earlier and stop screwing around with drug addicts."

I couldn't exactly deny that I'd been in a compromising position with Jackson, so I didn't try. "Look, Bart, if you called to lecture me on my morals, you missed the boat by a few decades. But for the record, that was just . . . that wasn't really . . . what it appeared to be. But anyway," I continued, to drown out his interruption, "it's beside the point. I'm supposed to be trying to get rest and keep my stress level down, which is tough enough to begin with. Getting phone calls in the middle of the night . . ." I trailed off to find a good substitute for 'is really goddamn irritating' and finally came up with a lame, "doesn't really help."

"Well, if you were here I wouldn't have to call you. I mean, if I were there, I'd be home when you got home."

I sat on the floor, my back against the wall by the fireplace, and set the phone on my legs. I could tell I was in for a long siege. Bart's last two calls were only about twenty-five minutes, but that was because he was more angry than drunk. The self-pity sessions tended to drag on forever. "Well, I'm not there, Bart," I said, "and I'm not going to be there, and these late night calls are bad for the baby."

"You think I don't care about the baby."

Damn right, asshole, I thought; but I said, "I'm sure you do, I just don't think you quite grasp how closely the baby and I are linked." God, I was starting to sound like Cal.

"And anyway, these calls aren't any worse for him than that Jackson guy you were making out with." The bitterness in his voice made it clear this was the real issue.

I thought hard for a minute, reviewing my own behavior, then summoned all the sympathy I could find. "Okay, Bart, you're right. I'm really sorry about that. I don't know what came over me, but it won't happen again. I promise." My heart cracked a little as I said these words, knowing I better stick to them. "Okay?"

He was silent for a moment, then sighed. "Okay."

"Okay. I'm going back to bed now. Please don't call so late anymore, okay?" No response. "Bart? Okay?"

More silence, and then, "I miss you, Max."

I sighed and dredged up some sympathy. "I'm sorry. Just . . . try to remember what a bitch I am, that should help."

It didn't help. On and on he went, over and over the same ground. It was like being stuck on one of those damned traffic rotaries they have in this stupid state. Every time you think you're going to be able to make your exit, along comes a semi and around you go again. The weirdest part was, he kept accusing me of planning to do stuff it had never even occurred to me to do, like never letting him see the baby or sneaking out of town in the dead of night without telling him where I was going. I tried to stick to Cal's advice and just kept repeating the same words over and over again — *No, I wouldn't do that to you or the baby; Yes, I'll put whatever you want on the birth certificate* — all the time wishing I could just hang up and unplug the phone.

I was so exhausted that keeping my voice low key and neutral wasn't too hard until about 3:20, when the tenth iteration of "you're-just-going-to-disappear-and-not-tell-the-baby-about-me" started up. Then something deep inside me that had been unraveling for the past weeks — some overstretched length of emotional elastic — finally gave. It didn't snap; it just kind of disintegrated like a cheap pair of panties. I struggled upright and realized my jaw ached from biting back the words that were, like it or not, about to be released, and I heard myself speaking in a deep, low growl. "You know something, Bart?"

He stopped in mid-whine, probably wondering who or what had taken the phone away from me. "Max?"

"When we started this conversation, running away with

the baby was something that had never even occurred to me. But" — my *Exorcist* voice continued its chilling takeover — "suddenly it sounds like a damn good idea. Thanks for suggesting it."

"I knew it! I knew you'd used me as a sperm bank!" There was an odd sort of triumph in Bart's voice.

"Oh, and another thing." My lungs filled with dark, heavy air as I prepared to finish him off. "If I'd wanted a sperm bank, I would have gone to a sperm bank. If I had been looking for decent genetic material, I most certainly would *not* have wasted a single second on you. Got that? Good."

I slammed the phone down and sat there, curled up like a serpent in the dark, eyes slitted with anger, my breath hissing hard through my nostrils. Even my skin was tense. I don't know how long this went on, but it was probably a good five or ten minutes of boiling, seething rage.

When I was able to follow my own thoughts again, the first one I grasped was that Bart may not have understood what I said, since it was a fairly complex insult and he wasn't particularly gifted at interpretation.

But if he didn't understand it, he probably would have called back, demanding an immediate explanation.

Then it occurred to me that Bart may have understood my insult very well and might now be on his way to my house with a loaded gun. Remember, this was Bart: woman-blamer, member of the NRA and the Hawk Marsh Huntsman's Club, the man who regretted that he hadn't "pulled an O.J." on his wife.

Maybe he'd make up for that missed opportunity with me.

My neighbor's dog suddenly started barking like crazy, which was bizarre at this time of night. I strained to hear over the dog's barking and my heart's banging. A soft sound on my porch made me scramble to my feet, switch off the lamp and squint through the darkness. Fury switched to terror in less than a second; the sides of my throat stuck together when I tried to swallow, and my heart slammed the brakes on its full-tilt gallop.

There it was again, a gentle bump just outside the window over the sofa. My rickety porch gave one of its familiar creaks under the weight of . . . who? what? It could just be a scavenging raccoon, or it could be a drunk, pissed-off two-time divorcé with a chip on his shoulder and a shotgun in his hands.

Wedged into a corner, peering fearfully through the dark living room, I nearly screamed out loud when I saw a pale face pressed against the window. I couldn't make out the features, but I didn't waste time trying. Without another thought, I launched myself toward the kitchen, grabbed the car keys from the card table, hurtled out the back door and around front into the truck. Thank God Molly started up quickly for a change; I slammed her into gear, spraying gravel as I peeled out of the driveway, and headed toward the main road — wearing nothing but a T-shirt and pajama bottoms.

For reasons I didn't care to think about, I headed straight back to Skiff Neck. My head justified that it was the closest lit-up place at this time of night, but my heart had another idea entirely.

As I pulled into the tiny village, I remembered with a jolt that Bart lived there too. What if he drove by and saw my truck? What the hell was I thinking? I screeched to a halt across from the WunderBar, struggled to my senses again and tried to calm myself down. My breath came in short, sharp gasps and every inch of me vibrated with adrenaline. After a few deep breaths, I started the truck up again.

A sudden rap on the passenger window sent me off the deep end. When the passenger door creaked open and a shadowy figure leaned into the cab, I jerked the truck into gear, floored it, and stalled it out. "OUCH! SHIT!" the ghost barked in a rough masculine voice.

Jackson. I almost threw up with relief. He rubbed his head, which had bounced off the dashboard, and scowled at me in the dim light. "Jesus Christ, Maddie, what the hell are you doing?"

I had to give that some thought. "I don't know," I said wearily. "I really have no idea."

Back on the musty mattress, wrapped in a blanket, I sipped herb tea. Jackson dried his hands on a ragged towel and sat beside me, caressing my shoulders. "Better now?" Yes, much better than a quarter of an hour before, when I could barely walk up the stairs to his room because my legs wouldn't cooperate. I gave him a weak smile. "Something had you really freaked. You wanna tell me what?"

I set the mug on the floor with still-unreliable fingers. "I don't know, I think I just spooked myself."

"What set you off? There had to be something, babe. You're not the spooky type."

"Oh, well, the baby's father called me in the middle of the night, drunk and stupid as usual, and I snapped. Then I got scared that he might come around and kill me. That's all, really. Hardly worth mentioning."

Jackson wasn't smiling. "Is he the type?"

I sighed, shaking my head. "I honestly don't know for sure. I suppose it's possible, but it seems improbable. Like I said, I just spooked myself. I should get back home."

"You're not going back there unless I go with you, and that's that. And I can't, 'cuz I got curfew, so you're staying here." Jackson picked up my mug and set it on a greasy milk crate. "Who is this guy, anyway? I wanna know what we're dealing with." I pursed my lips firmly. "Do I know him?" I shrugged. "Does he come to the bar?" I shrugged. Jackson sighed irritably. "Jesus, Maddie, it's not like I want to gossip about you or something. I just want to know who this dickhead is so I can kick his ass for him."

"Look, Jackson, he doesn't really need that done, okay? I mean, I can see why he's upset and stuff. I just wish he'd get over it and move on."

"It sounds to me like he's harassing you. That's grounds for an ass-kicking, in my book."

"Well, skip it. And anyhow, if I want someone's ass kicked, I do it myself." I tried to stand up, but the damn mattress was so low to the ground that I couldn't make it to my feet. After a few seconds of flailing, I looked at Jackson. "Help."

"You ain't goin' nowhere this time," Jackson growled, pushing me back onto the mattress. "Relax, babe, and try to get some sleep." He threw himself beside me and hauled me by the armpits up toward the pillows. "You already got your jammies on, anyhow."

"Where are yours?" I asked.

"Underneath this." He quickly stripped down to boxers and T-shirt, then pulled the long string on the ceiling light bulb and snuggled up next to me with an emphysemic grunt. "Nighty-night, hot shot."

I turned toward him and rested my head on his shoulder, trying to squash down the alien surge of happiness and grab a little sleep before I had to go to work.

I woke up a few hours later on Jackson's flat, mildewed mattress with a strange feeling that had little to do with Roz's morning aerobics. I knew Jackson was lying beside me; I could feel his heat. But I also felt some very strange vibes. I turned over to look at him; he was staring at the cobwebbed ceiling. He turned sullen gray eyes on me and I got a distinct chill.

"Hi," I said, just to test the waters. He observed me coldly for a moment longer, then grunted and sat up. Not a good start. "You okay?" I asked his rigid back, which was covered only by a threadbare muscle shirt. "Did you sleep at all?"

He lit a cigarette; God knows where he pulled it from. Immediately I felt myself getting queasy at the acrid odor, and he caught my grimace when he turned toward me. With a martyred air, he smashed the cigarette into an empty tunafish can on the crate next to the mattress. Welcome to Skid Row. The place looked even worse than it had the night before.

Before I managed to struggle to a sitting position myself, he emitted a growl that sounded like, "Why a hair?"

"Excuse me?"

He pissily over-enunciated, "I said, why are you here?"

I blinked a few times. It was pretty early in the day for sledgehammers. "Um . . . well, because you told me to stay. Why didn't you ask me to leave?"

He punched the mattress impatiently, eliciting a puff of damp dust. "I didn't say I wanted you to leave, I just asked why you were here."

Oh boy. "And I just told you why." I was finally on my feet without the aid of a crane. "So, what's going on? We were pals before I conked out last night. Did I do something really offensive in my sleep, or what?"

Jackson glared down at the street through the tiny window. "Don't be stupid."

I found my socks and pulled them on under my pajama bottoms. "So far today I've been asked why I'm here and told not to be stupid. And I've only been awake five minutes. Excuse me if I'm confused as hell." I found my slippers and dropped onto a crate to yank them on.

"Women."

Oh Christ. Not Jackson too. "What's that supposed to mean?"

"They make things so goddamned complicated. They ask a million questions, examine every word a man says and every move he makes under a fucking neutron microscope, then get all pissed off about what they see."

"Hm. I see your point. However, I have no idea what it has to do with me or anything I've done to you." I stood up and vertigo set in; the room went black and I plopped back down onto the crate. God damn it, I wanted to get out of there.

"Well, think about it, okay?" Jackson stomped around the room, an unlit cigarette hanging from his mouth.

"Go ahead and light it. I'm leaving anyway, and it might help you chill." My head still felt light and woozy, but I had to get away from this. I stood up and headed blindly for the door, walked directly into the jamb and banged the shit out of my elbow. "FUCK!"

"Jesus." Jackson came over to me and looked at my arm, then noticed my face. "Why the hell are you crying?"

"Because that hurt like a son of a bitch, okay?" A whiney little voice inside me sobbed, *And I thought we were friends and I thought you liked me and I thought you were different* . . . but I squelched it and forced my brows to furrow. "And what the hell is up with you? It's like I went to bed with Albert Schweitzer and woke up with Rush Limbaugh."

He laughed at that, anyway, a testy guffaw. "Well, anything broken?"

Just my heart, I thought absurdly. I bent my elbow a few times and shook my head, even though painful twinges shot up my arm. A couple of tears dripped down my face and I wiped them away. "Seems to be functional," I said as airily as

I could manage. Hell with him, anyway. What was it about me that brought out the raging chauvinist in every man I met?

"Well." He looked awkward and stupid now, which he damn well should have.

"Yeah. Well. I gotta get home and dress for work. And I'm supposed to meet with the principal about my contract for next year, so . . ." I pulled the door open, dying for him to apologize, to grab me and wrap me up in his bony arms and nuzzle me with his ragged face like he had the night before.

Needless to say, he didn't. "Well, sayonara, babe," he muttered and closed the door behind me.

"Well, what did you expect?" Libby berated me when I told her about Jackson's overnight personality change. The last bell had rung and we were alone in my tiny, cluttered office off the woodshop. "What *were* you doing there?" Libby leaned toward me over the desk, a knowing smirk dimpling her cherubic face. "You know he did Alison Shipwood, right? And it wasn't all that long ago."

I frowned. "Don't believe everything Cal says."

"This isn't from Cal. This is from Morris, my very own hubby. He walked into the pub and caught them together. Up against the wall behind the bar, he said." Libby sat back and preened.

I wiped at an ancient coffee mug ring with a crumpled late pass. "Well, it's history now."

"Don't be so sure." Libby shifted uneasily on the hard plastic chair, then reached underneath her and pulled out part of a socket wrench set. "Guess your cleaning spree hasn't reached the office yet, huh?"

"Well, whatever. It's moot now, I guess. I promised Bart I wouldn't see Jackson anymore, and then he was such a dick this morning it's not really a problem." I put my head in my hands, rubbing aching eyes with aching fingers. I could have fallen asleep on my desk right then. "I can't believe this. Last night I actually kept thinking, 'So this is what they mean by a soul-mate.' Corny, huh?"

Libby smiled and spoke with a curious tenderness, "Not at all, Max," she said, then frowned worriedly and added, "But I think you've made a pretty bizarre choice for a soul-mate. I mean, my God, he lives like a complete bum, he smells, he's ugly, and he's fresh out of prison. Sounds like the man of your dreams has arrived."

"He doesn't smell and he isn't ugly. Okay, he's not conventionally good-looking, but . . ."

Libby sighed. "God, this figures. Cal's right again."

"Right about what?"

"He thinks maybe you're really in love with Jackson, but you have this tendency to sexualize everything due to your past . . . you know, the rape and all."

"Cal thinks I'm in love?" This was scary. Cal was usually dead-on with me, and it was annoying as hell.

Libby's voice took on its most aggravated scolding-mom tone. "You've always had the weirdest taste in men. It's not like you haven't hit the bottom of the food chain before, but . . . well, usually they're harmless and stupid." She slammed her hands on my desk, causing papers to fly, and leaned in toward me further. "But this is all beside the point. Carrying on with some street person is not what you need to be doing right now. You're going to be a mother in a few months. Forget men; focus on motherhood."

I pushed my chair back with a loud squeak and struggled to get back into her face, but my body wouldn't let me. "You don't think that's consuming me right now?" I gasped. "God, that's about all I think about these days. I'm exhausted just from trying to figure out how the hell I'm going to afford this baby with no help from the father." I broke off as Principal Ron Gorman rapped on the open door and strode in. Christ. I wondered how much he overheard.

"I thought we had a meeting, Madeleine."

I looked at my clock to find it was after two. "Shit, I'm sorry."

A constipated smile pursed his lipless mouth. "No need for foul language." I made my own lips disappear and apologized. Gorman gazed at Libby and suggested, "Why don't we just meet here? This shouldn't take long."

I nodded, wondering how I was going to get a raise out of this weasel. Libby rose and excused herself, patting the chair invitingly. "Have a seat, Ron. It's all warmed up and everything."

I knew Gorman secretly lusted after Libby like every other guy in the school. The thought of parking his skinny butt where her lush tush had just been resting was probably about as exciting as his life got. He gave me another reptilian smile and sat.

Fired.

Well, okay, not fired exactly, but my contract would not be renewed. Too many complaints about me from parents, he said. I told the kids 'shut up' instead of 'be quiet' when they were noisy. I swore in front of them sometimes. I was lazy and unprofessional and altogether not the kind of person who should be working with The Youth of America.

The unspoken reason, most likely couched under the heading of "inappropriate behavior," had to be my affair with Nick Jurgliewicz. I could read it in Gorman's heavy-lidded, judgmental eyes when I asked him why I wasn't informed of the millions of parents' complaints before this. He didn't have an answer.

There was nothing I could do. My contract ran out at the end of the year anyway; it was a simple matter of non-renewal.

I was now officially, seriously, and absolutely *screwed*.

Chapter 14

And so the financial scrambling marathon commenced. More like a triathalon, actually, consisting of endless phone calls, job applications, and trying to sell my truck. All of which bore little fruit besides frustration and depression. Oh yeah, and that thing I was supposed to be avoiding: stress.

I'd suspected for a while that there was no aid for single mothers who wanted to keep working. It's work or welfare unless you're below the poverty level, and if your job doesn't pay you enough for childcare, you're basically up the proverbial paddle-free creek. There was no question I'd have to sell the house — a thought that brought on fits of violent, uncharacteristic weeping — although I wasn't sure I could find a rental cheaper than my mortgage unless it was a room in a flophouse. Childcare alone was at least seven hundred a month, almost half my take-home pay from teaching in this cheap-ass town. I called everywhere I could think of, argued, pleaded, even got around to sobbing pathetically . . . for nothing. Bureaucratic hearts are hard to break. It got to the point that after every call I had to lie down and take deep, calming breaths for about an hour before I could try the next place.

I steeled myself to job hunting, but the nature of my pregnancy had me severely limited for the near future. In a blue-collar profession like carpentry, no heavy lifting is a major drawback. Also, no one was thinking as many months ahead as I was. I finally narrowed the search down to custodial work at one of the marine science labs in Skiff Neck, due to bennies like subsidized daycare. I put in several applications and haunted their personnel offices like a demented fan. After a while the human resources staff wouldn't meet my eyes.

I had less than two months left on my teaching contract. My health insurance would continue through the summer, cutting out a few weeks before Roz was due.

For the first time in eons, I was scared shitless.

"As well you should be," Libby reassured me after I whined on her shoulder. We were going through her sumptuous discarded maternity wardrobe, marking some of the less frou-frou garments for me, the rest for the local charity. "You haven't exactly spent your life preparing for the joys of motherhood."

I didn't need to hear that, especially from Libby Libido, my partner in high school and college crime. "Yeah, like your acting career prepared you for this." I gesticulated to the oversized master bedroom and walk-in closet stuffed with designer clothes. "And like you didn't do some serious bed-hopping and partying before you turned into Yuppie-rella."

Glancing over her shoulder to make sure no stray toddlers or husbands had wandered into the room, Libby giggled and shrugged. "Point taken, bitch. But I have to say I've noticed an improvement in you already." She held a flowery Laura Ashley number up to my shoulders; it fell about a yard below my feet. "I'm very pleased your use of the F-word has dropped so dramatically. Even Morris noticed." She kissed my forehead before tossing the dress into the Salvation Army pile.

I frowned, embarrassed that my effort at self-improvement had been detected so easily. "Yeah, well . . . I keep picturing this little face looking up and me and saying, 'Mom, could you fucking change me? I shit myself big time.' It kinda gives one pause."

"And," Libby continued in her approving tone, "you've been so good about staying away from Jackson."

My frown deepened into a scowl. "Yeah, well . . ." Libby held up a pair of denim coveralls that looked like a possibility — until I spotted smiley-faced daisies embroidered on the bib. "God, why do they think just because you're going to have a baby, you want to dress like one? No offense, Lib, but . . . ick."

"Don't ignore what I just said." Libby dropped the coveralls and grabbed a huge shirt. "I never saw you like that with a guy before — you lit up whenever you talked to him. I never saw you do that with anyone. Many times I have wondered if you had a heart at all." Suddenly exhausted, I sat on the satiny bedspread and sighed. Libby sat next to me and put her arm around me. When I didn't bite her, she put her other hand on my belly and continued. "I think this is the most wonderful thing that could happen to you, Max. It changes your whole outlook, doesn't it? It's like you suddenly know what's really important."

I was chewing my lips hard and inhaling to try to keep back the tears, but it was pointless. I gave up and buried my face in Libby's shoulder. "Wow," she breathed, "I've never seen you do that before, either." She stroked and rocked me until I got it back together. "So you're scared. Good. If you weren't, I'd worry about you even more."

I wiped my eyes and tried to glare at Libby, but instead my mouth twitched and I heard my shaky voice saying, "More than anything, I'm scared she won't make it. I mean, the tumor is bigger than her and it could make her come out too early." My throat closed and I cleared it. "Libby, I love her so much it scares the hell out of me. I talk to her all the time. I can't keep my hand away from her. I'd do anything to protect her. I'm so afraid. If Roz doesn't make it, what'll I have?"

Libby pulled my head back onto her shoulder and this time my tears wouldn't stop.

The first time I pulled up to ~~Daisy's~~ Herb's Diner with the red-and-white FOR SALE sign in ~~Molly's~~ window, my old mentor Archy Kopp and a few of the guys were gathered on the sidewalk examining a dead seagull. Daisy stood just inside the diner's doorway, wringing her hands and trying not to look at the corpse. Their morbid curiosity switched to me at the sight of that sign.

"Jeez, Max, you selling your twin?" Archy wheezed as he followed me into the diner. He made the truck sound like an actual sibling, which she kind of was. Frankly, I would have preferred to sell Gabe.

My stomach growled and Roz kicked as I studied the grease-smeared pastry case wistfully. "Yeah, well." I shrugged, wondering if these guys knew my situation. Word gets around in Hawk Marsh, but just in case, I added, "I have to be able to pay for the baby." I parked my butt on a vinyl-covered stool at the counter and blew my nose on a napkin.

Archy's blank face answered my question. "The what?"

"Baby. She's due in September, I'm out of a job in a couple of months, and no one'll hire a pregnant lady." I gave him a wan smile. "So, in case you didn't know, you're gonna be a grandpa after all."

A small crowd had gathered around us. Few faces were as surprised as Archy's; he was apparently out of the dirty gossip loop these days. He sank onto a stool and mopped his brow with my discarded napkin. Ick. "Holy crap, Junior, you're old enough to know better. Who's the daddy?"

I shrugged again. "Deep dark secret, Arch. Sorry."

His watery eyes narrowed. "Do you *know* who the daddy is?"

Hey, even I can be insulted. "Of course I know, it's just no one's damn business," I snapped.

Del Fisher, an old beau, gaped at me. "You're pregnant? I just thought you were getting a little chunky." You can see why he didn't last long.

"Comes with the territory, Del. Yeah, I'm knocked-up. Almost five months along."

I felt like an alien among my cronies. I'd hung out with most of them since I was a teen, laughing and working, drinking and carousing, one of the guys — only built a little different and enjoying the hell out of that difference. Now I was going somewhere they couldn't follow. They looked at the floor, at their coffee cups, at the sign on my truck, at anything except me and my traitorous body.

Archy broke the silence. "Hey, Daisy, get my gal here some coffee and a number two over light when you get a sec."

I shook my head. "Can't do the heavy breakfast these days, or I'll be sorry later." I turned to Daisy. "How about an order of whole wheat toast?"

The crowd took a nervous step back and stared. Me not eating like a 300-pound trucker was front-page news. After a moment, Del cleared his throat. "You better have some O.J. with that, Max. My wife drank a lot of O.J. with our first. Got follicle acid in it or something."

"You shouldn't be drinking coffee, you know," Al Peters chimed in. "Bad for the baby."

"And you really oughta have oatmeal instead of toast," suggested Bernie Shackleford. "It's got that whole grain stuff in it. But it's gotta be real oatmeal, not instant."

"And lots of milk," Archy insisted. "You never would drink enough milk, which is why you're a runt. Daisy, get my gal a big glass of milk."

"Skim milk," Sy DeMello corrected. "Gotta watch the fat."

When I burst into tears under all this unexpected caretaking, five callused hands patted my shoulders and told me everything was going to be all right.

I'd looked up the value of my truck and inflated it to allow for haggling. Since Molly was an official antique and in excellent condition thanks to me, she was worth a nice chunk of change. A tiny ray of hope flickered on my otherwise bleak horizon. If I sold Molly, I might be able to survive without a job until Roz was two and a half months old, the earliest most local day care centers would take an infant.

I had to stop screening my calls so as not to miss a hot prospect, and that's how I ended up hearing from Nick more often than I ever wanted to. He whined and pleaded and wept all over my phone; I felt like wiping it off after every call.

I repeatedly hung up on him, so he ambushed me after work one day. I was in my office packing to leave; my back was to the door and I jumped about six feet when his unwelcome voice behind me said, "Please just give me a minute." I sank into my chair and inhaled deeply to calm my nerves. Nick's eyebrows arced worriedly. "What's wrong?"

I held up a finger — no, not that one, though I was tempted — and took a couple more breaths, my hand on Roz. "It's called stress, Nick," I gasped. "Your middle name. What is your problem? Can't you take a hint?"

"I only need a minute," he pleaded. "I want to give you this." He held out a cassette tape. "Promise me you'll listen to it." When I didn't reach out for it, he set it on my desk. It was labeled in artsy calligraphy, *Our Hearts Belong Together*. I considered puking. Nick continued, "I remembered how you gave me tapes of music you liked, and I thought maybe this would be a good way of saying how I feel since you won't talk to me."

The tapes I'd given him mostly contained filthy blues songs, but that obviously hadn't sunk in. "I'm talking to you now, so listen real, *real* hard." I looked him straight in the eye and enunciated clearly. "Get bent."

With a tearful wave, he faded back into the hall.

On the other hand, I didn't hear from Bart at all. Since the night I'd turned tail and fled my own house after seeing that face pressed against my window, he had gone silent. At first it felt like a reprieve — one less bonehead I had to deal with — but the more I thought about it, the more angry I got.

What made me more Roz's parent than him? What made her less his child than his other two daughters? Why was I selling my truck and most likely my house when he was making no sacrifices whatsoever to be sure she was taken care of? I held off on calling him for a while, to give us both time to chill, but instead my anger built with each passing day. The more I learned about how little help I could expect from official agencies, the more furious I became with Bart. And with Nick, who wouldn't leave me alone. And with Jackson, who ... well, I wouldn't even let myself think about that.

My little sister Gabe played a role in antagonizing me too. Well-meaning but with a very narrow worldview, Gabe called me at least once a week with advice on how to fix my life. Her most brilliant suggestion was that I should marry Bart. "It's not too late, Max," she urged me. "God forgives all who sincerely repent."

I silently wished I had a sister who lived on this planet. "And what should I be repenting, unless I was actually stupid enough to marry that moron?"

"But, Max, you had... um, *relations* with him . . . you must have felt *something* for him."

Great, my sister *and* my conscience were giving me the

same crap now. "Not necessarily, okay? Look, Gabe, once and for all, I don't buy the religious stuff. And anyway, if there is a God, he's going to have some major explaining to do before he gets anything out of me." I pictured myself standing on a cloud at the foot of a huge golden throne, hands on my hips, giving The Big G a celestial kneecapping. At least that made me smile.

Predictably, Gabe gasped with horror at my pagan remark. "Max, don't say that! What would Dad say if he could hear you?"

"He'd probably say, 'You little slut, I'm going to kill you,' or words to that effect," I responded. Which set off another round of you-need-Jesus-as-your-personal-savior and look-what-happened-to-Junie.

Speaking of Junie, Cal was back to speculating on what had happened there. I dropped into the WunderBar after work one day, when I was pretty sure Jackson would be out, and found Cal hanging a huge black-and-white print of Liza Minelli in *Cabaret* over the bar. "I don't know, Max," he mused, squinting at Liza, "but the more I think about it, the more far-fetched it seems that Junie beat himself to death out on the jetty." Liza peered back at Cal from under her bowler, looking almost as world-weary as I felt.

"So what do you think happened?"

Cal gave the frame's lower-left corner an upward nudge. "I don't know, but I talked to Alison and Jackson, and they both said he didn't seem particularly depressed — let alone suicidal — when he was in here an hour before you found him." I scowled at the mention of Jackson's name, but Cal was still staring at Liza and didn't notice. "Alison said he actually seemed unusually upbeat, and was flirting with her like crazy."

"He was trying to shmooze her for a drink."

"Of course, but she said he was fairly coherent and funny, for a change. What do you think, is she straight?"

I almost choked on a mini-pretzel. "You think Alison's gone dyke?"

Momentarily stumped, Cal gaped at me, then burst out laughing. "No, Mad Max, I meant is Liza straight? The picture. I know all too well Alison's hetero." He gave me a sly nudge and added, "Your pal Bart's been hitting on her, you know."

"Ooh, lucky her." But I had to admit that stung a little.

"Seriously, Max, what were you thinking? You've been with a lot of oafs, but that one . . . wow."

I sighed. "God, Cal, I don't know. I really don't. Maybe Libby's right and it's time for me to make an appointment."

Cal hunkered down on the bar and grabbed up a handful of pretzels. "Want my theory for free?"

"Why the hell not? I probably deserve to hear it."

"Well, I don't know about that, but I think your tendency has been to choose inferior men . . . men who are weaker than you, dumber than you, unavailable for whatever reason . . . men you couldn't possibly love." He pushed his bushy face next to mine and whispered, "Because that way you can't get hurt."

"I guess that would explain Bart." I closed my eyes. "Is he making any headway with Alison?"

Cal snorted. "Ally's being her usual gracious self to him, but . . . I don't think so. He's too boring." I threw a pretzel at him; he caught it and popped it into his mouth, crunching thoughtfully. "I don't know what's up with my partner lately, but I think it's love troubles. I mean, obviously Mr. Mystery is on the outs or she wouldn't have been riding the hobby horse with Jackson." A thump on the back stairs made Cal lower his voice. "Speak of the devil."

"Well, I gotta go." I slid hastily off the stool and hauled ass out the door, with a wave at the irritatingly omniscient Cal.

It got to the point where I was seriously considering fulfilling Bart's prophecy and disappearing without a trace, just to get away from everyone. At least Roz gave me a good excuse to become a hermit. Armed with the doctor's orders to rest with my feet up, I became a TV addict. I found most of the prime-time stuff as lame as ever, so I ended up watching reruns of *Mystery Science Theater 3000*. One Friday night around twelve-thirty in the morning I was curled up on the sofa with Booger and Hairball, watching the wisecracking robots demolish a 1950s teen horror movie, when the neighbor's dog started barking its scrawny haunches off.

I hit my favorite button on the remote — mute — and listened to see if it continued. It did. I hauled myself to my feet, prepared to kill my neighbor, when there was a sudden pause in the yelping and I thought I heard a soft sound on my porch. I froze, barely breathing, and listened more intently. Just before the dog recommenced barking, my porch gave one measured creak, then another.

There was no mistaking it. Someone was walking on my porch. My mind flashed back to that night a few weeks before and I scanned the picture window for a pale face peering in. Thank God, I saw nothing.

Possibly inspired by the intrepid teens in the movie, I waddled to the front door and flung it open with a bang. "Hey!" I shouted into the night. "Get the hell off my porch, creep!"

No one answered. I stepped cautiously outside, holding my breath and darting my eyes around, barely noticing the goose bumps popping up on my arms in the brisk spring air. In the dark I spotted the little turn at the end of the porch where it wrapped around the side of the kitchen.

Was someone hiding around that corner?

I don't know if I was being brave or stupid, but my adrenaline was pumping and I was in the mood to kick some butt. I sneaked across the worn boards toward the kitchen window, edging my way as quietly as possible across the ragged wood in my bare feet. Dizzy from breathing shallow and from my heart's nervous pounding, I staggered slightly and felt a huge splinter pierce the ball of my left foot. "OW!" I exploded, hopping sideways to lean against the house and examine the damage. It was tough to see in the dark and I wasn't very flexible those days, so I slid to the floor in an awkward position and squinted at my foot in the dim light spilling from the living room window.

After a moment, I heard a soft rustling around the corner, about a yard away. Again I froze. My attention span wasn't what it used to be; the pain had driven the prowler out of my mind. Cautiously I turned my eyes toward the darkness next to me and saw a shadowy form a few feet away. It was on two legs, so I assumed it was human. Beyond that, I couldn't say.

As my eyes started to scan up the legs, the figure sprang into action, flinging itself over the porch railing and pelting toward the trees behind my house. I tried to scream but could barely inhale, so I floundered to my feet in time to hear the distant snapping of twigs between my neighbor's dog's hysterical yaps. I slunk around the corner of the porch and peered toward the woods. The utter stillness scared me more than the noises had.

Now I knew. I had an official, bona fide, faceless, creepy stalker.

Which was exactly what I needed on top of everything else.

Chapter 15

As I headed to the Skiff Neck Library after school the next day, the jovial local weatherman chuckled, "Yes, folks, there's a late April blizzard warning for our area, but it looks like it'll pass well to our north before it blows out to sea. Keep those shovels handy, but don't get your hopes up for a snow day." All of which meant we'd get hit but good. Leave it to New England to have a blizzard in the spring. Well, maybe the weather guy would be right for once but those steel-gray skies looked damned ominous to me. Then again, what didn't?

I still hadn't heard a word from Bart. It dawned on me that he'd heard via Alison I'd lost my job, so he was probably afraid I'd really go after him for money now. He probably knew enough about welfare to realize the first thing they'd want to know was the father's name. I'd left a neutral message on his machine a couple of days before, then a somewhat more strident one that afternoon. If he hadn't returned my call by the time I got home that night, it was butt-kicking time.

My truck was still up for sale. Now my house was up too. Next came my ass.

Huddled in a carrel against the back wall of the library, I feverishly searched through a stack of books for something — anything — that would give me hope for supporting the baby on my own. Roz kicked repeatedly at her favorite target, the floating ribs on my right side. I tried leaning back in the chair but the hard plastic seat edge perforated my ass, and when I rested the book on my stomach Roz shook it rebelliously. I slammed the book, then my head, onto the cheesy desk.

Five months pregnant, plus the two pound tumor. I felt huge and awkward, and my feet and ankles were permanently puffy. One hand reached automatically for the bouncing Roz and I patted her, trying to summon strength from her feistiness and reassure her at the same time. "It's okay, sweetie," I whispered, "we'll think of something."

She paused for a moment, then jerked abruptly. Another pause, another jerk. I stared at the bump under my hand, watched my shirt tremble with each movement from Roz, and then I burst out laughing. "Aw, honey, do you have hiccups?" I cooed, smitten. A nearby browser turned her head to stare at the crazy woman talking to her belly. "Should Mommy drink a glass of water?" Roz jerked again and kicked my rib extra-hard, probably pissed I was laughing at her, but I couldn't help it. Maternal enchantment flooded my heart and I grabbed the books with renewed determination, still giggling a little each time Roz hiccuped. I was completely goofy about that kid, and she wasn't even born yet. I wondered if I was going to be the kind of mother who admires her baby's poop and stuff like that. God, I hoped not.

Someone sat beside me at the carrel. Jesus, the place was practically deserted; why bug me? I roused myself enough to tug my mountain of books out of their way, and looked up to scowl irritably.

It was Jackson.

We just stared at each other for a moment. His smile was wary, a little sad. "Hey," he rumbled.

"Hi." I couldn't figure out how I felt about seeing him. It had been a few weeks since that last crappy morning. To buy some time, I flipped open one of my books and thumbed through it blindly.

"Saw your truck out front," he whispered into my ear. "Where ya been?"

"I've been around." I shuffled the pages before me.

"I really wanted to, you know, explain."

The book made an embarrassingly loud noise as I smacked it shut. "You know what, Jackson? I'm on bullshit overload. I really don't need any more crap piled on top of what I'm already buried under. That's why you haven't seen me."

Sagging back in his chair, Jackson pulled one of my books toward him. "*Single Mothers By Choice* . . . What's this, a how-to manual?"

"I'm not in the mood for misogynistic sarcasm, jack-off." When I glared at him, he grinned.

"I love the way you talk, Maddie Maxwell. Half patrician, half trucker." Well, that pretty much summed up my genealogy. He leaned toward me again and took my hand. "Just listen to me for a minute, okay?"

God, he sounded like Nick Jurgliewicz. Yanking my hand back, I said in a martyred tone, "It's not like I can run away. Just make it quick."

He cleared his throat. "Well, okay, look." I looked. "I was a jerk. I'm sorry."

I waited, but he just sat there. "All done?" I asked.

"You said be quick. You want more, I got more." I didn't pull away when he took my hand this time. Suddenly he couldn't look at me; he fumbled words out as if trying to piece something together. "Sometimes I get kinda down, okay? I mean, that room doesn't look too great in the daylight . . . and I woke up and looked at you and looked at the room and felt like this . . . huge loser."

To my chagrin, I found myself feeling sorry for him. "Well, I wasn't there for the ambience."

He looked up sharply, then smiled a little. "Okay, yeah, I

guess I know that . . . but I mean, I'm literally about six feet away from sleeping in a Dumpster. And sometimes I get bummed thinking about stuff I don't have, missing things that are gone, that kinda thing."

"Like what?"

Big sigh. "Like the kitchen in my old apartment. Like my friends, who think I'm shit. Like money. Like my girlfriend. Like something resembling a life, I guess." A tight, controlled breath. "Like seven years of my life." He shrugged. "And a lotta silly little shit. A mattress that doesn't kill my back. A long, hot shower instead of sponging off over the sink. A big plate of pasta with my homemade sauce."

And zing, my super-sized mouth flapped open and words flew out without my permission. "Okay, so what are you doing tonight?"

His expression flitted from surprised to pleased to regretful in about two seconds. "Naw, I was just bitching. I mean, I was just trying to explain why I was such an asshole. I wasn't trying to hint . . ."

"I know, I just thought what the hell. Why not?" I pushed the books aside and leaned on my hand. "I may actually be living *in* that Dumpster pretty soon, so don't knock it. My contract at the school wasn't renewed, no one will hire a pregnant woman, and my only hope is selling my house. So I say let's enjoy it while we can."

"You're selling your house?"

"It's on the market." I chewed my lip and scowled back a tide of self-pity. "Hey, it's cool. It's worth more now, with the work I did on it, so I can pay off the mortgage and maybe have enough to see me through the first few months of motherhood. I mean, if it sells in time."

"You're due in the fall, right?" Thank God I was too tense to be vulnerable; the way he was stroking my arm would, under ordinary circumstances, have been enough to make me drag him under the table.

"If she waits that long. She's the freaking Tasmanian Devil lately." I put his hand on my bulging belly. "Check it out." Roz had stopped hiccupping and was in the midst of a gymnastics routine. Jackson gaped and smiled.

"Holy shit, check out little Maddie."

"Her name is Rosalind. Roz. And why do you call me Maddie? I hate that."

"It suits you," he said.

"Why?"

" 'Cause you're always pissed off about something." He smiled again and gave Roz a final pat, causing her to kick violently in his direction. "Damn. Like mother, like daughter, I guess."

"Well, I wish you'd call me Max."

"Can't. Sorry."

"Why not?"

"Oh you know, one of those, uh, TestosterZone things you're always raving about. I don't wanna be calling out a guy's name in a, um, passionate moment."

"You are such a pig." But my big mouth betrayed me, as usual; the corners strained upwards into a smile for the first time in weeks. "Let's get outta here."

We stepped outside to discover snow pelting down in huge soggy flakes. "Uh, Jackson, have you heard about this blizzard that's supposedly not coming here?"

"Cal said he might close the pub if it started to look bad." We peered across the street at the WunderBar, which was pretty damn dark. "Guess it looks bad."

"Then I'm making a dash to the grocery store before we go to my place. It'll be a zoo."

It was even worse than I imagined. The old folks were out

in force — Hawk Marsh and Skiff Neck both had immense old fogy populations — clogging the aisles to complain about prices and worry about the weather. God, I hoped I'd never get that boring. I made a mental note to strike it rich before I retired. If I had the opportunity to retire.

Choosing a hand-held basket over a cart, I bobbed and wove my way through the aisles and elderly patrons, my mind racing and nagging and chiding me the whole time: Lord, what the hell was I thinking? I could actually get snowed in with this man, for God knows how long.

Why did that idea make me smile?

Well, there I was with reliable gas heat, a functional kitchen, a working fireplace, a great big comfy bed . . . well, come on, I would have to be damned selfish to leave Jackson to his moldy storage room mattress. I grabbed the last few items and nabbed him in the magazine aisle. "C'mon, let's get out of here before it gets any worse."

Jackson admired my little house with flattering awe, especially the stuff I modestly admitted to having done myself. The two-story, four-room tour didn't take long, so when we reached the bathroom I offered him a long, hot shower and he gratefully accepted. I left him to enjoy the indulgence, and hauled my butt down to the living room to check my answering machine.

The only message was from Nick, asking me if I'd listened to the tape he'd given the other day. Needless to say, I hadn't, although it was sitting near my boom box. Bart still hadn't returned my calls.

The loser.

I glanced at the clock. It was almost six. Bart had been off work for at least an hour. I poked his number into my phone and drummed my fingers. Four rings, then the answering machine picked up and his voice announced his unavailability. I struggled to sound reasonable and succeeded for almost two sentences. "Hey, Bart, it's Max again. I'm just checking in, because, you know, we really need to talk. My job's ending. I'm selling Molly and my house. You need to get your head out of your ass and acknowledge you've got some responsibility here. I mean, Christ, do you seriously want your kid on welfare? Call me. And I mean *soon*, or I'll be over there with a gun." I slammed the receiver for added emphasis. So much for reasonable.

As I got a nice fire going, I heard the shower turn off and the happy sounds of Jackson singing Willie Dixon's *Back Door Man* as he dried off. Interesting choice. I looked out the window and noticed the snow had already stopped. Disappointed, I hustled into the kitchen to shelve groceries.

Jackson was examining my tape collection when I came back. "Jesus, Maddie, there's more to music than the blues."

"Yeah, but I don't have a big budget so I only buy the necessities."

He picked up the cassette Nick had forced on me. "*Our Hearts Belong Together*. What's this, your favorites by Julio Iglesias?"

"I have no idea." I shuddered. "It's from an ex. He gave it to me the other day. I haven't listened to it."

"The baby's father?" I shook my head but didn't elaborate. "You mind?" He shook the tape from its case and popped open the boom box. "I'm curious."

"Sure, go ahead. I have no idea what's on there."

Jackson slammed the cassette door shut and pressed Play. "I just gotta know how he justifies that title."

I grimaced. "He's romantic, but creepy."

"You kinda go for romantic but creepy, don't ya? God, I hope so." He grinned at me as Cyndi Lauper's *All Through the Night* filled the room with techno-pop romance. "Aw, hey, this is a great song." Jackson cranked the volume and tried to get me dancing. "C'mon, why not? A little belly-rubbing won't hurt."

I was afraid it might. Just the feel of his hands on my arms was raising the little hairs all over my body. Plus the song kind of choked me up, and vulnerable was not the way I wanted to feel while I was alone in my house . . . on a snowy evening . . . by the fireplace . . . with this guy who was one eye patch short of being the consummate black-hearted rogue.

Cyndi moaned, and so did I. "Okay," I said, "but just a little."

Ha.

Ninety minutes later Nick's barrage of musical mush clicked off during the cricket chorus of David Byrne's *Sometimes a Man Can Be Wrong* — God, tell me all about it. I somehow doubted that this was what Nick pictured when he thought of me listening to the tape: Jackson and I leaning against each other in front of the fireplace, barely swaying, his scratchy cheek brushing my smooth one. And I was thinking that this was among the top five erotic sensations, right up there with the pressure of his denim-covered hard-on against my belly.

I really had to keep myself from getting to number one on that chart.

"Damn," he whispered into my hair. I looked up at him. Mistake. He brushed my mouth with those knee-buckling whiskers just before he kissed me. And yeah, I kissed him back. For a while. For a long while. We sank onto the sofa, suctioned together at the lips, until his mouth moved down about a foot. I heard myself whispering *JacksonJackson-Jackson* like a moron. He looked up at me and smiled. "I think maybe we should . . . make dinner."

To clear my lust-blurred vision, I blinked. "Huh?"

"Well, I mean . . . yeah, it's getting late."

"But don't you want to . . ." I trailed off, remembering Roz.

He stood up, unbuckled his belt, unzipped his pants . . . and tucked in his shirt, the rotten bastard. "What do you think? But, you know, we can't, so . . . well, they say food's a good substitute." He zipped and buckled up. I stayed put, mulling over my disappointment. "What's up, Maddie?"

"How can you just . . . stop like that?" In my mind, his mouth was still nuzzling my matronly bra. I wanted it back there in reality.

"It's called self-control. I've had lotsa practice the last few years."

"But, well, there's more than one way to . . ." The expression 'skin a cat' didn't fit the moment, so I left it to his imagination.

"Yeah, but we can wait. Right?" I pouted, which I didn't even know I could do. He sat back down and put his arm around me. That was a start, anyway. "Look, Maddie, yeah, I wanna spend all night just . . ." He made complex gesture followed by a sharp sigh. "All over you. You know what I mean? The whole thing. Not just bits and pieces, okay?" I shook my head just because I wanted to hear more. He sighed again, looked at me a moment, then grabbed me by the shoulders and drilled his eyes into mine. "I wanna be able to look at you like this, okay? I don't wanna see the back of your head, I wanna see your face. I wanna kiss you on the mouth. I wanna feel you against my chest." My nipples jumped at the suggestion. "I don't know, I mean, I love all kinds of sex . . . but that's what I want with you." He looked down and grinned, a little embarrassed. "The first time, anyway." He glanced back up and touched my lips with his fingertip. "Don't you tell a soul what a sap I am, okay?"

My heart was bumping around in my chest like an engine on low-grade fuel. "Okay," I murmured, wondering what the hell that was about. All I wanted was for him to kiss me again, which he did . . . just before he stood up.

He put out a hand, which I reluctantly took and allowed him to haul me to my feet. "That's getting tough for you, isn't it?"

"Gonna need a crane soon," I grumbled.

He slapped my ass and winked. "You got me."

Jackson wouldn't let me do much in the kitchen, insisting that he had his own sauce secrets and that he loved to cook. I believed it once I saw him dicing up the garlic and onions; he was a pro, and my little-used galley took on a gourmet aroma. As he relaxed and made himself at home, his smile got bigger and happier and easier. Despite having hardly been able to bear human company lately, I found him a lot more fun than solitude.

And that's about the time I remembered my promise to Bart. You know, the one about not having anything to do with Jackson. It had become a moot point after our last encounter, but there I was, feeling like a marshmallow over a campfire every time the man brushed by me. "Uh," I said suddenly, backing away.

"What?"

"Oh . . . God, I kinda forgot I promised Roz's dad I wouldn't see you."

Jackson's forehead crinkled. "He knows about me?"

I back-pedaled. "I mean, um, I wouldn't see *anyone*."

"Oh." He frowned at the pot of sauce simmering on the stove. "Who the hell is he, that he can tell you what to do? I mean, isn't he bailing on the kid?"

"Not entirely, I mean . . . he wants to see her, he just . . . can't afford to help out, I guess." I'd worked on my empathy for Bart, but it sounded lame as hell, especially since he hadn't called me back.

"Bullshit," Jackson spat. "He wants the fun without the responsibility. What is he, one of your students?" I tried to slap him, but he caught my hand and kissed it. "Sorry, that didn't come out right. I just meant he sounds stunted. Jesus, what a lout."

"You or him?"

"Both."

We started laughing. And then this moment came — this uncomfortable moment that had nothing to do with sex or lust. We kept on laughing a little too long at something that wasn't all that funny, because the feeling under the laughter was scarily intense. Jackson stopped first, cleared his throat, looked away from me. "Oh, shit."

My heart corkscrewed around. "Shit what?" We both cracked up again at that, then he looked at me sideways, a little red-faced.

"You know shit what." I looked at him blankly, not sure if he was talking about what I was thinking. He covered his eyes with his hands and groaned. "Oh Christ, you're a woman."

"No duh."

"No, I mean you want everything in words, right? My parole officer would be thrilled." He looked at me so intensely that there was no mistaking his meaning now, and suddenly my feet got very, very cold.

"Uh, I don't need words. It's okay."

He studied me, puzzled, then reverted to swearing. "Shit, girl. What am I supposed to do about this?"

"About what?"

"About all this?" His gesture included me, the baby, and the world at large.

"Well . . ." I frowned, realizing for the millionth time that this was a pretty awkward situation. "You don't have to do anything."

"I know," he said, "but what if I want to?"

As I cuddled in Jackson's arms in front of the fireplace, I found myself wishing like hell he was Roz's father. I pushed the thought back roughly and shook myself. Jesus Christ. I couldn't be falling in love with this guy. I dragged up every argument I could think of, like our sexually charged encounters. It's all hormones, I lectured myself. Look at him. He's a mess. Fresh out of prison, not doing well financially, screwed up physically in ways I don't even know about, and he has a hellish temper. Bad enough to land him in prison. Bad enough to put someone in a wheelchair. Yeah, that's what I need hanging around my daughter.

And I'd thought I couldn't do any worse than I'd already done.

Think again, girl.

Chapter 16

I woke up stiff and cranky and alone on the floor in front of the hearth, with Roz somersaulting wildly inside me. Something wet whistled on my eyelid; I pried it open to see a gigantic calico cat face sniffing me. "Hey, Booger," I rasped as I struggled to sit up. A few embers glowed under the ashes in the fireplace; a freezing gale hooted down the chimney and coated the hearth with soot. I shivered, pulling the quilt tightly around me. "Jackson? You here?" The utter stillness told me I'd been abandoned. I walked to the picture window to look for clues.

The outside world had vanished behind swirls of snow and a sky the color of Jackson's eyes. A hypnotic barrage of flakes pelted onto the already substantial accumulation; my truck was a smooth mound of white. I went to flick on a light and nothing happened; of course, the power was out. No lights, no heat, no hot water. Desolation threatened to descend on me; I struggled against it and forced myself into the kitchen to forage. At least I had a gas stove. Maybe I could put my head in it later.

I discovered a scrawled note on the table:

Mady - 11 PM no blizerd yet — Your asleep — missed curfew — thanks, love J.

Something that could have been a heart or an arrowhead adorned the bottom, covering dirty pink eraser smudges.

I frowned at the smudges, trying to make out what he'd erased. I wanted, ridiculously, to put the note next to my heart, which felt like it was drowning in a gooey sea. The transition from last night's warm golden glow to today's chilly gray solitude was hard to take.

Sternly I shook off self-pity, grabbed some cereal straight of the box and revived the fire. I told myself Jackson was smart to get out while he could. I was trapped for the day, no doubt about it. I couldn't shovel myself out, since that might endanger Roz, and the snowplows rarely made it to my cul-de-sac before sundown.

I alternately slept, read, and lectured myself in front of the fire all day, with Hairball, Booger and Roz to keep me company. To combat the unsettling longing for Jackson, I left another message on Bart's machine. "It's Max again. Listen, I'm sorry for losing my cool. I'm under a shitload of pressure and, damn it, this is your kid too." I slammed the phone down before I could say anything more and recommenced lecturing myself. See? That's the kind of guy you choose. You think Jackson's any better?

Around five, I woke from a sound doze when my ancient gas furnace grumbled to life and lights popped on. Late afternoon sun strained through the snow-heaped trees, the road was clear, and someone had dug Molly out. "Who the hell did that?" I asked the cats, who had heaped themselves in front of the fire. Hairball blinked at me, yawned, and sprawled upside down in reply.

The phone hadn't rung all day. I picked it up to make sure it was working, and a mocking dial tone assured me of my unpopularity.

A sudden rush of anger propelled me out of my lethargy and into my truck. Goddamn Bart. I didn't give a shit about his hurt feelings; this baby was his, too, and he'd damn well better face it. If he wouldn't return my calls, I'd beard him in his lair and kick his ass in person.

Icy clods and chunks of asphalt covered the winding road

to Skiff Neck, but Molly crushed them. As I passed the WunderBar I struggled not to stop and hunt down Jackson. Deep down I knew I was upset that he'd left, and that I was about to take it out on Bart. But I'd already built up such a head of steam there was no stopping me.

Bart's driveway wasn't shoveled so I parked in a drift on the street and waded up to his porch. The sky darkened and it didn't feel like the storm was over anymore. I looked up at the menacing clouds and saw three turkey vultures circling over the harbor. Lights glowed through the curtains and I heard faint blues music. Not Bart's usual choice; he was more of a Lite FM man. I figured he had some serious cabin fever going.

My mittened hand thumped dully on the door once, then again. "Bart!" I yelled. Nothing. It was miserably cold out there and he was probably passed out from drinking. Jerk. I tried the doorknob and it turned easily, so I barged in, stomping the snow from my boots.

The house smelled stale and yeasty, like old beer. I must have guessed right; he must have drunk himself into a stupor and passed out. Typical.

"Bart?" I called. "Hello? It's Max. I know you're here. Wake up and smell reality, buddy. We've gotta talk." From the living room, a muted stereophonic voice informed me I was listening to Blue 102. I followed it and looked around the apparently deserted room. "Bart?"

I had this really sick feeling all of a sudden. Something felt wrong, and something smelled even worse. Everything looked okay, but . . . I decided to check the other side of the sofa. Heart hammering, stomach lurching, I peered over the sofa.

A sigh of relief escaped me when I saw Bart passed out peacefully on the floor between the sofa and the stereo. One hand curled over his head and his face nestled in the crook of his arm. "Jesus," I muttered, laughing at my jitters. "See? Typical."

My nose didn't agree. What did he do, shit himself? I noticed a moist stain stretching out from under his hips; I covered my mouth and gagged. "Oh, gross." Then I realized Bart's face was bluish-white.

And the stain on the floor was dark sticky red.

Everything became very concentrated as I moved around to the front of the sofa. The air shimmered before my eyes; glowing molecules parted to let me through. I tripped over a beer bottle and watched its contents pour onto the carpet and mix with some other unpleasant liquids: vomit . . . urine . . . blood. Mostly blood.

I fell backwards down some big black hole, or at least, my brain did. My body stood there, all functions frozen. Even Roz was strangely still. Dully I realized I was in shock, staring and staring at Bart, but I couldn't break the spell. On some level, I congratulated myself for not puking or screaming. This really didn't look good.

I pulled off a mitten and breathed through that to filter out the nauseating smell, then kneeled on the floor between equally disgusting stains. Bart definitely had some holes in him that weren't there the last time I looked. I forced myself to reach toward his blue-tinged neck and put my fingers nervously where the pulse should be. It wasn't there. And the skin felt snakelike.

You couldn't get much deader than this.

My oxygen-deprived brain somehow directed my leaden legs to the kitchen phone. I could barely lift my arm to pick up the receiver, to punch in numbers with huge, awkward fingers. Nine . . . One . . . Nothing happened, then I realized I forgot something . . . One.

I waited. A voice questioned me, crisp and professional, and I pulled myself together with a tremendous effort. "I'm reporting a dead body," I explained, fighting down a wave of déjà vu. "Could you send someone out here?" They asked where I was; I knitted my brows and dredged up the answer. "Skiff Neck. Uh, Sunset Lane, by the harbor. It's a dead end." The irony failed to amuse me. "Could you send help?" They explained that they needed a number. I yelled, "Jesus, I don't know. Bart's house. Bart Fulton. Whoever he's renting from. He's dead. Please." I hung up and wandered to the doorway to stare at Bart. How long had he been like that?

The red answering machine light blinked at me. When did he last check his messages? Were mine still on there? I tried to remember what I'd said. At the time they'd seemed understandably pissed off but harmless. Suddenly they seemed dark and threatening, the products of an unbalanced mind.

Where were the police? Would they mind if I left? They didn't know who'd called 911. They'd probably be mad that I spilled beer and used the phone. I wanted to call Libby. I wanted to have Jackson hold me. I wanted to wake Bart up and yell at him for being such an asshole about the baby.

None of this was possible, so I just stared at the corpse, waiting for the pulse of blue lights against the window.

I wondered which cops would show. Probably that asshole Yergins, who had made me identify my father and my brother even though he knew perfectly well who they were. He'd just wanted to see the town slut look at her dead, drunk family members, maybe as some kind of object lesson, maybe to give Yergins something to feel smug about. Old bitterness seethed inside me. At least my reaction hadn't satisfied his morbid curiosity. Fuck them. Fuck them all . . .

Roz woke up when a strong drumbeat pulsed from the stereo. She loved drums; they made her dance. I put a soothing hand on her, which was when the realization hit that her father was dead. Not just my asshole ex-boyfriend, not just some drunk who'd been giving me shit, but Roz's dad. And he hadn't known her name, or even that she was a girl.

I inhaled deeply to suppress the ache that pushed up my throat and against my eyes. No. I would not cry. I would keep it together.

"I'm really sorry," I said to Officer Gary Cullinane, who looked more boyish than ever in his oversized police parka. "I'm a little freaked." We shivered together on the street outside Bart's house, while the big boys turned the place inside out.

"God, Miss Maxwell, I don't blame you. He's majorly dead." Gary looked a bit green himself. "Was anyone with you when you found him?"

"No, I was alone."

"What were you doing here?"

Great thing to have to explain to an ex-student, especially one who admired me like Gary did. "Can we go into that later? I'm freezing." He looked confused. "Look, my friends live the next street over. The Langleys. Would it be okay if I went over and used their bathroom?"

The poor kid blushed furiously. "Uh, well, I better check with Yergins," he stammered.

Gary, the team rookie, ended up escorting me to the Langleys' tasteful front door. Libby's delighted welcome turned to confusion when she saw the baby cop behind me. "Don't ask me to explain, just let me pee," I said as I brushed by her.

When I came out, Gary was chatting away excitedly to wide-eyed Libby, while an unusually disheveled Morris hovered in the background with Tucker wailing in his arms. "Are you sure you should be telling us this?" Morris asked Gary sternly.

Gary slammed his mouth shut and thought this over. "Sorry. I've never seen a real murder before." I guessed Junie didn't count since they'd ruled his death a suicide.

"You don't even know it *is* a murder," said Morris, ever the lawyer.

Blinking, Gary considered this. "Well, it would be a hell of a way to kill yourself. I mean, you might be able to stab yourself once or twice, but . . ."

"That's enough," Morris barked, then turned a formally concerned face to me. "How are you, Max? This must have been an awful shock."

"It pretty much sucks," I admitted. "Not what I had in mind at all."

"Did you touch anything?"

Loaded question. I looked at Police Chief Yergins' mottled face across Libby's spotless dining room table and tried to suppress a few bad memories. "I tripped over a beer bottle. I also called 911 from the kitchen phone."

Yergins scrunched his purple lips and shook his head, causing his jowls to wobble menacingly. "Anything else?"

I swallowed, a bit queasy. "I checked for a pulse."

"I assume you didn't find one?" Yergins questioned dryly.

I shuddered at the memory of the lizard-like skin. "Nope. He was cold . . . and kinda slimy." Yergins wrote something on his pad.

"What were you doing there?"

Oh boy, here it came. "I needed to talk to Bart and he hadn't returned my phone calls."

"Talk to him about what?"

Well, Bart didn't want anyone to know, but now that he

was dead I guessed it didn't matter. I sighed. "Our kid."

Yergins' long-haired eyebrows fluttered like moths. "*You* have a kid?" The inflection was deliberately insulting.

My hackles rose. "Not yet."

He let out a little puff of air. "Well, they say all it takes is a viable sperm and a viable egg."

That did it. "Hey, bite me, Chief. Like you're some kind of paragon." I'd gone out with one of his sons in high school. It was only for a couple of weeks, but he'd told me some interesting stories. "Look, I just found the body of my baby's father. Do you think you could be a little more considerate?"

Yergins looked at me like I had to be joking, then cleared his throat and resumed questioning me. "So I take it you knew the deceased pretty well?"

"I'm pregnant by him, so I guess the answer would be yes." I knew I should tone it down, but really, how stupid could you be?

"One night stand?"

I bit my tongue this time. "We went out for a while."

"I thought Fulton was married."

"He's getting a divorce. That's why it was kind of hush-hush." Yergins scribbled a few more notes. "His wife's name is Irene," I added, wondering if she was the mad stabber. "And he's got another ex-wife, Nina, and . . ."

"Thanks, but let's focus on you right now, shall we?" My stomach went cold. I realized I was hungry, and Roz was probably pissed. "So why did you need to talk to Bart about the baby?"

"Well, because . . ." I licked my lips and hesitated. This wasn't going to sound good, but it'd be best if he heard it from me. "Because my teaching contract isn't being renewed, so I'm selling my truck and my house to be able to afford the baby, and Bart's not helping because he's all pissed at me for breaking up with him and it's like he doesn't even think of her as his kid." I stopped for breath and caught Gary's alarmed gaze.

Yergins had gone squinty-eyed. "So, you're under quite a bit of pressure, huh?" He forced a see-through sympathetic tone.

"I'll say."

"Hm, yes, I can imagine. Losing your job and your house, pregnant and single. And you've been pretty upset with Fulton?"

Suddenly I felt trapped, like I did when they questioned me about Junie. Was there some kind of conspiracy in this town to implicate me in a murder? "Uh, well, not upset enough to stab him, okay?"

"How'd you know he was stabbed?"

"Well, it looked like it to me, I guess."

Yergins studied me for a moment as if trying to decide his next move, which was to pull his hat on. "That's it for now." Gary stood up, relieved, as Yergins turned his bloodshot eyes on me once more. "You're not planning any trips in the near future, are you?"

In other words, don't leave town.

Chapter 17

I was pretty damn sure I'd be hearing from the cops again as soon as they listened to Bart's phone messages.

As I drove back down Skiff Neck's main drag, the WunderBar beckoned. I decided I could use a non-alcoholic drink. And maybe, my subconscious added, a little talk with Jackson. Molly parked herself and I lurched through the snow to the front door, my body vibrating with every slam of my heart. The shock was wearing off, that was for sure, and Roz kicked my rib sulkily. I was dizzy with hunger; I realized I hadn't eaten since that handful of cereal.

Jackson sat at the bar talking to Cal and Alison. He turned to see who came in and waved me over eagerly. Again, the place was empty except for those three. I intercepted a disgruntled grimace from Alison and hesitated. But Cal's hearty, "Hey, Max, how's the hellcat and her hellkitten?" got me moving again. Screw Alison. I needed comfort.

Jackson slid off his stool and limped over to me, bending so he could peer into my face. Whatever he saw there froze his smile. "Jesus, you all right?"

I looked at him from very, very far away. His voice sounded thin and muffled. "Yeah, I'm fine," I slurred just before I hit the floor.

I didn't go all the way out, just enough so that they had to help me to a booth. Cal held a shot of brandy to my lips. "Damn good imitation of your old man, Max," he murmured when my eyes opened. He tipped brandy into my mouth; I spat it at him.

"Up yours, Cal," I mumbled.

"She's all right. What's up, Junior? A touch of maternity?"

"I'm okay. Thanks." Jackson's worried face came into focus behind Cal. "Got any crackers?"

"Sure thing, little mama." Cal hustled back to the bar and brought back a few crinkly packets, then stood there expectantly.

Jackson and I gazed at each other under Alison and Cal's scrutiny. Finally Jackson turned to them. "Give us a minute, okay, guys?"

A miffed sigh and the click of expensive shoes signaled Alison's departure. Cal waited a moment, probably dying for some gossip, then patted my shoulder and took off as Jackson slid in next to me on the hardwood bench. "Jesus, you scared the hell out of me. What's up?"

To my embarrassment, what came out of my mouth had nothing to do with finding Bart dead. "Why'd you leave last night?"

He looked surprised. "I thought — well, you were asleep, I was wide awake, and it wasn't snowing." He grinned. "I'm s'posed to be home by ten, actually. Terms of my parole."

"So you walked three miles in the middle of a blizzard watch just so you wouldn't violate your parole?"

The grin faded. "I didn't think you'd be upset."

"I'm not upset. It just seems kind of extreme." God, I sounded like a . . . like a woman.

"Well, you sure seem upset."

I closed my eyes and forced myself to focus. "Okay, I'm upset, but not with you. It's just — been a weird day." To my annoyance, the tears I'd squashed down at Bart's now blinded me.

Jackson's arm wrapped around my shoulder and he pulled me to him. "What happened, Maddie? You're a mess." I glanced up toward the bar and saw Cal and Alison staring us down. They immediately turned away. "Is Roz okay?"

I sniffled. "You know Bart Fulton, right?" Jackson's arm tensed behind my neck. I pulled away to look at his face. "You know him, right?"

Jackson shrugged. "Yeah, a little. He comes in here every now and then." He wouldn't meet my eyes. "Why? Friend of yours?"

"Look at me, okay?" After a couple of misfires, the gun-colored eyes fixed resolutely on mine. "He's dead. I just found his body."

He didn't even blink, although his forehead creased. "What?"

"I stopped by his house a couple hours ago and found him. I think he was stabbed. A lot." I averted my face as the body floated before me. "It was gross."

"Bart Fulton? The guy who drives that delivery van?"

"Yeah."

"Jesus." Jackson let a puff of air out and fumbled for his cigarettes. "Jesus, Jesus. You found the body?"

"He's dead," I repeated, as the question 'why' flashed through my brain for the first time.

"Yeah. What were you doing there?"

"I had to talk to him and he didn't return my phone calls."

"Talk to him about what?" His tone sounded harsh and jealous?

"Jesus, Jackson, the guy's dead. Can you lighten up?"

"Sorry, sorry." He took a deep drag on his cigarette and ran one slender hand through his unkempt mane. "It's just weird. I mean, I was talking to him here at the pub yesterday afternoon, a little while before I ran into you."

He lit another cigarette with the one he was already smoking.

Ain't Nobody's Bizness

★ ★ ★ ★ ★

Teaching the next day was difficult, to say the least. Some of the kids had heard about the murder and discussed it excitedly, with inaccurate gory details I didn't bother to correct. Fortunately they didn't know I'd been there. Yet.

That was taken care of near the end of my mechanical drawing class. As I coached a particularly backward student in the use of a T-square, an uncharacteristic hush fell over the other kids. I figured one of them was whispering a dirty joke or something, until I heard a soft male voice say, "Miss Maxwell?"

"I'll get to you in a sec. We're almost done, right, Gillian?" Gillian gave me a nervous smile and stared behind me.

"No, Miss Maxwell . . . It's Gary Cullinane." I turned to see the chronically apologetic Gary in his Hawk Marsh Police regalia, with Yergins lurking behind him. "Um . . . we need to take you to the station for some questioning . . ." He paused to look back to Yergins, who nodded sternly for him to continue. Gary sighed and mumbled, "In regards to the murder of Bart Fulton . . . um, okay?"

My stomach churned. I'd been expecting this, but . . . "Now?"

"Yeah, now," Yergins huffed, "ready or not. We got your hall pass right here." He dangled handcuffs in front of my face. Cullinane and the kids stared, shocked. It struck me that Yergins had watched a few too many episodes of *Law & Order*. "We have a few things to clear up in Fulton's murder, and we think you might be able to help us." He smiled.

I grinned furiously at the goggle-eyed kids and chirped, "Sure thing, officers. Happy to cooperate. Did you want to cuff me now, or wait till we're in the cruiser?"

The dismissal bell rang, but the kids didn't move.

"Aw, that was just my little joke. There's nothing to worry about, Max, we just need to ask you a few questions about your relationship with Fulton."

Not surprisingly, Yergins' words didn't reassure me much. Neither did the green walls, black linoleum, and glaring lights of the Hawk Marsh interrogation room. Two visits in one year was a bit much. I sighed and longed, oddly, for a cigarette. "We dated for a couple of months. I told you that."

"And the baby you're carrying is his." Next to Yergins, Gary sighed audibly at the shenanigans of his former shop teacher.

"Yeah."

"Let us play a little message for you." In response to a commanding look from his chief, Gary hit a button on the cheap tape player and I heard my own white-hot voice threatening to rip Bart a new asshole and remove a few appendages while I was at it. Yergins nodded and Gary stopped the tape. "Can you identify the caller?"

"Yeah, that's me." I took a shaky sip of stale water from a minuscule Dixie cup.

Gary forwarded the tape and found the message where I threatened to show up at Bart's with a gun. "I take it you and Fulton weren't on very good terms," Yergins commented dryly.

I shrugged. "He was being kind of a jerk about the baby." I leaned back in the chair to give Roz a bit more room, and breathed deeply to calm my nerves.

Yergins frowned. "And this was your way of straightening things out?"

"I have a temper." Cullinane looked at me sharply, wondering perhaps if this was a confession. I hastened to reassure him. "No, no, it's not that bad, I just yell a lot."

Yergins cleared his throat. "Do you often threaten to cut off your boyfriends' balls or shoot them?"

"Only when provoked." I refrained from giving Yergins a measured glare. "Look, I'm halfway through a rough pregnancy, my teaching contract's not being renewed, and Bart was acting like everything was my fault. Like this was some kind of plot against him, instead of an honest mistake." No, no, *you're* not a mistake, I mentally reassured Roz, touching my belly for comfort.

"So you broke up with Fulton, huh?"

"The night I found Junie's body."

Yergins nodded wisely. "Seeing anyone now?"

"I'm a bit preoccupied, what with losing my job and being pregnant and all."

"So the answer is no, huh?"

I nodded.

"So you're not seeing Jackson O'Brien?"

My heart sped up a little. "Uh . . . not really, no."

"Why the hesitation?"

"I was just surprised. What's he got to do with this?"

"That's what we're trying to find out," Yergins said with irritating smugness. "Did you go see him right after you found the body?"

I sat upright and unkinked my shoulders. "I went to the WunderBar. He was there."

"You spoke to him alone?"

My eyes bugged out at this. Who the hell told him that? The answer roared back: Alison.

"Answer the question, please."

"Uh — yeah, I did."

"May I ask why?"

"I . . . he . . . we're friends and I wanted to talk to him."

"Aren't you also good friends with Cal Winters, who was also there? Why didn't you talk to him?" Yergin's eyes narrowed, while Gary's widened with dismay.

I breathed deeply again, trying to regain some semblance of cool. "It's not quite the same."

"Why not?"

"Well . . ." I mulled it over. "For one thing, Cal's gay."

Yergins jumped on that. "So you and O'Brien are lovers?"

I considered this. Were we? "Um . . . well, not technically, but . . ."

"Not technically? What the hell does that mean?"

My patience blew. "It means we haven't boinked, okay?"

"Miss Maxwell!" Gary gasped.

"Sorry. Look, I don't know what you're driving at, but Jackson and I . . . I just wanted . . ." I trailed off, not sure how to express what I had wanted without sounding like a complete sap. "I wanted to tell him what had happened," I finished.

"And how did he respond?"

"He was worried about me." As I recalled his reaction, I felt my forehead tense.

"And what else?" Yergins studied my face like a cat studies a birdcage.

I shook my head. "He just tried to calm me down."

"You better tell us what's on your mind," Yergins growled.

Thinking quickly, I shifted on the chair. "Sorry. The baby's getting a bit wild, and I'm starving. It's distracting me."

By the time they dropped me back at the school, the late buses were pulling out. Starved and drained, I dragged myself into Molly and aimed her homeward, slapping the tape deck off so I could hear myself think.

Who the hell would want to kill Bart? Okay, he was a jerk, but he wasn't evil or cruel, just ignorant and mildly abusive. Nothing I hadn't seen before in spades. Hardly worth killing.

When I pulled into my driveway, I was surprised to find Jackson lounging on my porch. "Hey, Maddie," he rumbled as I dragged myself toward him. "How was work?"

Disoriented, I looked around and realized the sun was still shining and the melting snow had turned my lawn to a mud hole. "Okay, I guess." I had to tell Jackson the police had asked about him, but couldn't figure out how to approach it. "Actually that's not where I just came from."

"No?"

"No. I got hauled in for questioning."

We strolled toward the porch. Jackson looked at my face worriedly; I must've looked like hell. "Was it rough?" he asked.

"It was weird. I don't know what to think." In fact, I was trying not to think at all about what it all meant.

"They don't think you did it, do they?"

I shrugged.

"Those assholes. What kinda shit they ask you?"

"I . . . um, left Bart a phone message they wondered about." For some stupid reason, I still didn't want to tell Jackson about Bart, even though I had a feeling he already knew, or at least suspected. Maybe I didn't want to have to explain. We entered my house in silence. Jackson was sunk deep in thought, so far away that trying to converse was pointless.

The single message on my answering machine didn't exactly brighten my day. "Hello, Madeleine, this is Ron Gorman. Look, I've had a few phone calls from concerned parents and I'm going to have to ask you to take a leave of absence until this police matter gets resolved. I'm sure you understand." Click, beep. What a dickhead.

Jackson stared at the machine for a moment, then walked back outside to the porch, lit up a Camel and stared at the setting sun. "Shit, Maddie," he muttered when I joined him.

I dropped onto the steps next to Jackson. "Unreal."

I shivered a little in the April breeze, and Jackson took off his threadbare flannel shirt and wrapped it around me. His tattered T-shirt looked too thin for the chilly air, but when I tried to object, Jackson shook his head and smiled at the sun on his tattooed arms. "Feels good." I pulled the sleeves around me and inhaled his scent, my eyes stinging with self-pity and fear. "So, Maddie, damn. What'd they ask about?"

I sighed, finally came out with it. "They asked me about you, for one thing."

Jackson squeezed his eyes shut and shivered in the sunlight. "What'd they ask?"

"Why I went to see you, why I wanted to be alone with you . . ." Jackson turned bewildered eyes on me. "How well I knew you, and so on."

"Damn Cal."

I shrugged. "Damn Alison, more likely."

He stood abruptly and limped away from me, around to my backyard. With a groan, I pushed myself up and waddled around the corner after him. For some reason I felt enormously pregnant; maybe Roz throve on crises, like her mother.

Jackson was leaning against my scraggly willow tree, pounding his fist against it rhythmically. He saw me coming and turned away, stuffing his fists into his pockets and scowling at the ground. I watched him, unaccountably sad on his behalf. His bony shoulders poked out pathetically under the worn T-shirt; his jeans hung off his hips as if discouraged.

He yanked a hand out of one pocket and thrust it through his hair, which stood up wildly on one side.

Okay, which was the real Jackson: the bad-ass lecher or the overgrown waif?

God knows I loved them both. I loved them — okay, I loved *him*, Jackson — in ways I didn't think were possible. At least for me. I wonderingly acknowledged it as I watched him agonize over whatever was bugging him, kept my distance while longing to hold him and help him. Wow.

The waif eventually wandered over to me, scuffing his sneakered feet in the dirt. "Okay, Maddie, I got a problem," he confessed. "A big one. I need your advice, okay?"

I nodded solemnly. Our hands met and clung together; I looked up at his worn face and he leaned his forehead against mine. "I was there."

"Where?"

"Bart's. Last night. Before I ran into you."

I swallowed. "Why?"

" 'Cuz he invited me. Said he had some records he wanted me to look at, so . . ." He sighed nervously. "Shit, Maddie, I gotta tell the cops, but . . . Jesus, you know they're gonna haul my ass straight to jail if they don't have anyone else. And they don't. I know you didn't do it, and who the hell else are they looking at?" He clonked his head against mine. "But shit. Jail. I'll kill myself before I spend anymore time inside. I swear to God I will."

Without a word I grabbed his hand, hauled him to my truck, and headed straight for Libby and Morris Langley's house.

Chapter 18

"Just pretend I'm a police officer, and this is the interrogation room." Morris had abandoned his stuffed shirt persona and seemed almost gleeful at the prospect of playing a role again, however small his audience.

We sat around the Langley's elegantly rustic dining room table, our steaming mugs on ceramic coasters. Libby aligned the spotless blue Williams Sonoma carafe with its matching sugar bowl and creamer, then placed herself on my right, across from her husband. My herbal tea smelled like old vase water next to the rich aroma of French Roast emanating from the carafe, but I had sworn off coffee for Roz's sake.

Jackson sat on my left, clearly uncomfortable but trying to appear undaunted as the cleft-chinned Morris uncapped his fountain pen and scratched a few neat strokes onto his pristine legal pad. "Okay, Jackson, just tell me what happened. Don't leave anything out. Would you prefer the ladies to leave?" I glared at him and hunkered down rebelliously as Libby obediently started to rise.

"Naw, 'course not," Jackson said.

Libby lowered herself back down.

"Go on, then."

"Okay, well." Slouching as well as he could in the rigid chair, Jackson started the story he would have to tell the police next. "I put in a few hours in the kitchen."

"At the *VhoonderBar?*" Morris had a German accent as impeccable as his wardrobe.

"Yeah. Then I went out to the bar and Bart Fulton was

there and he and Alison were talking."

"Alison Shipwood." Morris seemed to like saying the old-money name aloud; he scribbled it on his pad. Unseen by her husband, Libby wrinkled her nose.

"Yeah. Then the phone rings and Alison takes it in the kitchen. So Fulton calls me over and tells me he has some records he thought I might like, do I wanna come over and check 'em out? And I say sure, when, and he says how's now, and I say fine, so we go." He stared into his coffee mug.

"Did Cal or Alison know where you were going?"

Jackson shook his head. "I was off-duty, so I didn't report in. Anyway, it turned out he didn't have anything I was interested in, but he really wanted to talk to me for some reason, so I let him."

"Talk to you about what?"

"At first it was about his wives." Jackson kicked restlessly at the leg of the table; Libby winced but managed not to correct him. "He kept drinking beer — he was already pretty stinking, too — and telling me how awful his wives were to him and what a great guy he was. And then... well, he started in on Maddie. So I left."

Morris leaned toward him. "What did he tell you about her?"

"He started out saying she was a man-hating lesbian bitch, and it went downhill from there."

"Oh God." I couldn't help laughing. "Yeah, I must be a lesbian if I dumped him."

Morris frowned me into silence and turned back to Jackson. "What else?"

"I told him I had to get going. He offered to take me back, but there was no way I was gonna let him drive me anyplace ... so I said no thanks and got up and put on my coat..." His eyes slid toward me and away again. "And that's when he told me Maddie's baby was his." I took a loud swallow of tea and almost choked.

"How did you react to that?"

"Well, shit, I was surprised 'cuz frankly I couldn't see it. I guess I looked it, 'cuz he started in about how she tricked him and lied to him and what a psycho bitch she is. It sounded like a big load of crap to me, so I said good-bye again and walked out."

"And he was alive when you left, I presume?"

"Yeah. Drunk on his ass, but alive."

"Was it snowing when you left Bart's house?"

"Naw, it was still early — like around 6:30 or so. But it was pretty damn cold and damp — lotta sleet coming down. I got chilled as hell. I saw Maddie's truck at the library so I stopped in to say hi."

A sharp scream followed by a high keening sound issued from the TV room. "Excuse me," Libby murmured as she dutifully exited.

"Then?"

"Well. We talked a little and Maddie invited me over to, uh, weather the storm." The sad warmth of his weary grin hurt my throat.

"And you agreed."

"Shit, yeah . . . I mean, the idea of a snowy night with Maddie was pretty damn seductive." I couldn't look at him; I didn't want him to see my eyes right then.

Morris looked nauseated. "Did you tell her about seeing Bart?"

"No, no, no way."

As Libby tiptoed back in, Morris nodded at the coffeepot. Stepford Wife-like, she silently poured another round for the boys. As if they needed it. I sniffed the aroma longingly and stifled a yawn as Morris continued his questioning. "Why not tell Max?"

"Why should I upset her with his crap? I could see it for what it was."

Libby noticed my untouched mug of organic bilge. "You want something else, Max?" she whispered. "Milk? Orange juice?" I shook my head and she squeezed my arm.

"So you went to Max's house and?"

"Did what she said. Got the fireplace going, listened to music, made dinner, just kinda did normal stuff." Jackson stopped, burying his face in his coffee mug for a long moment. Morris and Libby looked away discreetly so I gave him my hand under the table. He gripped it hard, cleared his throat and went on. "And we talked a lot. And after a while I could tell she was sleepy, but she was being polite."

"Max?" Libby's amused tone pissed me off.

"Yeah." Jackson winked at me halfheartedly. "But we were wrapped up in a quilt by the fire, nice and cozy, and she finally conked out. So I covered her up and sat there a while, then I looked out and saw it still wasn't snowing all that hard. So I decided to walk home."

Morris's eyes narrowed. "What time was this?"

"Maybe eleven or so?"

"Why did you decide to walk home when a blizzard was forecast?"

Jack shrugged. "I was s'posed to be home by ten, really, but my parole officer'd probably forgive me if there was a blizzard. It started to look like maybe the weather people were wrong. It happens, y'know." He studied the pattern on the tablecloth. "And, well, Maddie was sound asleep and . . . well, I thought maybe if it did snow, she wouldn't want to be stuck with me for, like, days, y'know?"

"But she invited you."

"Yeah, well . . ." Jackson looked at me uncomfortably. I wondered what the hell this was about.

"Well what?"

"Look, man, I left her a note. I had some things to do," he said.

"Level with me, damn it," Morris commanded in what must have been his courtroom voice. "You think the police are going to let that go by?"

"I had to take something," Jackson blurted.

"What?"

"Drugs. Medication." At Morris's look, Jackson added, "Prescription stuff, nothing illegal."

"What, then, if it's not illegal?"

Jackson glared at me. What the hell did I do? "Antidepressants, okay? Mood-leveling shit."

Morris sat back in his chair, observing Jackson. "How often do you take this medication?"

"Couple times a day. And I missed my earlier dose, and I didn't want to skip two in a row."

"Why? What happens?"

Squirming a little, Jackson muttered, "I get cranky, okay?" He let go of my hand and gloomily sipped his coffee. Libby and Morris arched eyebrows at each other across the table. Ma and Pa Yuppie.

"When do you normally take the medication?"

"Around noon or whenever I get up, and after my gig, midnight or so."

"Twice a day, then. And why did you miss the earlier dose that day?"

"I woke up late, and had to haul ass downstairs to get the kitchen prep done. I just, y'know, forgot. And I don't carry the shit around with me." Jackson grabbed my hand back and said, "Maddie, remember that time you stayed over and I was such an asshole the next morning?"

"Vividly."

"Yeah, you said — what? It was like going to bed with Albert Schweitzer and waking up with . . ."

"Rush Limbaugh." I filled in the blank for him.

"Well, at least you didn't say Mike Tyson." He chuckled weakly and turned back to Morris. "That was 'cuz I missed my dose the night before."

Morris's chiseled chin pointed in my direction. "What was he like?"

I blinked. "Grouchy. Irritable. Critical."

"Violent?"

"No!" But I remembered how he'd stomped around and snapped at me about nothing — and that was after missing just one dose, not two.

Jackson saw the doubt on my face and sagged. "Fuck. Oh, fuck." With a sudden movement he stood. "Look, I need a piss and a smoke. I'll be back, okay?" The kitchen door banged behind him.

"Jesus," Libby breathed. For a second I thought she was worried Jackson was going to piss in her backyard. He probably was. But then I realized.

She thought he did it.

"This is *not* good." Morris frowned after Jackson. "The prosecution is going to kill him."

Chapter 19

I drove through the melting streets, Jackson slumped beside me. "They think I did it," he growled. "Did they say so to you?"

"Not in so many words, but I got that impression."

"Shit." He looked over at me. "Maddie?"

"Yeah?"

"Do you?"

"No, of course not," I said.

"Really? 'Cuz I thought you looked kinda, you know, doubtful for a while there."

I chewed my lower lip as we bumped down the dirt road to my house. "Well, I guess Morris is a good lawyer, and he was doing what we needed, playing devil's advocate. He had me looking at it from the other side. But I know you didn't do it."

"How do you know?"

I'd hoped he wouldn't ask me that. "It's a gut feeling. I just know."

"Well, he's right about one thing. A jury won't be that intuitive. I had motive, means, and opportunity. And a prison record, damn it, and a rotten temper, and I'm on psychotropic drugs. That's the kinda shit they look for. Circumstantially, I'm screwed." He slammed out of the truck and into the house.

When I plodded to the living room a minute or two later and collapsed onto the sofa to caress the entwined Hairball and Booger, Jackson was staring at my answering machine. "You been getting weird phone calls lately?"

"Nothing but, to tell you the truth. Why, did someone call?"

"Yeah. I walked in the room, the phone was ringing, the machine picked up, some guy said some weird shit then hung up." At my request, he pressed a couple of buttons, finally got the right one, and a tense whisper bleated from the tinny speaker.

"I love you so much. I'll do anything for you. But I guess you know that, right?" A sniffle, a sigh, then silence.

"Do you know who that is?" Jackson demanded as I covered my face with my hands.

"Nick. Nick Jurgliewicz. A teacher I had an affair with last year. We broke up last fall, but he started calling me again recently and no matter what I say he just doesn't get it."

Jackson sat on the arm of the sofa, mulling over Nick's words. "So he'd do anything for you, huh?"

We looked at each other, then I struggled to my feet and checked my new caller ID. "He was calling from the school. Must be working late." I grabbed my jacket and headed out. "Let's go talk to him."

I parked the truck a little ways down from the back door to the art room, near Nick's battered Escort. Yeah, it looked like one of our rendezvous, especially at that time of night, but I didn't want to park out front given my "time out" status. Jackson studied me as I took my time getting out of the truck. "You okay?"

"Yeah, sure, just . . . this is just weird." I fumbled, dropped my bag upside down on Molly's floor, and cursed. Jackson shoveled everything back into it and handed it to me. "Thanks." I groped around for my lip balm and killed some time putting that on. I knew this whole thing was stalling; Jackson was going to have to go to the police soon, or he was going to look guilty as hell if someone else knew he'd been at Bart's.

Clearly annoyed by my fooling around, Jackson said, "Why don't you stay out here? I'll talk to him."

I frowned and shook my head. "Naw, he's more likely to talk if I'm there."

When I peered in the window, I saw Nick seated at his desk, phone to his ear. He was listening zealously, his eyes glazed, his mouth slightly open. Like he used to look at me.

Holy shit.

I rapped the window almost hard enough to break it. With a guilty jump, Nick slammed the phone down as his head snapped up. My eyes snagged him like a fishhook; all he could do was stare. Jackson peered in over my head. "Jesus, what's the hold-up?" He rattled the doorknob angrily. Nick jumped up from his seat and came toward us; a few seconds and we were face to face.

"Max," he breathed.

Jackson pushed his way by me into the room. "Hi, I'm Jackson O'Brien. You Nick Jurgliewicz?"

Nick nodded, eyes still fastened on mine over Jackson's skinny shoulder.

"I'd like to ask you a few questions. Have a seat." Jackson guided Nick to a chair at one of the long tables, then dragged me to the other side of the table and straddled the chair next to mine. "I came with Maddie 'cuz she's pretty freaked out by these phone calls you've been making. I don't think she should be here at all, but she insisted."

No reaction from Nick, who stayed riveted on me. My guts were quaking as I forced myself to speak harshly. "Nick, you might want to listen to Jackson here."

"What?"

The absent-minded professor thing I used to find so appealing was really disturbing all of a sudden. I looked wide-eyed at Jackson, who grabbed my hand and leaned across the table toward Nick. "Listen, you friggin' space shot, I'm asking you about these weird-ass phone calls you've been making to Maddie. You hear me?"

Nick's eyes snapped to Jackson's hand holding mine. "Who are you?" he asked.

Again Jackson explained his presence as Nick glared at our clasped hands. "So first I wanna know exactly why you keep bugging Maddie when she's made it pretty fucking clear that your calls are unwanted."

"Don't talk to me like that." Well, well, meek little Nick seemed to have developed a spine sometime over the past few months.

Jackson surprised me. "Sorry, man. I gotta watch my language."

Nick's Bambi eyes turned back to me. "Why are my calls unwanted? What did I do?"

"You're not talking to her, Nick. You're talking to me, okay?" Jackson rumbled, but Nick barely acknowledged him before addressing me again.

"Is he the father?"

Jackson leaned across the table and pulled Nick's face in his direction. "No. The father's dead. Someone killed him. You know anything about that?"

Nick's eyes darted around like panicky fish. "What? It was *that* guy? Why would I know about it?"

"I don't know, Nick, suppose you tell us." I struggled for a neutral tone, but Nick suddenly seemed guilty as hell.

The darting fish flicked back toward me. "I don't understand why you were seeing anyone. I thought we'd get back together when things calmed down. I thought you'd wait."

"I thought you'd decided to stick to your wife. You never said . . ."

"I thought you'd just *know*. I thought you loved me!"

I swallowed queasily. "I guess I thought I loved you too."

A sharp whistle startled me. "Okay, folks, back to reality." Jackson smacked the table with his open hand.

I rode right over him. "But I guess I'm starting to realize I've never loved anyone. Until now." I patted my belly and felt Roz bump against my hand; my voice choked. "This is who I love, and there's nothing I won't do to take care of her. I asked you to stop calling and I explained why. So I guess I want to know —"

"What your fucking problem is," Jackson finished for me. "And incidentally, where were you this past Tuesday night?"

Nick studied Jackson coldly. "Is he with the police?"

"No, I'm not," Jackson said. "Not officially, anyway. I'm working for Maddie here. She wants to know who killed her baby's father."

"Not me. And why should I talk to you anyway?"

"Because Maddie's going to the police with some answering machine tapes with your voice on 'em. She thought she should let you know first. Personally, I think she should just hand 'em over. They're pretty interesting, and they sure as hell show you had a motive to kill Bart Fulton."

Every drop of color washed from Nick's face, stranding his vivid brown eyes in a featureless sea. "You're kidding," he whispered.

"No kidding, man. Talking to you in person is even creepier than listening to you on tape. You might want to think about getting some counseling pretty soon. You could probably cop the insanity plea and get off easy."

Nick licked his lips. "Look, I haven't called her that often. Just a few times."

Impulsively I pushed back my chair and strode to his desk, hit the speaker then redial buttons on his phone. After four tinny rings, my own crabby voice broadcast through the room. "Hi, this is Madeleine Maxwell. Leave a message and I'll . . ." I slapped the speaker button off and glared at Nick. "You called me about half an hour ago. You were calling me again when we got here. How many other times?"

His eyes threatened to fly out of his head. "God, I don't know." A sob interrupted him. "I — I know it's weird, but — I just wanted to hear your voice." Jackson's sympathetic nod surprised me again. "And when I call you won't talk to me, so . . . I call when I'm pretty sure you're out. I usually hang up before the beep. But sometimes I just . . . can't stop myself."

"Well, you might wanna stop yourself, bud, because right now you look like a prime suspect." Jackson paced to the other side of the table, where Nick sat with his head buried in his hands. Wayward wisps of hair stuck through his fingers. "You sound like a raving nut case on those tapes, you know that? I think you're having some kind of breakdown. You seeing a professional at all?"

"My wife," Nick sobbed.

"Your wife's a shrink?"

"She's seeing a psychiatrist. She's — Max — listen to me, please? That night she — she really hurt herself. I couldn't do anything. I had to be there. She — she took a knife and cut her arm to ribbons right in front of me." Nick shuddered at the memory and pushed up the right sleeve of his sweater. "Then she came after me."

Jackson's sullen silence on the way back oppressed me further, which I didn't think possible. Sickened by what we had just heard and seen, I waited for him to break the ice. Instead he added another layer as we pulled into my driveway. "Did you get what you wanted from that?"

I refused to acknowledge the implied insult. "I don't think he did it, do you?"

"I'm not convinced one way or the other." Jackson slumped in his seat as I cut the engine. "Jesus, Maddie, where do you find these assholes?"

"They're everywhere. How do you avoid them, is more like it."

"How long did you carry on with that one?"

I shivered as the early spring chill seeped through my jacket. "Is this relevant?"

"He's lying." Jackson's voice was sharp as the air. "He's lying about something. He lied about how much he called you until you caught him. How do we know his wife cut him like that? How do we know it's not the other way around?"

"Heather's got a whaddyacallit, a syndrome. When she feels hurt or angry, she cuts herself open."

"Says Nick."

"I'm pretty sure it's true." I recounted the research I did for Nick when he first confided Heather's behavior to me. "I forget the specific name for it, but it's common with women who were abused as kids. I think it numbs them when the emotional pain gets to be too much." I huddled down inside my sweatshirt, drawing my arms partway up the sleeves. "It's weird she went after him, though."

"Hell, I'd like to stab him, and I've only known him ten minutes." My stomach writhed at that. "I'd love to know what you saw in that wimp."

That did it. "What the hell is this about?"

"What?"

I flapped my semi-straight-jacketed arms. "All this pissiness about Nick. I thought we were looking for the truth here, not dissecting my past."

Jackson slammed out of the truck and stomped up the porch steps.

I found him in the kitchen, loudly making tea. Drawers banged, silverware clattered, mugs clunked. Ears flattened back on her head, Booger trotted from the kitchen and sought refuge with me in the living room.

To drown him out, I shuffled to the hearth to build a fire, clanking the damper, crackling newspaper, thumping logs. Disgusted by all these moody humans, Booger took off for the bedroom. Of course, no matter what I did, the damn fire wouldn't light. Instead of using my brain, I sat on the hearth, cursing and crashing, until Jackson came in with a steaming mug of tea and took over for me.

"I can do it," I muttered testily.

"I know." My tolerant friend was back, quickly and competently lighting the fire. We sat together and stared into the flames for a while. "I'm sorry."

"Yeah?"

"Yeah. I got stupid on you," he said.

"You sounded jealous."

"I was." He blew on his tea and gave me a rueful wink. "I am."

"I thought you hated jealousy."

"I do." He smiled tightly. "Now you know why."

I pushed myself back against the sofa, willing the cramps out of my shoulders. "Yeah, it's pretty pointless, isn't it? I was so jealous of Nick's wife, and look at what a mess she is."

"Jealousy is a damn useless thing, for sure." Jackson's eyes were like antique silver in the firelight. "Alison gave me a little taste of my own medicine. That should've cured me, huh?"

I tensed up even more at the mention of Alison's name. "The ice queen got jealous on you?"

Jackson leaned forward and poked the fire. "Oh, a tad," he muttered.

Speaking of jealousy. Jesus. My head felt like it was going to blow off if I didn't ask the question, so I finally snapped it out. "If there was nothing going on between you two, why was she jealous?"

Jackson whacked a glowing log with the poker and watched the sparks dance. "Okay, okay, I guess I should explain what happened. But I don't get it either, so maybe you can shed a little feminine intuition on this whole stupid thing." I tried to unclench my jaw as I waited.

"Okay, here it is. A week or so after I got here, Alison and I were closing up the place. Cal was long gone. She'd been drinking pretty steadily, and I figured that was why she started coming on to me." So far, I could deal. In fact I liked the idea of Alison shitfaced and horny; it was so different from the usual image she presented. "At first I was thinking, hey, what the hell, it had been so damn long I didn't even know if things were still, you know, working." His look challenged me to find fault with that. Given my own tendencies, I really couldn't, so he continued.

"Anyway, then I started thinking . . . shit, she's my boss, it's gonna be awkward as hell if we go through with this. So I said that to her. And that's when things got weird." He leaned back, resting his head against the sofa. "I mean, for a while she seemed pretty understanding, but then a few weeks later we were working behind the bar and it was like she suddenly decided to attack. Whammo, she pinned me up against the wall and like *glued* her face to mine. I couldn't even come up for air."

I was trying not to crack up at this picture, but it sure put Alison's alleged affair with Jackson in a very different light. He noticed my smirk and smiled back. "Yeah, no kidding. It was bizarre. And the weirdest thing was, I thought I heard Cal come in the back door while we were, um, liplocked. I tried to get away to, y'know, take a look, but she grabbed me by the front of my shirt and held me there. I couldn't move. That's one strong woman," he mused.

"So, did you file sexual harassment charges?" I sneered.

"Naw, 'course not. She apologized the next day, said she was drunk, and we kinda made a joke out of it. But then I dunno, things were okay for a little while, we even kinda got friendly, then she threw herself at me again. This time when I turned her down she was upset. I mean, outside she acted real dignified, no problem and all, but she seemed upset underneath. And then she saw me with you that night in the alley and it's been a friggin' soap opera ever since."

I frowned. "I thought she had a lover."

"Yeah, Mr. Mystery. Cal loves to quiz her about him, but she ain't talkin'."

"You think he's still around, even though she's mooning after you?"

"Yeah, he calls a lot. I think he's married or something."

To my chagrin, I felt a little sympathy for snooty Alison. "Hmph. Sounds familiar."

"Yeah, no kidding. Anyhow, my guess is he pissed her off — maybe flirted with someone else . . ."

"Or paid too much attention to his wife," I put in, speaking from experience.

". . . and she decided two could play at that game. She thought she'd have a dirty little affair with the hired help."

"Guess that backfired on her, huh?"

"Yeah, she was blown away by my irresistible charm and suaveness," he said. "Not really, but . . . yeah, I hafta say she seems to have a major thing for me. Go figure. I think she was surprised by it — maybe horrified is more like it — and tried to act like it was nothing. But after she saw you and me together, she started up with this desperate shit."

"Meaning what?" My nerves tingled.

"She promised me all kinds of crap. She offered me a partnership in the pub. She even had your pal Morris draw up an agreement. I don't think Cal was too pleased, but she's got the purse strings, so . . ." With a shrug, Jackson dismissed the power of the wealthy. "She presented it like I'd be doing her some big favor by accepting and being in charge of the entertainment. When I said I didn't want to be tied down like that, she got all weepy and asked me what you had that she didn't have, or something along those lines."

"You're kidding me. She asked *that?*"

Jackson had a sudden, acute interest in drinking in his tea. "Yeah." He set the empty mug on the coffee table and looked at me resolutely. "And now it's time for me to do my, uh, civic duty and talk to the cops."

Chapter 20

I woke up late the day of Bart's funeral — it was Saturday morning, for God's sake — so I hustled into shower, clothes, truck. The only dark stuff I found that still fit was black leggings and an oversized purple chenille sweater. I hoped it wasn't too flashy for my baby's father's funeral, but I bet the Stiff Neckers would be surprised I didn't show up in scarlet.

I drove to the WunderBar to pick up Jackson, who had been interviewed, then interrogated, then reluctantly released by Hawk Marsh's finest the day before. I was cautiously optimistic that his voluntary visit would make him look better; Jackson, on the other hand, figured it was just a matter of time before he was behind bars again. We both hoped the funeral would provide a few missing insights into who would want Bart dead. Other than us.

Roz wriggled rebelliously against the seatbelt strapped across my stomach. She was less eel and more baby every day; my hand frequently rested on my abdomen to detect her almost constant motion. A bump that could be a head or a butt occasionally pushed its way across my belly when I was showering. I still didn't actually look pregnant, just chunky and busty. As I was only five months along, I guess I should have been grateful I wasn't a blimp, but, perverse as ever, I longed for the unmistakable swelling belly. I wanted my body to brag for me.

My oversized grin faded as I recalled where I was going. Jesus, here I was smiling like a fool and Roz's father was dead.

Well I might as well admit it. I wasn't really all that sorry.

God, I was loathsome.

We were too late for the indoor mass, which was fine by me. Catholic churches creep me out more than Protestant ones, with all the gross-out statuary. As we waited outside for the graveside ceremony — the cemetery was right next to the church — I studied the stone Nativity figures on the lawn with amusement. The stone Baby Jesus' arms were raised in a helpless gesture, and Mary also stood in open-handed bewilderment; both seemed to be saying, "Hey, what do you want from me?" Joseph just stared.

Needless to say, Jackson and I got a lot of sour looks in the cemetery. Even Cal and Alison frowned upon Jackson's presence. They both seemed genuinely upset at Bart's passing. Guess they didn't know him too well. Or maybe I'd been too damn busy justifying my own selfishness.

We decided to sit near the back, even though a damp, chill breeze was flowing through that end of the tent. The little plastic folding chairs looked like they were designed for third graders, so we opted to stand.

It was a mercifully brief ceremony, most of which we couldn't hear because of the breeze, which bore the priest's voice away. I tried to see up front, but there were too many people in front of me and I'm too damned short. Long-legged Jackson could have told me plenty if he weren't so sunk into melancholy that it was pointless to ask him.

As we headed back toward the church I asked anyway. "Could you tell who the wives were?"

"Huh? Oh. Yeah, think so." Hands stuffed deep in his pockets, Jackson frowned at the ground. "There's a little dark woman with two young girls. She was putting on a big show with her hankie."

"First wife. Nina."

"And there was this other one, redhead, really hot, with a Hell's Angels-type guy. She didn't seem too upset."

"Irene. Either one look guilty?"

"Come on, Maddie. No one's gonna be all shifty-eyed at their victim's funeral." He hastened his shuffling gait. "I wanna skip the reception thing, okay?"

I stopped. "But Jackson, that's where we can learn the most!"

"Skip it. It's not gonna work, Maddie. Just take me back to the pub, okay?"

Hastily I cooked up a good lie. Not a total lie, but an exaggeration. "I have to pee."

"You can pee at the pub."

"But the church is right over there, and the pub is like ten minutes away." I crossed my legs for effect.

He didn't buy it entirely, I could tell, but he didn't want to be mean. "Oh, all right," he snapped. "Just run in and whiz fast so we can duck out again, okay?"

That wouldn't work. "Come with me."

"Why? You can find a ladies room on your own."

"But — well, I need moral support. Some of these people are really giving me the evil eye." God, I sounded like a paranoid whiner. But it worked; Jackson grabbed my elbow and dragged me roughly to the church basement.

Turned out the tiny fluffy ladies room was an emotional minefield. In the full-length mirror behind the door, Alison Shipwood reapplied tear-smudged eyeliner and straightened her wind-blown hair. She froze when we locked eyes in the mirror. Sniffing angrily, she redoubled her cosmetic efforts and almost jabbed her eye out.

A very pretty Latino-looking woman sobbed at the sink as a very unpretty teenage girl consoled her — a teenage girl with goldfish eyes, big braces, and no chin.

This had to be Rachel: Bart's eldest, Roz's half-sister. That made the crying woman Nina.

By now I really had to pee, so I tried to open the stall. "I'm in here!" a little girl yipped. Good God, that had to be Sally, Bart's youngest. I leaned against the wall, wishing I could just walk out again.

"Sally, hurry up in there, this lady needs to go." A sad smile crinkled Nina's huge dark eyes. "Hi, I'm Nina Fulton. Did you know my husband?"

Hm. Nina seemed to have forgotten she was divorced. "I'm Madeleine, um, Maxwell. Uh — yeah, I saw him at the, um, coffee shop. Uh, sometimes." If I tripped over my tongue much more, I wouldn't be able to talk at all. "I'm, um, really sorry."

A loud flush drowned out this untruth and a tiny replica of Nina — Sally Fulton, age ten — banged out of the stall and glared at me. "She knows him. She used to go out with him."

"What? Wherever did you get that idea, baby?" Nina turned on the water tap for Sally and shoved soap into her hand.

"I *know*. She dumped him. Daddy was really upset. He had her picture and everything."

Suddenly I was thanking God my pregnancy didn't show yet. I shrugged at Nina, and caught a glimpse of Alison's mirrored expression as I slipped into the stall.

If I could have laughed, I'd have joined her.

"What? Sarah Rebecca, stop being so silly! Daddy wouldn't go out with *her;* he loved *me!*" With that questionable remark, Nina left, children in tow.

I was surprised to find Jackson in the lush, well-appointed reception area, sipping black coffee and looking around curiously. "Well, I know you wanted to do some snooping, so what the hell," he explained. "Plus, this is pretty interesting. Check out the broads."

The two widows couldn't have been more different. Nina, dressed in appropriate sobriety with sexy undertones, dabbed her eye with a black-laced hankie as mourners stopped to offer condolences. She kept nasty little Sally close to her side, while the sincerely sad Rachel moped behind her. Bart had implied Nina had a few screws loose, and from what I'd just witnessed he hadn't been exaggerating for once.

Irene, on the other hand, didn't even bother to affect sorrow. A skin-tight black leather dress was her only concession to grief. She beamed at various guests, took generous bites from a huge blueberry muffin, and laughed happily when her muscular, longhaired escort whispered in her ear. Maybe the relief of being rid of Bart for good was making her giddy. No messy divorce needed now; she could fire her lawyer and move her lover in. Hm again.

I noticed Rachel watching Irene with a look of bewildered, grave disappointment. When I caught her eye, her thin lips pursed over the bulge of her braces and her face grew thoughtful. She murmured something to her mother, who ignored her, and started walking straight toward me.

Yikes.

"Hi," she said shyly, her basset hound eyes widening nervously. "Um. Sally said — um, did you really used to go out with my dad?" Again she folded her lips over her braces, rendering herself even more fishy and distorted.

"Uh . . ." I wasn't sure what to say. The poor kid. She deserved the truth. Well, depending on how you define 'deserve.' Or 'truth,' for that matter. At any rate, I gave it to her. "Yeah, we went out for a little while."

She blinked and a tear ran down her face. "Why'd you

stop?" she demanded, smearing the tear awkwardly across her freckled cheek.

I was surprised and strangely pleased. Maybe my own daughter wouldn't be spineless despite her father, even if she was chinless. "It just . . . we just . . . didn't work out."

"Why not?" Her voice tightened but remained firm, and I felt a sudden rush of pity for this girl trying to make sense of her father's terrible luck with women. It was obvious Irene had left him for another man; he'd implied several times Nina left him for a few men, and he'd hinted darkly at a woman as well.

I took Rachel by the arm and gently tugged her away from the crowd, toward a huge white statue of Mary that adorned the nearest corner. I looked up at her face — thirteen years old and she was already taller than me — and wondered if my daughter would resemble her. She wasn't bad up close. My eyes stung with poignant sympathy; hey, I'd been an ugly teen with an adorable little sister and an unsympathetic mom. We had more in common than her father's DNA. I cleared my throat and gave her a tentative pat.

"Look, Rachel, I'm sorry about your dad. I mean about him dying and about his crappy luck. Sometimes it takes a really long time to find someone you can work things out with. Sometimes you never find them at all. It doesn't have anything to do with whether someone's good or bad or deserves to be loved or not. It's just . . ."

"Didn't you love him?" Her hunger for reassurance quivered between us.

I sighed, frustrated with my inability to comfort her. "Look, your dad was a really, um, nice guy, okay?" Rachel's face threatened to crumble, but she sternly forced it into tense, trembling lines. "Frankly, I'm *not* really a nice person. I'm trouble. And I like trouble. And your dad had enough trouble already. And that's all I can say that you might understand right now."

Tears flooded her face and she blurted between hiccups, "If he was so nice . . . why did . . . someone . . . kill him?" Her features fell into dripping ruin.

"What the hell are you saying to her?" A strong hand spun me around. I stared up at the stunning, green-eyed, red-haired Irene, who pushed me aside and rushed to comfort Rachel. "Rache, honey, what'd she say?"

"Leave me alone, you slut!" Rachel's uncontrolled scream tore the room as she spit angry words at her stepmother. "You killed him, didn't you? You and your whore boyfriend! You fucking bitch! I hate you!"

And the ugly duckling smashed the gorgeous swan across the face and ran for the door. When her mother, sister, and stepmother all just stood there staring, I took off after her.

I found Rachel behind the church, crumpled at the muddy base of a tree and sobbing wretchedly. She resisted my efforts to help her up so I let her lie there. Jackson crept up to us and settled down next to me, lighting a cigarette. "Cat fight starting inside," he muttered as he flung the match away.

Rachel jerked up at the sound of his voice, then rubbed her slimy nose across her rough woolen sleeve and stared at him round-eyed. "Who are you?"

"Name's Jackson."

"Did you know my dad?" she asked pathetically.

"Your dad? Yeah, a little." Jackson seemed strangely comfortable in the surreal situation. "We talked music when he came in for a drink after work, that sorta thing."

"He liked music. I play piano."

"Hey, cool, so do I." Jackson pulled a battered but clean handkerchief from his pocket and handed it to Rachel. "Feel better?"

Her nose honked wetly into the hankie. "I was mean to Irene." Rachel scowled. "But she shouldn't be laughing."

"No, maybe not, but sometimes it's weird. People laugh when they're upset 'cuz they don't know what else to do." He waved away the sticky handkerchief Rachel tried to return. "Death freaks people out and they say and do things they don't mean. I mean, you don't *really* think she killed him, do you?"

Damned if Jackson wasn't cutting right to the chase, the devious bastard. Rachel considered his question carefully as she tugged at tiny grass spikes poking through the mud. "Well, I don't know. I guess not." She scowled again. "But I don't like her boyfriend. And I bet he did it."

"Oh, really? Why do you think that?" He shook out a pack of unfiltered Camels and offered her one; she started to giggle and covered her mouth, embarrassed.

"I can't smoke; my dad would kill me." The words lay there for a minute, then Rachel started laughing for real. Like her screaming, it was out of control, but at least it was a release.

Jackson grinned and started to say something, but around the corner a door slammed and a woman swore shrilly. "That fucking bitch! She stole him from me and then she killed him!"

"Mrs. Fulton, try to calm down." A male voice, placating, commanding. Sounded like Morris Langley to me.

"Mama." Rachel leaped to her feet, tense as a pointer dog.

"Stay here a minute, babe," Jackson whispered, placing a firm hand on her shoulder. "Your mama's having a meltdown and she might not want you to see it."

"What?" Rachel sounded surprised. "No, she gets like this a lot. It's okay. I should go to her. She likes to have me there when she's upset." Rachel paused long enough to give

Jackson a shy, tight-lipped smile. "Thanks for the hankie, Jackson." She shoved it into her pocket and ran off.

Good God, that was the quickest crush development I'd ever seen. At least the girl had taste.

"Jesus, that poor kid." Jackson muttered as Nina's shrieks continued. "She's probably been taking care of her crazy mother for a while, huh?" He took a final drag on his Camel, tossed it to the ground, and crushed it with a size twelve sneaker. "Hey, anyone else you wanna scope out, or can we leave? I'm getting depressed."

"Can you talk to the boyfriend? Rachel suspects him."

"Yeah, well, he broke up her happy home, right?" But he started back toward the church anyway. I followed, suddenly exhausted. Roz wiggled a little to cheer me up. It worked.

I joined the spectators at Nina's breakdown. Irene stood alone, near the back. Muscle boy was nowhere in sight. Jackson headed into the hall and I gave Irene a daring tap.

She whirled around. Her dazzling smile and glowing eyes faded as soon as she saw me. "Oh. I thought . . ." She looked around hastily and frowned. "What do you want?"

"Look, I just wanted to clear the air. I wasn't saying anything to hurt Rachel. She was crying because her father's dead."

My blunt tone disarmed her. "Well, I guess I knew that. Who are you, anyway?"

"Madeleine Maxwell. Bart and I were seeing each other a couple months back."

Strong eyebrows arched. "Oh? I didn't realize . . ." She stopped, shrugged. "Well, I guess it doesn't matter now. Look, I'm sorry I jumped on you like that. I love Rache to bits and feel like . . . God, I don't know. Like I really let her down." Irene chewed her lip ruefully. "She's such a great kid. And look at how Nina treats her. It's a crime." We glanced over to where Rachel was rubbing her mother's shoulders from behind, while tiny Sally glowered on the side. "But what the hell could I do? I mean . . . well, you said you *used* to date Bart, right?"

"Oh yeah. It was over."

"And you ended it?"

"Yeah," I said.

"Why?"

Those intense green eyes challenged me to tell the truth. I needed her to trust me, so what the hell. "Well, I guess he seemed nice at first . . . but then, well . . ." I hesitated for effect. "Well, this is going to sound harsh, but — I really think he hated women."

Irene's lovely face relaxed and she pulled me a little further away from the crowd. "God, thank you for saying that," she whispered. "He does — he did hate women. And the worst thing was he thought he was so liberal!"

Smothering a smile, I nodded. "No argument there."

"He just didn't get it, did he?" She gave me a little conspiratorial grin. "I mean sex. He thought it was all about him." Her vivacious face hardened at a memory. "God, I mean . . . after I met Gus and fell in love with him . . . it was so awful, I felt terrible because the kids loved me, so I *tried* to stick with Bart. But — God, he would insist on having sex even though I told him I couldn't enjoy it. I would lie there and cry and he'd just pump away until he was done. Unbelievable. He was so mad at me for crying. Like I could help it! Finally I just couldn't stand it anymore." A rueful smile pinched her lips. "God, wasn't he awful in bed?"

I shrugged, unable to remember much except the pressure to get there. "He wasn't memorable, that's for sure."

At that, we giggled a little too loudly, and Alison, Sally, Morris, and Nina shot visual daggers in our direction.

Chapter 21

"So whaddya got?" I asked Jackson as we pulled out of the church parking lot.

He frowned and sunk further into the tattered passenger seat of my truck. "I got that we had no damn business being there." Looking out the window, he added, "Especially me."

"Screw that. What do they know?"

"They know I've been interrogated, that's for damn sure. Someone's been talking." He stared gloomily at the passing landscape. "Y'know, Maddie, I love Cal, but I wish he'd shut the hell up."

I was exhausted. I was drained. I was starving. I didn't want to think about this anymore. But the voice in my head wouldn't shut up any more than Cal would. "We've got to talk about this, Jackson. We've got to try to figure it out before it's too late. Yeah, they're looking for someone to blame. Who better than the town drunk's slutty kid and an ex-con outsider?"

Jackson covered his face with long, shaky fingers and rubbed his eyes hard. "Yeah, I know you're right."

"So, you wanna go home, or you wanna go back to my place?"

He smiled jaggedly. "I don't think you really have to ask that, do you?"

My throat hurt as I smiled back, wishing it was a few days ago and this would be a time to look forward to. Now we didn't know how much longer we had . . . and we certainly didn't have time to enjoy each other anymore, to relish the slow unfolding of romance. Now everything just sucked.

In my itty-bitty kitchen, we slapped together a couple of sandwiches and started to make a list of possible suspects. I divided it into people who knew Bart well with clear reasons to kill him, and other people who had the opportunity but whose motives were more elusive.

I started with Nina, Bart's unbalanced first wife. Jackson frowned when I wrote her name down. "Well, yeah, she looks like a bitch, but . . ."

"And she's nuts, and I know she's been pissed at Bart lately, despite the grieving widow act." In my imagination, Nina glared at me with snapping black pupils, her compact, curvaceous body tense. There was a big chip on her shoulder for sure. "She probably has the temper to stab a guy to death, but does she have the smarts to cover her tracks so well?"

Jackson shook his head. "The second wife, that redhead . . . she seems more the type. Gotta look out for redheads." He didn't bother to explain his sad smile.

I scribbled Irene's name reluctantly under Nina's. "But I don't think she cared enough to stab him to death." I visualized her defiant but humorous green eyes. "Okay, yeah, she's strong and smart enough — God knows what she was ever doing with Bart — and she didn't seem at all sorry he was dead. But stabbing the crap out of someone takes passion, and I just don't see it."

"But if she didn't care about him, she'd have no problem killing him, don't you think?"

I thought about it. "I'd trust her less if she made a big show of grief, like Nina. Plus, Irene's so wrapped up in her lover I can't imagine her bothering with much else."

"Speaking of . . ."

"Yeah, what's his name again?"

"Gus," Jackson said around a mouthful of sandwich.

I gulped down some milk for Roz's sake and wrote *Gus* on the paper. "Is he as big a sleaze as he looks?"

Jackson chewed his sandwich, then said, "Well, actually, he seemed like a pretty nice guy, just . . . y'know, young and goofy." He took another big bite. He must have been starving.

"Could be an act." Tattooed, leather-clad Gus looked like a great candidate to me. I remembered his sneer when Irene confronted me at the funeral. "I don't think he's such a nice guy. Too bad a woman like Irene went from goofball to sleazeball." I got a sudden image of a glass house, and brushed it away hastily. "I wonder if the police talked to him yet. Maybe an anonymous tip?"

Jackson was shaking his head and chewing throughout my rambling. He swallowed vigorously. "No, I'm telling you, no. Gus is kinda stupid, but he seems like a pretty nice guy."

"Really?" I was sorry to hear that, especially from Jackson.

"Really. Trust me. Anyway," he added, "he has a pretty good alibi for that night. He brought it up all by himself."

"Well . . ." I gnawed at the pencil. "I'm not crossing him off the list. He's got a damn good motive." Jackson conceded, and I moved on. "How about Bart's kids?"

Jackson almost spat out his soda. "What? They're . . . kids!"

"Yeah, I know," I said, "but one's a neglected teenager. Maybe it's like a poltergeist thing." When I saw Jackson's reaction, I felt stupid, which made me get defensive, of course. "Rachel obviously loved that undeserving bastard. She was probably dying for just a scrap of the attention that nasty little Sally gets."

I was strangely enchanted by this theory. Could Bart's dismissal of Rachel have gotten her upset enough to kill him? Or was I over-identifying with the ugly duckling older sister?

There were times I wanted to kill both my parents for the way they doted on blonde-haired, blue-eyed Gabrielle. Well, at least Gabe was nice. Sally was a rat.

"And what about Sally?" I continued out loud.

"God, what is she, nine years old? Come off it, Max, you're getting nuts." Jackson gave me a playful little slap.

I sighed. "Okay. Maybe in *The Bad Seed*, but not here." But the thought made me smile. In my mind, petite, dark Sally glared at me as I considered her as the killer. He was right; it was nuts. I crossed her off the list regretfully. "Too bad. Can't you just picture Sally and her nasty hypocrite mother knifing the crap out of Bart?"

Jackson cleared the dishes and his throat. "Moving right along," he announced, "who else knows Bart well enough to want to kill him?"

I had to say it. "Me."

Not a whole lot taller than Sally, I stood at the end of my own imaginary line-up with my usual bad posture, out to here with Bart's love child. The child he refused to support. The child he made late-night, drunken, accusing phone calls about. The child I threatened to castrate him over.

Jackson sat down and put an arm around me. "No way."

"We have to consider it. You do, anyway. What if I set this up and you're my patsy, or whatever they call it?" Then I came out with my own darkest fear. "Could I have had some kind of hormonal aberration, driven over to Skiff Neck, killed Bart, and conveniently blanked out the whole thing?"

Jackson's head wagged back and forth throughout this speech, too. "You don't really think that, do you?"

I thought about it seriously. Very seriously. "I don't think I was mad enough at him to do that. Even when he totally pissed me off, I had a *little* sympathy for him, mainly because he was such an idiot he couldn't help himself. I mean, I think he was simply incapable of seeing beyond his own problems." I chewed the pencil again and Jackson took it away from me. "But the question is, am I? I mean, I tried to put myself in his shoes. I tried it a lot, just to make sure I wasn't being unreasonable or crazy. But maybe I was after all. Maybe I'm so nuts I killed him and don't remember it."

I tried to picture myself, knife in hand, stabbing away at Bart. Oh, wait, I had to beat him up first. Not hard, if he was as blasted as Jackson said. Okay, so there I was, kicking and pummeling the crap out of a sozzled Bart. Then I grabbed that knife or whatever and plunged it into his doughy gut. Then I drew it out and plunged it in again . . . and again . . . and . . .

"What the hell are you thinking about?" Jackson asked, amused. "You look like whatsername, Bette Davis, in one of those black and white horror flicks, with her eyes all bugging out." He snapped his fingers in front of my face. "Whoa, hey, Maddie! Come back, okay?"

I brought myself back to reality with a shudder. I had the temper, undoubtedly. I learned I was capable of murder at the age fourteen, but I'd been too damned small to kill that 270-pound rapist.

But would I have killed Bart?

No. No matter how lame and stupid and annoying he was, I had never wished him dead.

"So . . . what have we got so far?" I forced myself to focus on the list again. "Okay, so, those are the people that might want to rid the world of Bart for obvious reasons. Anyone else?"

Jackson snorted. "Yeah. How about your old boyfriend — Nick, was it?"

My hackles rose. "Come on. He's a pussy."

"He may be a pussy, but he's a psycho pussy."

Nick's disturbing gaze riveted my inner eye and I sighed. "Okay, he's out there, that's for sure — and he knew about Bart because I told him. I mean, I didn't tell him who it was, but he could have found out easily enough. But I don't think he did it." I brightened up as another suspect occurred to me. "How about Nick's wife? She's a bona fide nutcase, and she likes knives."

Jackson scowled. "Nick seems more likely to me."

"Well, Gus and Nick's wife seem more likely to me." We glared at each other for a moment in a standoff for our favorite murderer. Then the phone rang, and I grunted up out of my chair and limped into the living room to grab it. "Hello?"

"Hello, I'm looking for Jackson O'Brien." The woman's voice was briskly formal but familiar.

"Who is this?" I asked.

Frost came through the wires. "This is his employer calling."

"Oh, for God's sake, Alison, lighten up or buy yourself bigger size panties." Jackson looked up, startled, as I handed the phone to him. "It's Shipwood, badly in need of an enema," I announced loud enough for Alison to hear me.

I busied myself at the sink, pretending not to eavesdrop on Jackson's mostly monosyllabic responses. "Yeah . . . No . . . Well, yeah . . ." A heavy sigh. "Fuck . . . Well, no I understand, but . . ." Jackson's fist hit the table and his voice got louder. "Okay. Fine. Yeah, bye." He continued to sit at the table, glowering at the saltshaker as the phone started quacking. I wrestled it from his clenched hand and hung it up.

"Problem?"

He picked up the pencil, pulled the list of suspects toward him and scrawled "J. O'Brien" under Nick's name. "There's a knife missing from the kitchen at the pub. It's one I use a lot, to chop stuff up. And Alison says she doesn't want me back there until this mess is straightened out." He stared at his name on the list. "She says it sounds like I already have a place to stay anyway."

"She's right." I put my arms around him, but he remained rigid and unresponsive. "So now we're both unemployed. Gives us more time to figure this out." I grabbed the list from him and sat back down. "Okay, why'd you do it?"

"Easy," he growled. "I'm nuts about you, he told me he was your kid's father, he dissed you, and I forgot to take my medication."

"But I got pregnant by him way before I met you."

"Doesn't matter. I'm a jealous son of a bitch with a nasty temper."

He was sinking fast. I saw a straw and grasped it. "What about Alison?"

"What about her?" he snapped. "Vindictive bitch."

"Exactly." I grabbed the pencil from him and printed her name in big letters under his.

Jackson didn't follow my thinking, but at least he looked up. "Why? I mean . . . huh?"

I thought fast. "She's nuts about you, and is completely pissed that you're with me. Maybe she saw this as a way to get rid of both of us." To my surprise, this made a lot of sense. Well, to me, anyway. "And I'm pretty sure she knew this is Bart's kid, because they were always giving each other these looks when I was at the bar." I liked this idea a little too much, since it made Alison the bad guy.

Jackson didn't look convinced, but he politely considered it. "And the missing knife — she could've got that as easy as me. Easier, really. It's her place." He frowned. " 'Course, that might just be a coincidence. It's not like it turned up at Bart's or anything. It's just missing." His eyes flickered down again. "She said she had to report it. Just in case."

I slammed my open hand on the table, causing the chomped-on pencil to jump and roll onto the floor. Hairball materialized and pounced on it, chasing it around the kitchen. "Jesus, that clinches it. Think about it. Okay, she's all obsessed with you and you reject her for me, right? She knows my kid is Bart's, and she knows Bart and I aren't getting along too well, so she kills Bart with a knife from the WunderBar — one you use a lot so it's got your prints — then she . . ."

"Whoa, whoa, Maddie. Time out here."

I wasn't stopping for anything. "Then she plants it somewhere, then pretends to notice it's missing so she can tell the police . . ." God, I was brilliant. "And then —"

Jackson reached across the table and put his hand over my mouth. "You're overlooking something kinda important, okay? Alison and Bart were *friends*, Maddie. They were pretty good friends." He cautiously started to remove his hand, but when my mouth opened he put it back. "I even think Bart had a thing for Alison, but she wasn't interested in him that way. But she talked to him a lot, about his divorce and shit, and she definitely felt sorry for the guy. She wouldn't kill him. Certainly not because of me."

Jackson took his hand away and I talked fast. "Yeah, and Cal said Bart was hitting on Alison. He could be pushy, you know. Maybe he pushed her a little too hard and —"

He rolled his eyes and fought a grin, then stood up and stretched. "I need a smoke."

I picked our suspect list up off the floor and followed him out to the porch. April sunshine dappled the trees and made everything look strangely fresh, except the paint peeling off the house. "Maybe Alison wanted to pin the murder on me, then, figuring if I had access to you then I'd have access to the knife . . ."

Jackson lit a Camel and gave me a dire glare. "Maddie, read my lips. Alison — wouldn't — kill — Bart." With a half-hearted wink, he added, "Not even to put you away."

The phone rang. I waddled back inside and answered it irritably. "What?"

"Hello to you too, sunshine," Cal murmured. "Max, dear, I have to talk fast because Alison's having a breakdown. The police are on their way over to your house. They're looking for Jackson."

My guts avalanched into my shoes. "God, why?"

"They found the murder weapon. It was under a drift in Bart's backyard, which melted today. Guess it didn't occur to them to dig."

My stomach clenched hard. "And?"

"It's the knife. Jackson's favorite slicing and dicing knife from our very own kitchen." I sank into a chair. "When Alison called about our missing knife, they made the connection right away."

Jackson poked his head in the door, ashen and shaking. "The police are here," he croaked.

"They're here, Cal. I'll talk to you soon." I dropped the phone and went straight to Jackson, who put his arms around me. We held onto each other as Yergins and Cullinane came up the porch steps.

Chapter 22

"What the fuck, Cal?" I yelped, forgetting my no-swearing resolution as I slid onto a barstool at the Wonder Bra. "They put Jackson in jail and they don't even have prints or anything yet."

Solemnly wiping a shot glass, Cal shook his head. "Tell me the whole dreary story," he sighed. "Jackson's gone to jail. Alison's gone to pieces, the business is going to hell. I'm hanging on by a thread, but that's okay, because no one's coming in. In my humble opinion, we ought to just close the blessed place."

"What do you think? I mean, you know he didn't do it, right?"

Cal looked at me pityingly. "Oh my dear, not you too."

"Not me too what?" Barely grammatical, but it was the best I could do under the circumstances.

"You think he's innocent? So does Alison. What does he have, some kind of magic wand penis? He waves it at a woman and she thinks he's not bad, just misunderstood?" Cal's dishtowel seemed bent on destruction.

"So you think he did it."

"To quote the eternally eloquent Madeleine Maxwell: no duh. I hate to say it, but it looks like a crime of passion to me. Alison said he was here talking to Bart, she went in the kitchen, when she came back they were both gone, and the next morning Bart's dead. Jackson must have figured out Bart was the father of your child, and we've all seen him mooning around you like the big bad wolf in sheep's clothing.

Last but far from least, the man's got a nasty temper and a prison record to prove it." Cal squirted ginger ale into glasses, tossed in lime wedges and ice. "Standard soap opera *merde,* trite but true. Why, what's your theory?"

I shook my head. "I dunno. I had it figured that Alison did it in some kind of jealous rage over Jackson."

Cal leaned on the counter, intrigued. "To frame you, you mean?"

"Me or Jackson or both. Now it just sounds stupid."

"Not entirely." He sipped his ginger ale and mopped the gleaming counter some more. "Hm, or maybe I did it to frame Jackson. Alison offered him a piece of this place, did you know that?"

I sipped my soda. "Yeah, he mentioned it to me. What the hell was that about?"

Cal rolled his eyes. "That was about Alison trying to keep Jackson under her thumb. She had Morris redraft our partnership agreement to cut Jackson in. I stood to lose if he'd agreed to it." Cal shrugged. "But he turned it down, so I guess that lets me off the hook." He buffed the bronze beer taps and frowned. "You're right about one thing: she's nuts about him. And I mean literally. I've seen cases of obsession, but hers runs deep. Midlife crisis deep."

"Yeah, I noticed." I sipped my soda and waited for Cal to lumber around the bar and sit next to me. "But — listen, I know what you think, but give me your professional opinion about this. Okay?"

"Anything for you, little mama."

"You say Alison is obsessed with Jackson."

"Double scoop, with a cherry on top," Cal said.

"Do you think Jackson is obsessed with me?"

Cal mulled that over, fingering his curly beard. "Well . . . I wouldn't say obsessed, no."

"So why would he kill Bart over me?"

"Hm, good question." His eyes squinted thoughtfully. "Maybe he hides it well. He's got that macho bluff act down pat, but you've seen him pour on the pathos when he's performing, haven't you? He's capable of feeling a lot more than he lets on." Leaning on his hand, Cal studied me. "And you seem to have the ability to dredge up surprising emotions in men. Alison was lamenting that the other day, saying she and Jackson were doing great until he set eyes on you."

I shook my head at that. "Jackson's version is pretty different. He thought maybe she was using him to make Mr. Mystery jealous. Plus Jackson says nothing actually happened between him and Alison, that he nipped it in the bud."

Cal clucked skeptically. "My, my, whom to believe?" He twisted a cocktail straw around one pudgy finger. "I'd thought Alison's affair with Mr. Mystery was over, and I thought Jackson was the reason, but . . . well, he's still calling here as often as ever."

Aiming for casual, I asked, "Do you have any idea who it is yet?"

"No idea. Sorry, Sherlock." Cal chuckled and squeezed my hand. "I'm pretty sure he's from out of town. At least, they meet out of town. One phone call and Alison's out the door, saying she'll be back in a few days. They carried on for a heck of a long time without anyone really knowing about it." He took a delicate sip of ginger ale and sighed. "Even those of us near and dear to La Shipwood remain in the dark."

"Did you ever answer the phone when he called?"

Cal nodded. "I couldn't recognize his voice, though. I think he disguised it." He cocked his head quizzically. "In fact, the calls I've picked up here that turned out to be him, he sounded different every time. For a while I thought she had a few men."

Bizarre, but maybe he was a celebrity, someone who had a recognizable voice. I switched gears. "Cal, remember Nick Jurgliewicz?"

"The little Walter Mitty art teacher who was calling you?"

"Yeah. You think he's capable of murder?"

Cal heaved an enormous sigh and shoved his face into mine, holding my shoulders firmly. "Max, come off it. Jackson did it. And you know what else? I think he killed Junie, too." My mouth dropped open and Cal popped a plump hand over it. What was it with men covering my mouth these days? "No, no, you will listen to the voice of sweet reason for once, Mad Max. No murders in Skiff Neck for years, then the same day Jackson O'Brien arrives here we have a dead body on the beach, right outside his place of employment. Someone who angered him. Someone who flirted with Alison," he stressed. "Then a few weeks later, another dead body. Someone he was with the night of their murder. Someone who flirted with Alison. Hm, do you see a pattern here?" He removed his hand and chucked me under the chin affectionately. "Look at the facts, think about your baby and, to use the your former favorite word, move the fuck on."

I started to snap back at him when the front door swung open hard enough to knock over the specials board. Alison Shipwood swayed in on unsteady legs, lurching toward us like a drunken ostrich until Cal raced to her rescue. "What did we take, sweetums?"

"Just a little Valium. Oh God, I can't . . ." I'd never seen Alison like this. Make-up streaked down her face, hair fluffed wildly on one side and lay flat on the other, clothing drooped from her thin frame. She squinted in my direction. "Oh for God's sake, what the hell is she doing here?" So much for breeding.

"Max and I are having a little chat. Come join us, won't you?"

Cal guided her to the bar and managed to anchor her onto a stool. She collapsed forward onto the counter, head resting on her arms. "Drink?" she implored.

"No way, princess. Not with that stuff in your system." He shoved his ginger ale at her and rubbed her shoulders.

"What the hell is Max doing here?" Alison asked the bar.

"How much Valium did we take?"

"Not enough, God damn it." She sobbed weakly. "God, I should never have told them about that knife. Maybe if they'd just found it, they wouldn't have figured out where it came from." She smacked herself in the forehead and wailed, "They won't let me bail him out, Cal."

"I know, I know," he murmured. "Don't worry, he'll be okay if he's innocent."

She just sobbed harder.

"Alison." She jerked her head up at the sound of my voice and observed me with drugged loathing. "Look, I know you hate my guts. I'm not crazy about yours either. But I'm trying to help. I don't believe Jackson did it. In fact, I know he didn't."

Her jaw tensed. "How do you *know?*"

"Call it a hunch, intuition, whatever. I just know in my gut he didn't do it, and I'm trying to figure out who did." Alison glanced questioningly at Cal, who gave her a solemn nod. "So, look, and pardon me if this is really impertinent or whatever, but — Jackson told me you have a lover stashed away somewhere." Her eyes snapped into focus and bulged angrily. "Tell me, is there any way — I mean, given your relationship with Jackson and all — that this guy would go nuts, kill Bart and try to make it look like Jackson did it?"

After a moment of blank staring Alison started to laugh, a

weak, humorless cawing. "No, Max," she gasped. "I don't seem to inspire the kind of alpha male behavior you do. I envy you your power, I really do."

Could Jackson have killed Junie and Bart?

I sat on the jetty where I'd found Junie's body a few months ago, watching the sun wink on the dappled water and the gulls wheel overhead. The huge rocks were cold and damp with spray, and my butt was freezing, but the day was a stunning contrast to the blizzard of just a few days before. Spring had returned to Hawk Marsh. Which was nice and all, but it didn't help me out a bit.

God and all my friends knew my choices in men were pretty damned awful. Both Cal and Libby had given me a million warnings as I'd embarked on a million affairs, and they'd been right a million times. No exaggeration there. I honestly didn't have a single affair I could look back on with warm nostalgia; there wasn't a man in my so-called romantic history who made me wish I'd stuck around a little longer or made a commitment to something more lasting.

So why should I trust my judgment where Jackson was concerned?

"Hey, Max." I barely reacted to Libby's voice, even though I hadn't heard her come up behind me. Guess I was too numb to be startled. She leaned against the boulder next to me and put her arm around me. "Shitty week, huh?" I had nothing to add, so I just nodded. "You out here doing some thinking?"

"For a change, yeah, I guess I am."

"May I ask?"

Picking up a pebble from the jetty, I hurled it out to the glittering waves, where it sunk straight to the bottom. "I'm an idiot when it comes to men." Wisely, Libby kept her mouth shut. "Seriously, what's your take on Jackson?"

"Honestly?"

"Yeah, honestly."

Libby pushed away from the jetty and brushed off her jeans, then took my arm and pulled me into a stroll along the shore. "Honestly, Max." She sighed. "I can totally see why you're attracted to him. He's talented, he's smart, he's funny, and . . ." With a little whoosh of breath, she added, "Okay, and he's sexy."

I couldn't help grinning. "Yeah, he is, isn't he?"

Libby rolled her eyes moonily. "He's devastating. He's the first man you ever picked that I would even consider trying to steal away from you. But!" she continued before I could smack her. "Sexy does not equal good. And, Max, you really have to look at the facts."

God, this sounded familiar. "You been talking to Cal?" She gave me a sidelong, teasing smile. "Yeah, I thought so. Well, I'm trying, okay?"

Monday morning I drove to the prison. After making some depressing jokes about how many girlfriends Jackson had, the guard ushered me to a battered metal table in the visiting area, then brought Jackson in. And the second I saw him, all my resolve to see him as the bad guy flew right out the window.

Lanky, brash, colorful Jackson was diminished, washed out by the fluorescent glare and the over-bright orange jumpsuit. He looked like he'd been hit by a wrecking ball. His face had crumbled — there's no other way to describe it — and his slate gray eyes had darkened to black. He looked at me from the bottom of some dank, emotionless well and didn't say a word.

Desperate to cheer him and myself up, I babbled on and

on about leads I felt might go somewhere, winding up with, "If we could just figure out who Alison's lover is, I could maybe track him down and . . ."

"Maddie?"

Wow, he was talking. "Yeah?"

Jackson took a weighted breath and leaned toward me. "I want you to do me a favor, babe, okay?"

"Sure, yeah, whatever."

"Okay." He sighed and looked me in the eye. "Promise me you'll do this, please."

My heels dug in at that. "I'm not promising anything till I know what it is."

"Humor me, huh?" One side of his mouth quirked a little as he tried to smile. It didn't work. "Shit. Okay, look. This is good-bye. Got that?" I didn't get it. He sighed again, staring at some unreadable Magic Marker graffiti on the table. "See, look. I'm screwed and I know it. I'm not getting out this time. Even my attorney thinks I'm guilty as hell, and that's because the evidence and my record are against me. I'm toast. And I been working on trying to accept that, okay?" His eyes slid toward mine, then fell again as if they were too heavy to hold up. "The thing that's making it hard is, well, you."

My mouth moved, but nothing came out at first. Then I croaked, "Why?"

Jackson's face tensed as he stared at the table. "I worry about you. The baby. You should be taking care of that, not worrying about me. And . . . well, you make me think of . . . things I shouldn't waste my time thinking of anymore." He looked up and drilled his eyes into mine with surprising intensity, given how weary he sounded. "So don't come here again, okay? I don't wanna see you. I don't wanna be reminded. Just leave me alone." There was no anger in his voice, just resignation.

"Jackson, we've got to get you out of here."

"It ain't gonna happen."

"I'm working on it."

"Well, stop. It's pointless. You got other things to think about. I don't want you working on this anymore, and I don't want you coming here. Just forget me and think about your baby, for Christ's sake."

My chin stuck out in a way my father used to hate and I barked, "Tell me what you know about Alison's lover."

"Not a Goddamn thing, and it doesn't matter anyway. I was born to die in jail. Just let me, okay?" My eyes watered and my larynx felt too big for my throat. Jackson shrugged impatiently. "Look, babe, all you gotta worry about right now is yourself and your kid. Listen to me — this is important. There's no way you're gonna get me outta here. There's nothing you can do."

The magic words. My perverse streak shot forward at the phrase "no way." My eyes dried up and my jaw tightened. Jackson looked at me and sighed again, his brows furrowed deeper and his voice took on a commanding tone. "Maddie, listen. I mean it. This is dangerous shit, you understand? You're asking for trouble. And if you keep looking you're gonna find it. Do you hear me?" He studied my stubborn look and his voice roughened. "Don't you give a shit if something happens to your baby? 'Cuz I sure do. Jesus, how do you think I'd feel if I heard you got hurt 'cuz of me? Listen to me. Stop it. Forget it."

He studied me a moment longer with stern, pleading eyes, then stood up so fast he knocked his chair over. The guard stepped quickly to his side, alert to danger, but Jackson just nodded at me sadly. "Bye, Maddie. Don't come back 'cuz I won't be here."

He turned to the guard. I jumped up and yelled, "I'll see

you at the trial. They want me to testify."

"For the prosecution?" I nodded. He considered this, then shrugged. "Well, don't worry about it. There's not gonna be a trial."

He turned his back to me, nodded to the guard, and walked away without looking back.

Chapter 23

Driving home in the twilight, I wondered if I should have warned the prison guard to put Jackson on suicide watch. But for all I knew, they might have handed him the sharp instrument then and there, so I kept my mouth shut.

My shoulders, arms and neck were so tight they felt like high-tension wires. Every inch of me ached and Roz was going ballistic against my ribs. Food. I hadn't eaten all day. Jesus, Jackson was right. I was neglecting the most important thing in the world because of all this bullshit. I found myself thinking that maybe I should just drop it all.

Yeah, right.

When I got home, the answering machine's red light blinked at me. I grabbed a banana to appease the pissed-off Roz, then fell onto the sofa next to Hairball and hit "Play." First up was Principal Gorman calling to tell me he needed that leave-of-absence paperwork he'd sent me ASAP. "Oh yeah? Come and get it, dickweed," I snarled at the machine. Next, my little sister Gabe wanted to know how I was doing now that the second trimester was almost over, although everyone knew that was the best three months of any pregnancy. "Yeah, well, try it with a two-pound tumor, a dead father and a lover in jail." Libby was worried about me going up to the jail to see Jackson. Was I forgetting what we'd talked about the other day? "Thanks for the support, pal." Then the phone rang and I grabbed it. "Hello?"

"Max?" My skin turned icy at the sound of the timid, quavering whisper. "It's me. Um — look, I know I shouldn't be calling you but — I can't help it." Little electrical shocks pricked my scalp and I shivered. "Max, I love you. I hope you're not seeing that Jackson guy. He looks — really mean. I wouldn't put anything past him." My heart jabbed my ribs and I realized I had stopped breathing. I gasped air into my lungs with a high, tight sound and tried to hang up the phone, but I was shaking so hard I had no motor control. Was this fury . . . or terror? "Max? Are you there?"

"I — I told you — not to — call me," I managed to wheeze into the phone. Hairball looked at me worriedly, his yellow eyes probing my face.

"Why not?" Nick wailed.

"The baby — the baby, you moron!" My voice was so breathy and high I didn't know if he'd understand me. "Let me explain again. This is a high-risk pregnancy. I'm supposed to avoid stress. Something about you freaks me the fuck out. Listen to me; I'm hysterical. This kind of stress could kill the baby. That would make you a murderer. So. Leave. Me. The. Fuck. *Alone.*"

I managed to hang up the phone before bursting into tears. I cried and cried and cried until my face swelled up, until my sinuses were packed, until my head pounded with misery. Then I dragged myself into the kitchen, wheezing and choking, with Hairball and Booger in anxious pursuit. They were probably hoping I'd feed them.

I wandered back into the living room. As I honked my nose into a paper towel, trying to ease some of the terrible pressure in my head, I caught sight of someone outside the screen door. I was too numb to be scared as I tried to make out the tall form looking at me through the twilight, or to protest when it pulled open the door and entered my house uninvited.

"Max? You okay?" For a moment I thought it was Jackson,

then I remembered where he was. I blinked stupidly up at the shadow. "It's Morris. Why are you in the dark?" I couldn't think of an answer to such a portentous-sounding question, so I turned on a lamp. "Uh . . . Libby sent me over with some chili for you. She's afraid you're not eating." He spotted my kitchen — he'd never been to my house before, but the fact that it was the only other room on the floor made it easy to find — and wandered in, swinging a sleek, expensive-looking metallic thermos and looking around vaguely. "Got a saucepan I can heat this up in?"

"I'm not hungry right now. You can leave it." He turned and looked at me, growing uncomfortable at the obvious traces of emotion. "Don't worry, I'm okay, I just want to be by myself."

Morris ignored that and pulled a pan out of the drain. "Libby's afraid you're going to worry yourself sick and hurt the baby. She doesn't think you should be alone right now."

"Well, Libby's more cautious than I am."

"She didn't like you going to see Jackson today. She thinks you're in love with him." He smiled quizzically. "Seems like every woman around here is in love with him. Quite a popular guy for a career criminal."

"He didn't do it, Morris," I snapped. Mainly I was pissed because I thought I'd finished crying but now I felt little worms of grief squirming around my heart again. In an effort to distract myself and act hospitable, I grabbed the kettle from the stovetop and filled it. "Want some tea or something?" I gulped air into my aching chest, tamping down the heartache until he went away.

"Why do you say he didn't do it? The circumstantial evidence . . ."

"Is just that: circumstantial. Someone could've planted it."

Morris smiled sympathetically. "Come on, Max. Why would anyone do that?"

"Because they were jealous of him. Like you said, all the women around here are in love with him." A sudden thought struck me. "Do you know anything about Alison Shipwood's lover?"

Morris looked puzzled for a moment, then comprehension dawned. "Cal's Mr. Mystery? Nope, sorry." He dumped the thermos contents into the saucepan and lit the burner as Hairball and Booger wrapped themselves around his ankles. "Why, do you think he did it?" he asked, irritably shaking cats from his feet and fussily dusting fur from his perfectly creased trousers.

I shrugged. "Seems like the most likely candidate to me."

Morris adjusted the flame and turned to me. "Max, listen. Jackson is the most likely candidate. And that's because he did it. End of story." I felt my eyes swell with tears again, and his voice grew kinder. "You look exhausted, Max. Libby was right; you need food and rest. Why don't you go wash your face while I heat this up for you?"

"I'm not hungry."

"You need to eat for the baby's sake."

I sniffled. "Yeah, maybe I should."

"Libby also sent over some sleeping pills for you. She said half of one would be enough." Morris frowned. "Personally I don't think it's a good idea when you're pregnant."

I didn't either. "Did Libby take them when she was pregnant?"

"Apparently she did with Tucker. She never told me about it at the time, probably because she knew I wouldn't approve. I read the printout and they haven't done pregnancy testing on this one. But Tucker turned out fine, so I guess . . ." He pulled a small vial out of his pocket and set it on the table.

"After you eat." I stared at the vial, entranced with the idea of temporary oblivion. It had been so long since I'd even had a drink . . .

He turned back to the stove, where the chili was already bubbling away. After a couple of brisk stirs, he snapped the burner off, dumped the chili into a bowl and placed it in front of me on the card table. "I'm supposed to watch you eat this. Libby's orders. She's very worried."

Spicy vegetarian chili was one of Libby's specialties. It smelled fantastic, and suddenly I was hungry. Starving. This was comfort food, and God and Libby knew I needed comfort. I shoveled it in, then felt guilty for enjoying it. "Morris, do you think there's any hope for Jackson?"

Leaning against my hideous counter, Morris frowned and stopped short of patting my arm. "I don't see it. They might be able to get him off on a technicality, but like I said, the circumstantial evidence is pretty strong, and he had motive, means and opportunity." He shrugged a shoulder. "Not to mention his fingerprints are on the murder weapon."

"It was a knife he used all the time at work."

"But his were the only clear prints on it, so it's more than likely he was the last one to use it. And it was unquestionably the murder weapon." Morris crossed his arms over his chest smug and satisfied with his analysis.

So Jackson was right. I wondered how he was going to do himself in. I was pretty sure I knew how I'd do it, if I were so inclined. I looked at the little vial of pills on the table and wondered if I could smuggle them into the jail.

"I guess you were hungry after all." Morris smiled as he took the bowl away and rinsed it quickly, then scrubbed out the empty saucepan and thermos. "Is there anything you need?"

I shook my head, exhausted. "No, I don't think so. I'll just grab one of those pills and hit the couch."

Morris handed me the vial and a glass of water. "Just half of one, now," he reminded me in his father-knows-best voice. "I should be getting back home. You okay?" I nodded and put my head down on the table. God, I felt like an overcooked noodle. "Hey, let me help you to the sofa. You don't look too good."

I was barely aware of moving into the living room. Morris threw a blanket over me and turned on a lamp. "Get some rest," he whispered from an enormous distance. I thought he was gone. I knew I was.

Someone's fingers were down my throat. I gagged weakly and tried to turn over, but my muscles wouldn't cooperate. "Come on, come on, come on," the fingers' owner whispered urgently. I obliged by throwing up all over them. It burned like mad. Libby's spicy vegetarian chili.

Everything started coming in snapshots, like there was a strobe light on reality. Someone was dragging me, holding me upright and forcing me forward. I couldn't tell who it was, but his scent was warm and familiar and comforting and it made me want to keep breathing so I could smell him. He held me tightly, muttering spasmodically like he was having trouble catching his breath. Sounded like he was saying, "I'm sorry, I'm sorry," over and over and over. Cold water struck my numb face. I tried to get my limbs to move, my mouth to open and protest, but exhaustion rendered me utterly immobile, like one of those a waking dreams. With a huge effort I got my voice to come out at last, the words slurred together like a drunk's. "Hoozzah?" And I fell flat on my face. Was that grass sticking up my nose?

I was freezing and the grass was wet. Someone was telling me to hold on. His voice sounded tinny and far away. I tried to ask him what was happening but this time I couldn't get my mouth to move at all.

More vague sounds and sensations followed. Someone lifted me onto something and wheeled me around. A siren wailed. I knew I was in a hospital by the nauseating chemical smell and over-bright lights that pierced my eyelids. Hushed voices murmured incomprehensible words in reassuring tones. I was falling backwards through the bed.

When I came back, I was scared and everything was grayish yellow and my legs were flailing around uncontrollably. Someone told me it was a normal reaction, not to worry, I was in the recovery room, I was doing great. Oh really?

I heard a child's voice, a little girl, wailing, "Mommy! Mommy!" right next to me. Tears flooded my ears and I tried to call back to Rosalind until I heard a woman's voice saying what I wanted to say: "I'm here, sweetie, Mommy's here."

Then I threw up again and the gray turned to black.

Chapter 24

"Max? By God, I think she's coming around." My eyes cracked open and Cal, next to my bed, smiled hugely at me, which didn't fool me a bit. "Hello, Mad One. Shit, girlfriend, you've looked better."

I found my voice at last. "What the fuck?" I asked querulously, not really wanting an answer. Hazily I took in an enormous bouquet on the nightstand, the flimsy pull-around curtain, and the bland pinky-beige décor. "God, I hate hospitals."

"Ah, she's back with us for sure. Hardly the maiden in distress now, are we?"

Next to Cal, Libby dabbed her eyes with a battered tissue. She looked terrible. "Oh, Max," she sobbed, squeezing my hand. "Why?"

"Watch the I.V., Bette Davis," Cal chided her before turning back to me. "So, you want to tell me about it?"

"What?"

"You took a shitload of zaleplon. Where'd you get it?"

Libby's eyes were solemn. "Did you steal that bottle from me?"

"You mean the sleeping pills?" I squeezed my aching brain for information. "Um, I only took half of one. Morris gave it to me."

Libby looked startled. "What?"

"Morris," I repeated. Cal and Libby exchanged puzzled glances. "When he brought over your chili." I was aware of some very sore sensations in my abdomen and ribs. "God, I ache all over."

"Not surprising. You've spent most of the evening puking your brains out."

"Oh yeah." I closed my eyes at the memory, then they flew open again. My heart slammed into my diaphragm and I grabbed my belly protectively. "How's Roz?"

Cal and Libby spoke together. "She's fine."

"You sure?"

"Yes, thank God. The doctors are keeping an eye on her, but you threw up most of it before you even got here so it never reached her."

I relaxed, then remembered my mysterious rescuer. "How'd I get here? Was that you, Cal?"

Another exchange of glances. "You called nine-one-one," Cal explained tentatively. "Don't you remember?"

I remembered something entirely different. "No, someone came in the house and stuck his fingers down my throat. Then I was in an ambulance, I guess."

"Yes. The one you called."

This was damned annoying. "No, no, I didn't call it. It must have been . . . whoever was there. Morris?"

Cal's brows arched. "You were alone when the ambulance got there. No one came with you. The only reason we're here is Libby's name was on the bottle of pills."

Libby burst out, "Why'd you do it, Max? If you were that depressed, couldn't you call me?" Her big eyes swam with tears.

Cal gave her a squeeze. "Come on, lighten up on her, Lib. She's had a crappy day."

I was lost. "What the hell are you talking about?" They looked at each other again, concerned. "Come on, talk to me, for God's sake. I've been kinda out of it for a while."

Turned out everyone was under the impression I'd tried to kill myself by taking a bunch of sleeping pills. "But that's nuts!" I objected. "I took half of one measly pill. What's that, five milligrams? How's that gonna kill me, Cal?"

He was shaking his big furry head, perplexed. "You had a hell of a lot more than five milligrams in there, Max. They checked your vomit." I swallowed queasily. "You'd taken a pretty hefty dose. If you hadn't induced vomiting, you wouldn't be in very good shape right now."

"But I didn't induce vomiting, someone else did. Some guy. I thought I knew him, but . . . and I didn't even know I'd taken that much." This was too weird. My brain flipped around, an empty Rolodex, until I hit something. "The chili. The chili you sent over," I said to the blank-eyed Libby, who turned to Cal for interpretation. "Along with those sleeping pills."

"Yes, it was mixed in with chili, but they found an empty can in your wastebasket."

I grimaced. "I wouldn't eat canned chili. Blech."

Libby's lips pursed. "Well, I didn't send any over, and Morris is out of town tonight."

I stared at her. "What are you talking about? He was at my house around sunset with a thermos full of chili."

Anxiously she insisted, "He's at a meeting in Boston, Max. Has been since noon." She turned to Cal. "Is this normal? Is she hallucinating or something?"

I couldn't believe this. "Libby, he was at my house a few hours ago!"

Cal eyed me sympathetically and spoke with his best soothing bedside voice, the one he used on crazy people. "Max, you've been under an unbelievable amount of stress this week. You're exhausted, your life feels out of control, and you're probably scared to death but you'd never admit that. In a moment of weakness you stole some pills and took a few more than you should have. Fortunately you realized what you'd done, called nine-one-one, and stuck a finger down your throat before any real damage occurred. No doubt you had a few wild dreams in the ambulance . . ."

My head whipped back and forth so hard I almost puked again. "Goddamn it, Cal, I wouldn't have done that!"

"But you did." He gave me a sad-but-wise smile that made me want to slap him.

"I did NOT!" I snapped.

Libby choked, "It's okay, Max, we understand. I mean, my God, Junie's dead, Bart's dead, Jackson's in jail, your house is . . ."

"Jesus Christ, think for a minute!" She pinched her mouth up again and looked at me with a pained expression. "Think, guys. Come on. Would I do that to Rosalind?"

My nurse chose that moment to appear, ripping the curtain aside and insinuating himself into the crowded space. He shoved me back in the bed and checked a few things, then turned to my confused visitors. "Time to go, folks. She needs rest, not stress."

Libby leaned forward and kissed me, her mouth still pursed when she turned away. Cal put a hand on my arm and gazed at me from under his bushy eyebrows. "Think about it, Cal," I growled. He gave my arm a reassuring squeeze before he left.

"You have got to rest, girl," the nurse chided. "Maybe you'll think twice about poisoning yourself next time. Tossing your cookies for three hours is exhausting, isn't it?"

"Not as exhausting as bullshit." But I lay back on the pillow, stifling a yawn. "And for your information, I didn't poison myself."

"Is that right?" Nursie asked sweetly. "Well, how the heck did all that bad shit get in your tummy?"

A thought lurking at the back of my mind crystallized, and

a tingling rush shoved me bolt upright in a panic. "Jesus H. Christ, someone tried to kill me!"

Nursie contemplated my hysterical outburst with warm brown eyes. "Oh dear," he murmured. "Maybe we should be in E wing." Again he shoved me back on my pillow. "Now you get a nice rest, honey. It'll all look better in the morning." With a little wink, he left me alone with my revelation.

Someone had tried to kill me.

But why?

And who had saved me?

I grabbed the phone next to the bed, gritting my teeth against my body's objections. Damned if the police number wasn't stickered right onto the phone. I dialed madly and asked for Yergins or Cullinane. Unfortunately I got Yergins, who took on a tone of sarcastic friendliness when I announced myself.

"Well, hello, Max. Sorry we had to nab your boyfriend like that, but he really needs to learn to control that temper."

I barely succeeded in controlling mine. "Listen, Yergins, I don't want to play games. I'm in the hospital. Someone tried to poison me, make it look like a suicide attempt. I'm pretty sure I know who it was, but . . ."

Yergins whistled softly on his end. "You don't say. Someone finally tried to off you, huh? Too bad they didn't succeed."

I took a deep breath as nausea and anger threatened to overwhelm common sense. "Look, Yergins, I know you don't like me. I'm not crazy about you either. But we're talking about a serial killer now. He might have killed Junie, he definitely killed Bart Fulton, he framed Jackson O'Brien, and he's made an attempt on me. Now what are you going to do about it?"

Yergins cleared his throat and spoke with infuriating calm.

"Not a damn thing, Maxwell, and here's why. Your boyfriend killed Bart Fulton and you know it. I think maybe he killed your brother too, for practice. I think maybe you even helped him, and what I'm looking for right now is a way to tie you into the murder. Smart of you to stage an attempt on your own life to make us think we have the wrong guy, and damned convenient you didn't die. But don't forget . . . I know you, and I know what kind of people you come from. You can't fool me."

And he hung up.

I stared at the quacking receiver for a good fifteen seconds before I realized someone had pushed through the curtain and was standing beside the bed. My heart jumped as I looked up and recognized . . .

"Nick?"

"Max," he whispered.

I stared, attempting to gather my wits before I let him have it. It didn't work. "You asshole, what the hell are you doing here?"

He looked bewildered. "What did I do now?"

I couldn't believe this wiener. "Jesus, you really are out of touch, aren't you?"

He swallowed nervously. "Ssh. I shouldn't be here."

"You can say that again. Christ, you harass me to the point that I freak out, and then you wonder why I'm pissed at you?" No comprehension lit his puzzled eyes. "Hello? Remember that last phone call? The one where I could hardly breathe because I was so pissed?"

"You mean last week?"

"No, I mean this afternoon. Jesus, what does it take to make a point with you?"

"But I haven't called you since . . . since you and that tough guy came to see me."

Great, now he was so far gone he was blanking out. "Bullshit, Nick. You just called me a few hours ago." But now I wasn't even sure. My brain felt fog-bound, dull and exhausted.

"No, that was . . . last Wednesday, I think." He sank into the vinyl chair next to the bed and took my hand. "But I only called because I care about you. And I'd heard you were laid off or whatever because of the murder, and I wanted to talk to you." Tears brimmed in his puppy-brown eyes. "All I've been able to think about is getting you back. But after you came to the school with that tattooed guy, I realized it was hopeless. All I want is for you to be happy."

I couldn't take any more of this crap. "Then leave me alone. If the pills didn't kill me, all this bullshit will. Jesus Christ, I'm supposed to be avoiding stress, not getting buried in it!" I glared at him. "And you've contributed more than your share. Now get the hell out before I call the cops." Empty threat, but he didn't know that.

Nick's bewildered eyes fastened on my face, then dropped to the floor, suddenly embarrassed. "But . . ."

"What?"

He looked back up at me. "But I saved your life," he blurted.

I sat up at that. "What? When?"

"Tonight." His chin went up defiantly. "I was there. I made you throw up, and I called nine-one-one."

This was a bit much for my befogged brain to process. "Wait . . . what were you doing there?"

The determination faltered a little. "Well, I . . . I come by your house sometimes . . . just to . . . you know, feel close to you. I . . . park down the road and walk . . ." He swallowed, blushing under my gape. "I'm sorry, I just can't help it. I want to see you. I want to know you're all right."

Memories of muffled bumps on the porch at night rushed at me. "You come up on my porch and look in my windows, don't you?"

He pushed a shaky hand through his mussed hair and sighed. "Yeah, sometimes."

"You're a psycho, you know that? You're a stalker." But I couldn't subdue a question. "How the hell do you manage to get away from your wife?"

"She takes stuff to sleep at night now. It really knocks her out. If I slip out for an hour, she never knows." He had the decency to look ashamed.

My eyes narrowed. "Stuff to sleep, huh? How do I know you didn't give me some?"

"I would never do that, Max." He shifted restlessly on the vinyl, causing it to squeak. "And tonight she had her support group, so I dropped her off and decided to check on you. I saw this car in your driveway and, well, I wondered who it was . . . so I parked on the side of the road and waited. Then I saw this guy come out of your house and get in the car. I waited for him to leave, but he didn't. Not right away."

Holy shit, a witness. "Sharp-looking guy?"

Nick frowned. "Yeah. Looked like a CEO or something. He sat there for a few minutes, then he got out again and went back in." He blushed furiously. "So I sneaked up to the window and — it was so weird, he was dragging you from the sofa and he wasn't being very gentle, either. You were completely limp, like you'd passed out or something. He kind of dropped you on the floor, then he went in the kitchen so I couldn't see him. He took off pretty quickly after that. I ran in there and tried to wake you up, then I noticed this pill bottle lying near you . . . zaleplon." He smiled ruefully. "That's what Heather uses to sleep, and she overdosed once. I made her throw it up, so I did the same for you. Then I called for the ambulance and carried you out to the lawn and hid on the porch until they got there." He looked ashamed. "I had to rush home and change, hide my clothes . . . and I really had to race to get back in time to pick up Heather."

My head reeled with information overload. "Jesus, Nick, if you weren't stalking me, I'd be in bad shape."

"I was so scared," he whimpered. "I thought you were going to die in my arms. I didn't understand what was going on, I just knew I had to help you. But I couldn't have Heather know I was there so . . . I left after the ambulance came. I ran. God, I'm such a coward."

My brain had started working again; it was racing so fast I barely heard him. "Look, Nick, I know you don't want to be involved, but I may need your help in proving something." His eyes expanded some more. "That guy you saw tried to kill me and make it look like suicide. He succeeded; even my best friends think I'm crazy now. And since he's a respected family man who lives in Skiff Neck, and I'm the Hawk Marsh town slut, who do you think they're going to believe?"

"Max, don't say that."

"Why not? It's true; I don't care." I leaned forward and grabbed his hand, giving him the full eyeball treatment. "But now I have a witness. You were there; you can back me up. If I called the police chief, would you tell him what you saw?"

For a few seconds, the spaniel eyes shone with excitement at the idea of helping me out. His mouth opened and he took a breath, and I got ready to hit the redial button on the phone. But at the last minute, the breath rushed out again and he whined, "I can't."

I almost smacked him with the phone. "Why not, for Christ's sake?"

He shrugged and whimpered, "Heather." The look on my face must have been pretty scary, because he winced when he saw it. "Come on, Max, she'd kill herself."

So he *was* a wienie. Guess I knew that. It didn't make what I had to do any easier. "Just go away so I can think," I growled. As he moped his way to the door I added, "And hey, thanks for making me puke."

He gave me a regretful smile and skulked away.

Why would Morris try to kill me? There was only one answer to that question. I was getting too damn close. What had I guessed? That Alison Shipwood's mystery lover was the killer . . . which meant . . .

Of course.

Damn, Libby would hit the roof.

Getting the hospital to release me was surprisingly difficult, given my vague insurance situation. "But I did *not* try to kill myself," I said for the zillionth time as the doctor explained why Roz and I needed to stay overnight for observation. "And I couldn't possibly have any of that shit still in me. All I want is to get the hell out of here. I have things to do."

His eyebrows raised at that. "Like what?"

"Like straighten out some stuff. Like see my friends. Like find a new job. Okay?"

"One night can't hurt. We need to keep an eye on you; you've been through quite an ordeal, and there's the baby to think of."

Nursie walked in at that moment, and I appealed to him. "Would you talk to this bozo and tell him I'm not suicidal?"

"Well, when a girl downs twenty or so sleeping pills with four-alarm chili, it does tend to make one think she doesn't hold life very dear."

So I was forced to play along with them, pretending to resign myself to a night in the hospital. They finally left, congratulating themselves on their persuasive powers.

Grateful that the other bed in the room was empty, I waited until their voices faded down the echoing hallway before I swung out onto the floor and grabbed my clothing out of the nightstand. Despite nearly passing out as I dressed, I got myself together in record time, slipped the door open a crack, peered down the empty hallway, and discharged myself.

Chapter 25

I was still pretty shaky from all the puking, but my unbridled fury pumped enough adrenaline through my system to keep me going. After the cab dropped me off at my place, I headed straight for Libby and Morris's house, banging Molly along the dark road at well over the speed limit and not even worrying about the cops for once. Hell, if they chased me, maybe I could get some help. Seemed like the only way I could get any help these days was to get in trouble first. As long as they didn't talk to Yergins . . .

What the hell was I going to say when I got there? Jesus. I had to accuse my best friend's husband of trying to kill me and actually killing Bart and maybe Junie. Libby's cushy lifestyle was circling the drain and I was willing to bet she had no idea.

As I approached the WunderBar, I noticed Alison's car parked outside. Business as usual? That seemed unlikely, given her condition the other day. Maybe she was just drinking herself into a stupor. If so, I couldn't blame her.

My chest tightened with grief. There was no way I could stay here if I couldn't prove my story. Too many reminders, too much pain. I braked Molly so she drifted softly by the WunderBar and, lump in my throat, I found myself looking toward the alley where Jackson and I had first groped each other. I craned my neck for a glimpse of the fence next to the Dumpster where he had sniffed me for perfume. Then my foot hit the brake so hard I stalled the truck in the middle of the street.

What was that white thing next to the Dumpster?

It looked like part of a car . . . and I had a feeling I knew whose car it was.

Hastily I restarted Molly, turned her lights down, and guided her as quietly as possible down the alley. She barely fit, but I managed not to scrape the building as I parked behind Morris's shiny white BMW. It was almost completely out of sight from the street; if I hadn't been indulging the odd attack of nostalgia I would never have noticed it. What the hell was it doing here at this time of night?

I shook my head roughly to clear the leftover sleeping pill fog from my brain, and reviewed my theory for holes. I was positive Morris was the killer. He'd always loathed Junie; maybe he'd just practiced on him, as Yergins suggested Jackson had done. He lived right around the corner from Bart, and as Alison's lawyer he had easy access to the WunderBar. And I was sure he'd tried to kill me, calling beforehand to make sure I was home, imitating Nick as he'd heard him on that answering machine tape.

Jackson had some kind of affair with Alison . . . Bart was flirting with her . . . Junie was flirting with her . . . I was sure Alison's lover was the killer.

I had to be right.

And I had said as much to Alison, which meant . . .

My hand yanked on the door handle and I squeezed myself out of the cab through the narrow opening. Barely breathing, I inched up the fire escape and carefully turned the broken knob to the upstairs hallway, right outside Jackson's room. My heart ricocheted around my ribcage as I felt my way toward the inside back stairs in the pitch dark. I'd never been so scared in my life. When a floorboard creaked under my foot, I about peed my pants; I squirmed, scowled, listened fearfully, and kept on sneaking.

Down the back stairs to the bar I crept, trying to hear over the violent pounding in my chest, until I could discern voices coming through the door to the kitchen area. One angry male voice, one soothing female voice. Morris and Alison. Sidling up to the kitchen door, my back tight against the wall, I focused on Morris's angry ranting.

". . . because I want to know, that's why. I want to know what you see in that filthy scumbag. Christ, Alison, if you'd just waited a little longer I would have left Libby . . . but no, you had to fuck that scuzzy bum, didn't you?"

Alison's cultured voice shook, but sounded surprisingly dignified. "I swear, Mo, Jackson and I never made love —"

Morris interrupted, furious. "Damn straight you didn't 'make love'! All that kind of scum can do is *fuck!*"

Gently, Alison corrected herself. "I'm sorry, sweetie. You know I . . . I don't like that word. We never did it, did anything, I promise. I just told you that to make you jealous, because I was so hurt. Honey, you don't really think I'd do that with him, do you?"

Smart girl, Alison. She was telling Morris what he wanted to hear to keep him from killing her. God, why was I cheering for that bitch all of a sudden?

"Don't lie to me. I saw you kissing him. I saw you two groping each other behind the bar. You didn't know I was there."

"I knew you were there, Mo. I knew you'd be dropping by and I heard you come in. That's why I was kissing him. I wanted to make you jealous." Alison's voice splintered. "It was a stupid thing to do, but I thought . . . maybe you'd finally . . ." She sniffled.

Morris's voice softened, but he still sounded skeptical. "Then why did you want him in the partnership?"

To my amazement, Alison laughed, an affectionate sound

that seemed slightly forced. "Aw, Mo-mo, is that what's bothering you? I wanted him in the partnership because he was good for business. That's all, I swear! For goodness sake, Morris, this *is* a business!" She laughed again. "Come here, you silly thing, let me give you a hug . . ."

She must have taken a step toward him, because there was a sharp scream and Morris barked, "Stay back! Stay over there! Don't come near me."

Nervous as hell, I edged toward the swinging kitchen door and strained to peek through the tiny window. First I saw Alison backed against the oven, her face pale and strained. I shifted carefully and located Morris a few feet away from the door, with his back to me. And aiming a gun at Alison's head.

"Okay, okay, okay," Alison panted, her elegant hands waving nervously in the air. "I'll stay right here, Mo, honey, I'll do whatever you want. I promise."

"Okay," Morris agreed in an over-the-top reasonable voice. "Here's what I want, sweetheart. I want you to write a little note saying your lover went to jail for murder and you just can't stand to go on living. Then I want you to turn on the gas to that oven and put your pretty little head in there until you die." He gave the final word a chirpy, upbeat inflection and cocked his head charmingly. "Okay, lover?"

Alison's knees gave slightly; she grabbed the edge of the oven for support.

Morris laughed. "Write the note first, darling, then stick your head in the oven. Go to the desk over there, go on." He gestured with the gun; Alison's eyes started to roll back in her head and she slid to a sitting position on the floor. Furious, Morris aimed the gun at her and screamed, "Do what I say, you dumb bitch! Do it now! Get up off the floor and stop that crap this minute!"

As Morris bellowed more abuse at the foundering Alison,

something told me it was time to act. Fast.

I steeled my jittery nerves, launched myself through the swinging door and tackled Morris from behind, knocking him facedown onto the floor. A deafening, heart-stopping explosion issued from the gun as it flew from his hand. Straddling Morris's back, I squeezed his ribs with my knees, grabbed his head with both hands and beat his forehead against the floor. Hard. Gallons of adrenaline pumped through my veins; I was wide-awake now, and yeah, I was capable of murder.

Libby will kill me, I thought inanely as I knocked her husband unconscious.

"Alison, wake up!" I screamed. "Wake up and call the police, you useless twat!"

Alison's eyes came back into focus slowly and fixed on me, then grew puzzled. "For God's sake, Max, stop screaming," she commanded in a scarily calm, reproving voice. "And how dare you call me a twat?" Her eyes rolled back again and she hit the floor like a sack of flour.

She was out cold and the phone was all the way out in the bar. I looked around frantically, hoping to spot an extension in the kitchen, but no luck, as usual. "Oh for God's sake," I muttered, whacking Morris's head against the cement floor a couple more times — just to be safe — before I stood up on legs that felt like twin earthquakes. At least I had the brains to retrieve Morris's gun from under the sink, where it had slid after it went off. I quaked out to the bar and dialed nine-one-one.

This time I remembered the whole number.

"Hi, I'm calling from the Wonder Bra . . . um, the WunderBar in Skiff Neck, and I'd like to report an attempted murder." I could tell the dispatcher was already skeptical due to my slip of the tongue, but I babbled on. "Look, I'm sorry, this is serious. He's killed one person and tried to kill another.

Two others, actually. So please . . ."

Alison staggered out of the kitchen, her face so pale it looked like someone had erased her features; the whites of her eyes blended with her washed out skin and bloodless lips. I started to shoo her back into the kitchen to keep an eye on Morris, but decided it was pointless and turned my attention back to the phone. "Yeah, he's out cold right now, but you better send someone right away. Chief Yergins, if possible." I actually smirked at the idea of rubbing Yergins' smug bulldog face in this.

When I hung up, Alison's pasty lips parted and she croaked, "You killed him."

"No, Alison, I just knocked him out."

"No, he's dead. There's . . . blood. Oh my God." She raised her hands to her face, and that's when I noticed the tiny gun she was holding. I froze.

"Alison, what's the gun for?"

She looked at it as if surprised to see it, then her pale blue eyes widened further and she gave me a chilling smile. "Morris told me he'd killed you," she explained. "He thought he'd taken care of you already, but I guess you're just too tough." She gave the last word insulting emphasis. "But now you've killed him, so I guess *I'm* going to have to kill you." She had the nerve to sound martyred.

"For God's sake, why?" I felt completely wrung out at.

She smiled again. "Jackson's going to be released now, isn't he? Now I know Morris killed Bart and framed Jackson. If you're out of the way, Jackson will come back to me."

I snarled. "Don't bet on it."

She cocked the gun and aimed at me, smiling broadly. "I never liked you," she explained in the understatement of the year.

I'd put Morris's gun down next to the phone. If I backed

up a bit, I could grab it and maybe blow that condescending smirk off Alison Shipwood's face for good. "You've snapped," I informed her. "You don't know what you're doing. I just saved your life and now you're trying to kill me. Does that make sense?"

Alison was shaking pretty hard by now. She pointed the gun at me, but couldn't aim for shit because her arms were trembling so badly. Her breath came in big, jagged gulps; her thin shoulders jerked sharply as she pleaded with me. "But I love him," she keened in a high, thin whisper. "My God, Max, you don't know how much I love him."

"I'm getting the idea." Somehow I felt sorry for her as she poked the gun awkwardly in front of her and took another step toward me. "Look, Alison," I stammered, fighting for time, "I understand, okay? Life isn't fair. You can't always have what you want. So . . . just deal with it, okay?"

Big tears dripped down Alison's pale cheeks. "But with you out of the way I've got a better chance," she whispered, bracing her pathetic shoulders and aiming straight for my head.

Behind her, the kitchen door banged open and a horrifyingly bloodied Morris lurched out sideways. Jesus, did I do that? Alison swung around wildly as I grabbed the gun from next to the phone. We shot at him almost simultaneously, me a split second after Alison. The backlash or whatever you call it from the gun knocked me on my ass. The porthole window in the kitchen door shattered and Morris jerked back violently, dark blood jetting from his neck. As he dropped to the floor, half in and half out of the kitchen, the door swung shut, clonking him on the head for one final insult.

Alison and I were still standing there, two statues aiming guns at a corpse, when the police broke down the front door.

Yergins took in the scene, walked over to Morris and checked him out. "You can put the guns down, ladies; I think you've made your point."

Slowly, we lowered our arms and looked at each other. "I could really use a drink," Alison observed in a quaver.

"Well, we're in the right place." I smiled at her weakly and tottered behind the bar. "Jack Daniels okay with you?"

Yergins's beefy face turned the color of steak tartar when he saw me wielding the bottle. "Jesus Christ, Maxwell," he spluttered. "Are you drunk again?"

"Not even a tiny bit, Yergins." I raised the bottle to him, then indicated Morris's still form. "Oh, and by the way, there's Bart Fulton's murderer."

"He killed Junie Maxwell, too," Alison added. She looked at me glassy-eyed, realization dawning. The shock was wearing off and she wasn't feeling too proud of herself.

I nodded at her, then back to Yergins. "You can release Jackson O'Brien and take that dead piece of shit away."

Yergins scowled at my arrogant tone; who could blame him? "Don't go anywhere, okay? You both have some explaining to do."

The police got busy securing the crime scene while Alison and I shivered at the bar. When Yergins moved away from us, she turned anxious eyes on me. I whispered, "Don't worry about it. I understand, and I'd probably have done the same to you given half the chance."

She stared at me bug-eyed. "You're not going to tell them?"

I shook my head. "You were stressed out and in shock. Anyway, they'd never believe me, so forget it. Did Morris tell you he killed Junie?"

Alison took a deep swallow of the whiskey and licked her lips. "He was here that night with some clients. He saw Junie flirting with me, and waited outside until Jackson threw him out." A thin tear ran down her pale cheek. "He told me all he did was ask Junie how he dared show his face around here. That's all. But Junie was dead an hour later." She polished off the shot and grabbed the bottle. "I know you won't believe me, but I liked your brother. I don't know if Morris killed him or not, but if not, he made him feel bad enough to kill himself." Topping off the glass, she added, "He was good that way."

Cal burst in the front door, wide-eyed and disheveled, wearing an ancient Skiff Neck Marina sweatshirt over enormous drawstring pants. I recognized the outfit as his jammies. "Jesus God," he breathed when he saw what was left of Morris. "What happened?"

"I'm still trying to figure it out." Alison tossed back her third Jack Daniels and poured another with shaky hands. "Got any Valium?" she asked him hopefully.

I closed my eyes at the thought of pharmaceuticals. "God, stay away from that shit. I just spent the night puking some crap out of my system. Morris tried to kill me." I gave Cal a dirty look. "Told ya."

"Morris?" Cal was completely lost, but I decided to leave it up to Alison to enlighten him. He listened, transfixed with horror, finally nodding as his psychotherapist mind pieced it together. "Of course. He was Mr. Mystery, right?" Alison nodded, trying not to look at the body of her former lover. "And we all know how ambitious Morris is . . . was. When he saw two men both getting a little too friendly with you, he found a neat way to get rid of both of them." Cal shook his head. "Good Lord, who knew Morris had that much on the ball?" Alison finished off her fifth shot without a word.

"Who's gonna tell Libby?" I asked.

"Leave that to the cops, I guess." Cal frowned. "But I'll tag along."

Something was still wrong here, and I couldn't figure out what it was.

Then I realized my abdomen kept tightening and relaxing. It was slight, didn't hurt at all, but it was regular.

And Roz wasn't moving at all.

"Cal," I said, trying to sound as steady as I could. "Could you take me back to the hospital? I think I'm in labor."

Chapter 26

I'll keep this short.

Rosalind Maxwell was born at 3:40 in the morning at Brigham & Women's Hospital in Boston, where Dr. Geary had shipped us via ambulance when he saw I had a serious infection and Roz was head-down with a rapid heartbeat. Now she was in the Neonatal Intensive Care Unit, lying on a little pad, hooked up to machines, a tube in her mouth to help her breathe, a needle in her hand for antibiotics.

She was tiny, but not as small as I'd expected. A full twelve inches, one and three quarter pounds. Pretty hefty for over three months premature, they reassured me. Her lungs weren't developed yet, but she was a girl; that meant she was a fighter. Like I didn't know that.

And she was beautiful. Unbelievably beautiful. Dark hair, ski-slope nose, perfect little mouth, strong chin. And a fifty percent chance of surviving. Up from forty percent earlier that day. They talked about her like she was a stock market share.

They told me her premature birth was not caused by the tumor or the sleeping pills. I had something called Group B Strep, a very common bacteria which flares up under stress. Gee, wonder what could've set that off? Somehow it crossed the placental barrier and infected Roz. My body decided to expel her. I had no choice, they told me; she had to be born right away, or both of us could die.

I went through hellish childbirth. The drugs didn't take because of the tumor, but that probably wouldn't have eliminated the real source of my pain anyway. I screamed myself hoarse all through the labor; four nurses had to hold me down. They thought it was because of the contractions. Morons.

The second Roz plopped out onto the bed, my screams stopped and I heard myself whispering, "Is she okay?" The doctors bundled her into an oxygen tent and worked on her as I lay on my back with tears pouring into my ears.

After a few moments a nurse held up a tiny blanketed figure and said, "Miss Maxwell, take a quick look at your baby. We have to take her upstairs right away." I looked up in time to see Roz open her eyes and stare, I swear, right at me. Then they took her away and I didn't see her again for hours.

When I did see her, it wrenched my heart to see the tiny thing so still and helpless on the miniature bed. Oddly, she wasn't in an incubator, but on a flat surface in the open air, with machinery surrounding her. I looked at her and felt like I was going crazy. How could this have happened? The nurse wheeled me back to my room and made me get back in bed.

There was an almost constant parade of hospital personnel through my room after her birth. Single mother of premie in room 412! Call in the counselors, call in the clergy, call in the unwed mother's brigade! "Where's the baby's father, Ms. Maxwell?" "Oh, my best friend's husband stabbed him to death, framed my ex-con boyfriend, and tried to kill me, but I blew him away in a bar last night. Hey, when can I take my baby home?"

My nurse, Hilda, came in and looked at my untouched lunch tray. "You should eat something, Max," she said. God, they were all so nice. It made me want to cry. Everything made me want to cry. Hard to believe I'd blown the head off a serial killer the night before. Hilda frowned and asked, "Is there anything I can do?"

"Can I see my baby again?" I asked in a thin voice.

Hilda smiled, picked up the phone, punched numbers, spoke sweetly. "Hi, Phil, it's Hilda. I'm with Rosalind Maxwell's mom. She wants to know if she can come visit?" She gave me a reassuring wink, then her smile froze. "Oh?" I strained to hear what Phil was saying and I was positive I caught the phrase "not responding."

"Okay, I'll tell her," Hilda said cheerfully, then hung up the phone, smile still intact. "You can't go down there at the moment, but Phil will call as soon as it's okay."

"What's wrong?" I demanded.

"They're just trying to increase her chances. Try to get some rest." And Hilda left quickly. If I'd had the energy, I would have started screaming again. Instead I settled for throwing my Jell-O across the room.

Soon a line of hospital types filed in, led by Roz's nurse Phil. They arranged themselves around my bed like pallbearers.

I had a really bad feeling.

"Max," Phil said gently, "Rosalind isn't doing so well anymore. If she lives, she'll be a vegetable, only able to stay alive by being hooked up to machines. If you want us to do that, we'll keep on with it. If not, let us know now. I'll wait until you come down to take her off the machines, and you can hold her." He blinked behind his steel-rimmed glasses. "What do you think?"

My heart shut down. No more. I didn't even have to think about it; the words jumped out. "Take her off. Let her go."

The crowd around my bed breathed a sigh of relief. "I think that's best," Phil said, and they all nodded.

When I got to the NICU, Phil held Roz out to me in his two hands. "Her heart's still beating," he whispered. I took her into my arms for the first time and studied the tiny, perfect face peeking out from under the little cap. "You can go in there." Phil guided us to a small room with a rocking chair, closing the door silently as he left.

I can't describe this. I was saying good-bye to someone I'd only known a few months, someone I'd loved more than I thought possible, someone who had changed my life dramatically.

Someone who had changed me forever.

Someone who had lived inside me, who kicked and pummeled and somersaulted and hiccuped as long as she was part of me, who hadn't moved since she was separated from me.

I couldn't say good-bye. I couldn't cry. I just sat and stared at her on my lap. I touched doll-sized fingers and lips and nose. I hugged her to me and kissed her tiny face, imagining a miraculous Technicolor moment in which the tiny fingers stirred, the bruised eyelids fluttered open, and my baby drew breath unaided, brought back to life by the sheer force of my love.

I begged her to come back.

She didn't.

Chapter 27

The bullet that killed Morris Langley came from his own gun. That piece of information kinda threw me, even though I'd been pretty sure I was the one who fired the fatal shot; I didn't think Alison's little pussy gun could've done that to Morris. I tried to figure out how I felt about shooting my best friend's husband, but all I could think was, he deserved it. It didn't seem real to me. Yet. Or maybe it just didn't matter.

By the time the hospital and the police released me, Libby had packed up her three kiddies and fled to her parents' condo in Miami. I didn't blame her; I only wished I had the same option.

I couldn't face my own empty house so I checked into Abneyville Shores, a turn-of-the-century beachfront inn with efficiency cottages. I rented the tiniest cottage, as close to the ocean as I could safely get. I stared at the waves for hours, often too numb to move. I read, I walked, I thought deep and hard about my life and all the dead people in it. Was I some kind of death magnet?

At first the pain of losing Roz was unbearable. My arms ached to hold her and my allegedly nonexistent heart broke over and over again. A firm believer in cremation, I was bewildered by my reluctance to do that to my baby, but finances dictated the necessity. I attended her funeral alone, unwilling to let anyone see my raw grief.

The doctors had told me the postpartum bleeding would stop in a few days, but they were wrong. It got worse, to the point that I was just about hemorrhaging. Reluctantly I dragged myself to Dr. Geary, who gave me gentle pats and told me Curly the tumor would have to come out as soon as possible. Meantime, he prescribed birth control pills to control the bleeding.

I couldn't keep from asking myself over and over, why did that monster survive and Roz die? What did that say about me, that my body successfully nurtured and supplied blood to a useless mass of tissue, but sickened and ultimately rejected a human being? I tried not to dwell on the apparent symbolism, but nightmares took over for my conscience and I woke up to my own wracking sobs and wails.

Ironically, I managed to sell both my truck and my house within a couple of weeks of Roz's birth. I didn't want to sell them when I had to, and now that it was no longer necessary I was happy to see them go. At the least, I was indifferent instead of heartbroken. Since the house buyer was in a hurry, I asked some of the guys to clean the place out for me. I didn't want to have to go back there too much, and I didn't want any of my old stuff. I told them to take whatever they wanted and dump the rest. I tried to pay them, but Archy shamed them into turning it down.

I didn't tell anyone where I was, but I didn't need to. It's a small peninsula and word gets around. Cal tracked me down within two weeks and left a message on my voice mail: "You can run, but you can't hide. Arthur and Cal's annual Memorial Day party starts this Friday night and continues all weekend. You may contribute your usual case of Sam Adams and your presence. That's all I ask. By the way, Miss Libido has returned from her exile, so I hope Mad Max will do so as well." After a moment, he added, "We've told Jackson you're going to be there, so you'd better be."

Memorial Day. Unexpected words and phrases carried a sting now, and going to a party so soon after Roz's death felt overwhelming. I wasn't sure about this, although I knew Cal would be hurt if I ignored the invitation.

I was even less sure about seeing Jackson. I hadn't even spoken to him since he'd been released. The last words he'd said to me were about killing himself, and now I could understand exactly how he'd felt. I wished I'd been cremated along with Roz. Her handful of ashes lay in a wooden box I'd made for her, which I kept next to my bed. My heart might as well have been in there with her.

But when twilight came that Friday, I found myself taking a cab to the Hawk Marsh package store, picking up a couple of cases of Sam Adams, and proceeding on to Skiff Neck.

"Big party out there, huh?" the cabby asked. "You know some rich people?"

"Yeah."

He smirked. "They're not so special. Some lawyer out there killed a guy a few weeks back, you know. Then some broad blew his head off. Served the asshole right."

I squeezed my eyes shut as I realized the buzz was still going. I had a choice here. I took the brash road, to practice for the party. "Yeah, actually, I'm the broad who blew his head off." It sounded flat and colorless.

He looked sharply at me in the rearview mirror. "You're kidding me, right?"

"No, actually, I'm not."

His eyes narrowed as they slid down my figure. "Papers said you were pregnant."

Ouch. "I was." I took a breath and forced it out. "She was born later that night. Three months early. She lived ten hours." My forehead furrowed and I stared out the window hard.

"Jeez, I'm sorry. I didn't mean to . . ."

"No, it's okay, it's cool. I have to get used to saying it."

"My wife lost our first. We had five more. You'll be fine." He pulled into Cal's driveway. "I better take those cases in for you, huh?"

When I climbed out of the cab, I recognized Libby's silver Miata and I suddenly felt awkward. "Maybe we should just drop 'em off and you can take me back home, okay?"

"Back to the motel? How come?"

I didn't get a chance to answer. Cal swooped out of the house, a Zeppelin in a Hawaiian shirt, and lifted me right off my feet. "Mad Max, I can't believe it. You came."

The embrace made me feel even worse. "Yeah, Cal, I don't know about this."

"She's getting nervous," the cabby explained.

Cal set me down and put his hands on his hips. "About what, for God's sake? You're among friends."

"Well . . ." Before I could explain further, the answer to his question wandered out of the house. I hadn't seen Libby since I shot her husband. I wasn't too sure how she felt about me anymore. And I was even less sure I was ready to find out.

We stared at each other a moment. She was changed by all the crazy shit she'd been through — paler, a little subdued, she'd lost some weight (which probably thrilled her), and she was wearing black, which she hated. Okay, it was a tight black dress that drew attention to her glorious bosom, but it was still out of character.

She looked me up and down, crossed her arms and said evenly, "You shot my husband, you bitch."

"Your fucking husband poisoned me, what did you expect?" I snapped back, trying to sound like my old self.

A small crowd gathered as we eyed each other a little longer, letting the tension build like something out of *High Noon* . . . then we couldn't keep it up any longer. We both burst out laughing — okay, it was a bit edgy — and hugged and sniffled. I hadn't realized how much I'd missed her until then, how afraid I'd been our friendship was history. And how desperately I needed my friends, despite my lone wolf approach to mourning.

Cal cleared his throat and clapped his hands. "Okay, everyone, the beer has arrived. Let's put it on ice."

Libby dragged me away from the house toward the beach, so we could talk in private. She linked her arm through mine like she used to when we were kids. "So, Jesus, Max, how've you been?"

"Shitty. And you?"

"Shitty. But at least I've got the kids, so . . ." She trailed off, embarrassed. "Sorry. God, I'm sorry."

I shrugged and watched a seagull skim overhead. "It's okay. How are the kids handling it?"

"They don't really understand what happened, thank God. I left them with my parents in Florida for a while." Libby kicked at some sea foam bubbling on the sand. "It's funny. I thought Morris was such a good father, but they don't seem to miss him. In fact, they seem a lot less tense."

I could understand that. "How about you?"

She shrugged. "I'm still waiting to miss him. Maybe it's shock, or maybe it's . . ." She looked around nervously and whispered, "relief?"

I could understand that too, given Morris' ultra-tight Jockeys. "So are you gonna stay around here, or . . ."

She looked puzzled. "Of course. Where else would I go? Anyway, it's not my fault my husband turned psycho. He did that all by himself. That stupid bastard was unfaithful to me — with Alison Shipwood!" She kicked at a shell on the sand and sent it flying. "He *killed* for Alison Shipwood. That son of a bitch." Obviously, this fact upset Libby more than her husband's killing spree or violent death at her best friend's hands.

"Money and power, babe," I sighed.

"Speak of the devil." Libby clutched my arm. Alison herself was walking toward us along the shore, her L.L. Bean shorts hanging off her lanky frame, her hair windblown and stringy as mine. "Oh, crap," Libby growled, then brightened. "Hey, Mr. Social Climber is dead. I don't have to be nice to her anymore."

I was sure Alison would go out of her way to avoid us, but instead she looked at us warily, then gave a weak wave and continued straight toward us. "What the hell," I muttered, not too happy about the idea of talking to her. Maybe I should've told the cops she threatened to shoot me. But there was no getting away now; she was close enough to hear anything we said. Libby assumed a stone cold expression and folded her arms across her chest. I stood next to her in pretty much the same attitude. Alison studied us, then burst out laughing.

"Good God, some things never change. Look at you two, the tough girls from high school all grown up." Her tone was lofty, as usual, but there was a hint of friendliness in there.

"Yeah, well, we see you still have that pole up your ass," Libby said sweetly.

Alison turned those flat blue eyes on Libby, who tried to get taller by lifting her chin and lengthening her neck. She was still a few inches shorter than Alison, but she looked almost as tough as she did at fourteen, before she discovered beauty products and movie stars.

Alison looked at her steadily for a moment, then down at the sand. "Look, I'm sorry about everything. I mean, I didn't do it to hurt you."

"Ha!"

Alison considered this response. "Okay, maybe I did, at first," she conceded. "But I . . . I can't believe how things turned out. It's a nightmare. I never thought he'd do anything like that."

Libby tossed her hair. "It wasn't just because of you, you know," she preened, ever the competitor.

"Well, killing Bart certainly was. I mean, I was definitely leading Bart on, hoping to get a rise out of Jackson. And I took up with Jackson hoping to get a rise out of . . . well, you know. Guess it worked, huh?" She shook her head sorrowfully. "Stupid games, and look where it got me." Alison shrugged and squinted at Libby again. "Anyway, maybe it's an odd thing for me to do, but I really wanted to apologize. I mean, my God, your kids and all."

To my surprise, Libby snapped, "It's not your fault. Morris made his own choices, and he did a number on us all. Look what he did to Max."

Alison smiled weakly. "Well, hell, look what Max did to him."

Libby paled a little. "Yeah. I only wish it'd been me with that gun."

"You and me both," Alison muttered. We all headed back toward Cal's together, me in the middle. Alison turned her head toward me. "You seen Jackson yet?"

My heart gave a hard little thud, but I just shook my head. "No, not since . . ." I grimaced as I remembered our last meeting. "Not since I visited him in jail." Alison nodded and looked satisfied.

"Is he coming tonight or what?" Libby demanded, with a sidelong glance at me.

"He was invited. Don't know if he'll actually come, but . . ."

We were back at Cal's porch, where Alison and Libby got detoured by other friends. When a drum-heavy tune started up on the stereo, I felt a familiar kick in my abdomen and smiled, automatically putting a hand on my belly . . . then took a deep breath, a squaring of my shoulders. I started to go inside in search of a beer, but a baby's lusty wail hit me like a wet towel and I lost the ability to walk.

Thinking about how Roz never even had the chance to cry, I stood in the doorway for a moment as wrenching grief flooded my chest and arms, then I forced myself to turn and walk back toward the jetty where I'd found Junie. Where the whole chain reaction of jealousy and death had started, it seemed to me.

The salt breeze blew my hair stiff and stringy, but I kept staring at the ocean. I thought about walking straight out there until the gray-blue waves closed over my head, until time stopped for me and I could hold my daughter again. Hypnotized by the whitecaps, arms and heart aching for Roz, I took the first step toward the ocean, then the second.

A hand grabbed my arm and a rough voice broke through the fog. "Where you goin'?"

I snapped out of my trance and stared into Jackson's stormy eyes, the same color as the water. "Hey," he said. "Jesus, you look like shit." Gently he pulled me away from the water's edge and sat me on the jetty. "You okay?"

My chest felt ragged when I laughed at his innocent question. "Hardly."

"Yeah, stupid thing to ask, huh?" His eyes stayed on me, anxious and hungry. I turned away and folded my arms across my breasts, acting a lot colder than I felt. "I thought you were . . . well, I been looking around for you." He shifted toward me, trying to get back in my line of vision, but I found an interesting shell. "I never got to thank you."

"For what?"

He laughed sharply. "Saving my ass, what else? Jesus, if it wasn't for you . . . well, a couple more of us would be dead, and that asshole would probably still be alive and prospering."

Dead. Alive. I crushed the shell against the rock and shrugged. "I didn't do it on purpose. And if I had it to do over . . ." I realized how that sounded. "I mean, I'm glad you're out and alive and all, but . . ."

Jackson shoved his hands in his pockets. "Shit, yeah. I had a feeling that might've hurt the baby."

"Yeah, a bit." I got up and wandered toward the shore again, fighting down the tears that threatened to drown me. Maybe I wouldn't need the ocean after all.

Jackson followed at a respectful distance. "So, what's up now?"

"Major surgery." I shrugged; it seemed pretty insignificant. "The tumor's giving me problems again. Then I have to think about where I'm going to live, what I'm going to do for a living, what I'm going to drive, whether or not I want to stick around this place any longer."

"I'm kinda stuck here till my parole's over." Jackson found a rock and threw it at the ocean, hard. "So, Maddie, where the hell you been?"

"Around. I needed some time alone."

"I been wantin' to talk to you, see how you are and stuff."

"Sorry."

Jackson sighed. "No, I'm sorry. Debi'd kill me if she heard me right now. I'm not being very sensitive." He kicked at some seaweed and exploded. "But damn it, how long do I sit on this?"

I looked at the slimy green glob stuck to his sneaker. "I wouldn't sit on that at all if I were you." When in doubt, make a stupid joke.

He looked at his foot. "Stop screwing around, Maddie. I'm serious here." After scuffing the seaweed off onto the sand, he started to reach for me, then stuffed his hands in his pockets instead. "Okay, no, I'm sorry. You really don't need to hear this, do ya? I know you got a lot going on right now and I think what I wanna do is let you know, y'know, I'm here. That's all. And I don't want you to be . . ." He hesitated, then pushed the word out: "Dead."

I stared out at the water again. "How were you going to do it? You know, when you thought you were stuck in jail for the rest of your life?"

He scowled. "I hadn't figured it out. You listening to me?"

"Yeah. You said you don't want me to be dead." A large wave curled toward us, shrunk abruptly and melted harmlessly onto the sand. "Well, I am kinda dead, at least for now," I confessed. "But I'm pretty sure I'll be back."

Epilogue

The question hovers over me like a wasp. No baby, no job, no home, no plans, no reason to live. So now what? Even Curly the tumor's gone, removed by a successful surgery that left my reproductive organs intact in case I want to take another stab at motherhood. Who knows?

I'm all cried out, at least for now; those months of hormonal wackiness seem to have made up for years of not crying. I'm sure tears will sneak up on me at inconvenient moments for the rest of my life, but for now the well's dry and I'm looking ahead. About time, too.

Awed by my newly acquired "local hero" status, Principal Gorman offered me my teaching job back in the fall. I told him exactly where he could put his contract and precisely how hard he could blow it out of there, which wasn't anywhere near as satisfying as I'd imagined. Guess I no longer get that smart-ass satisfaction from my barbed bon mots. My thirty-year adolescence has finally ended; now I have to figure out what I want to do with my adulthood.

The Abneyville Shores manager offered me a small stipend plus this cottage for free if I stick around and do maintenance during the tourist season, through Labor Day and probably beyond. I told him sure, as long as I could have my cats.

So now I'm sitting at the breakfast nook, watching Hairball blissfully groom his huge gut in the morning sun. Booger exits the litter box looking supremely grossed out. Guess I should clean that, huh? I reach my hand toward her and she runs to me, rubbing her wet nose against my palm and purring spasmodically before leaping into my lap, where she settles with much ecstatic vibrating. I pat her some more and turn back to the table.

Roz's little box of ashes and the two Polaroids her nurse gave me lie next to my coffee and this morning's paper, which is opened to an ad for a private investigator class I might take. Past, present, future.

Why did she come? That's the biggest mystery of all. Why did I get pregnant after being told I couldn't, and discover it days before a hysterectomy — which sure as hell seemed like one of those "meant to be" miracles? And why did she die only after surviving such enormous odds?

What the hell was that about?

People have tried to talk to me about it, but I have to come to my own conclusions. My little sister Gabe, the born-again Christian, believes everything happens for a reason because her "good father God" has some grand plan for everyone's lives. I don't know about that; my experience with fathers has pretty much sucked. Plus, the whole thing with Roz sometimes feels like the ultimate cosmic practical joke. Good one, God. You really had me going for a while there, big guy . . .

I study the ad, sip coffee, touch Roz's little box. I realize I'm smiling. The memory isn't all bad, even though it ended that way. She gave me stuff I never knew I was missing, stuff I didn't even know I wanted. Like my heart, for instance. So many parts of myself I didn't know existed.

I push aside the paper and grab the pictures, studying the tiny face, wishing I could hold her again. Then I grab the box, dump Booger onto the floor, and stride outdoors onto the beach.

The sun is warm, but a strong breeze stirs up waves. I take a deep breath before I climb onto the jetty and walk to the very end. After watching the waves a few moments longer, I carefully ease the lid open and stare down at what's left of Roz. Then I hold the box up to the sun and tilt it so the wind carries her gently out to the ocean. I can't repress a sharp sob as I watch her float away, and whisper an endearment to the breeze: "I love you, baby. I'll always love you."

I feel a flutter in my womb. She'll never be gone. Neither will Mom and Dad and Junie, but Roz was . . . Roz *is* different, set apart from all the other dead people in my life. She's a positive force. She started pushing me forward. And by God I will keep moving — but I won't leave her behind.

And someday, maybe, I'll figure this mystery out.